BLADE
of the
SAMURAI

ALSO BY SUSAN SPANN

Claws of the Cat

BLADE
of the
SAMURAI

A SHINOBI MYSTERY

Susan Spann

MINOTAUR BOOKS
A THOMAS DUNNE BOOK
New York

This is a work of fiction. All of the characters, organizations, and events por-
trayed in this novel are either products of the author's imagination or are used
fictitiously.

A THOMAS DUNNE BOOK FOR MINOTAUR BOOKS.
An imprint of St. Martin's Publishing Group.

www.thomasdunnebooks.com
www.minotaurbooks.com

LIBRARY OF CONGRESS CATALOGING-IN-PUBLICATION DATA

Spann, Susan.
    Blade of the samurai : a Shinobi mystery / Susan Spann. — First edition.
        p. cm. — (; 2)
    ISBN 978-1-250-02705-4 (hardcover)
    ISBN 978-1-250-02704-7 (e-book)
    1. Ninja—Fiction.   2. Samurai—Fiction.   3. Murder—Investigation—
Fiction.   I. Title.
    PS3619.P3436B53 2014
    813'.6—dc23

                                                        2014008766

Minotaur books may be purchased for educational, business, or
promotional use. For information on bulk purchases, please contact
Macmillan Corporate and Premium Sales Department at 1-800-221-7945,
extension 5442, or write specialmarkets@macmillan.com.

First Edition: July 2014

10 9 8 7 6 5 4 3 2 1

For Michael, for too many reasons to mention—
but mostly, because I love you

Acknowledgments

If I wrote a thousand novels, I still wouldn't have sufficient space to thank everyone who helped and supported me along the way. The list grows longer with every book I write. But, as always, some people require special mention.

To my husband, Michael, and my son, Christopher—thank you for constant love, support, and reinforcement. You keep my dreams focused and my butt in the chair.

To my incomparable agent, Sandra Bond, and my fantastic editor, Toni Kirkpatrick—thank you for believing in Hiro and in me. Working with you is an honor and a pleasure for which I continue to be grateful every day.

To my peer editors, David, Heather, and Amanda—thank you for your time, skills, friendship, and support. You make me better than I am alone.

To the amazing ladies of my critique group, the infamous SFWG—Heather Webb, Candie Campbell, L. J. Cohen, Julianne Douglas, Marci Jefferson, Amanda Orr, DeAnn Smith, Janet Taylor, and Arabella Stokes—I value each of you more than words can express.

To Dana Bate, Kelly Harms, Amy Sue Nathan, and Kerry Schafer, my fellow debut authors from the Debutante Ball blog's "Class of 2013"—thank you for your friendship and support. It was an honor and a pleasure to celebrate each of your novels, and to have your help in celebrating mine.

Thanks to my family: Paula, Spencer, Robert, Lola, Spencer (III), Anna, Matteo, Gene, Marcie, and Bob—your support, as always, gives me strength and joy.

Thank you to Joe, Master of the Interwebz, for everything from designing and maintaining my Web site to helping me figure out that the cat has reset my function keys.

Arigato gozaimasu to Tomoko Yoshihara for helping with my research and identifying the proper location of the Ashikaga Shogunate in 1565.

And last, but certainly not least, thank you to Erika, Laura, Wing, Peter, Michelle, and all of the other friends—online and off—who encourage me and support this crazy dream come true.

The name on the cover is mine, but I could not do this without your friendship and support.

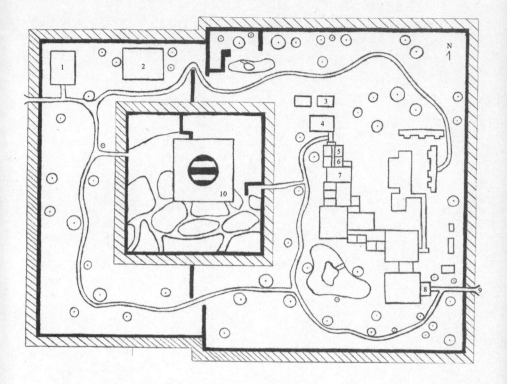

ASHIKAGA SHOGUNATE MAP KEY

 1 Stable
 2 Sparring Grounds
 3 Storehouse
 4 Kitchen
 5 Private Office of Ashikaga Saburo
 6 Outer Office of Ashikaga Saburo
      (Shared By Ito Kazu)
 7 Audience Hall (Under Construction)
 8 *Bakufu* Mansion Entry/Waiting Room
 9 East Gate
10 Shogun Ashikaga's Private Residence

Chapter 1

Hiro opened his eyes in darkness.

Night enveloped the room like a shroud, broken only by the beam of moonlight streaming through the open veranda door. The still air and the moonbeam's angle told Hiro that dawn was still an hour away.

In most Kyoto houses an open shoji represented a dangerous oversight. For Hiro, a *shinobi* assassin turned bodyguard, the door was an early warning system that had just paid off.

He strained his ears, listening for the sound that woke him. He heard only silence.

A weight shifted atop Hiro's feet as his kitten, Gato, twitched in her sleep. The shinobi found that reassuring. Gato's ears were sharper than his own, and the cat never slept through sounds she didn't recognize.

Hiro yawned and closed his eyes to weigh the merits of early-morning exercise against two more hours of sleep.

A board creaked outside the veranda door.

Hiro's eyes flashed open. The kitten raised her head, ears pricked toward the sound.

The loose board sat between Hiro's door and the one to the adjacent room, where Father Mateo slept. The Jesuit had wanted to fix the squeaky timber, but Hiro insisted the board stay loose to help the shinobi protect his Portuguese charge.

Hiro slipped out from beneath his quilt and pulled on a pair of baggy trousers. As he tied the ankle straps to keep his cuffs from tangling in a fight, he listened for the second creak that would tell him when the intruder stepped off the board.

He heard nothing.

A surge of adrenaline loosened Hiro's muscles. Only another shinobi could move with sufficient stealth to prevent the board from creaking a second time.

He wasted no time wondering why an assassin had come. Hiro's clan, the Iga *ryu*, had ordered him to defend the Jesuit's life at any cost, and Hiro would not allow himself to fail. He grabbed a dagger from his desk and scurried up the built-in shelves on the southern wall of the room. He was glad he had reinforced them to hold his weight.

The wall ended at rafter height, leaving plenty of space for a man to crouch beneath the peaked thatch roof. Hiro crawled onto the nearest rafter and glanced over the wall into Father Mateo's room. The Jesuit slept soundly.

A shadow blotted out the moonlight as a human form appeared in Hiro's doorway. The intruder paused only a moment, then stepped inside.

Gato arched her back and hissed before vanishing into the shadows.

The assassin wore a cowl that hid his face. He moved across the floor with an inward twist of the toes that Hiro recognized as a hallmark of the Iga *ryu*.

This killer had not come for the Portuguese priest.

Hiro gripped his dagger and readied himself to jump. As he drew a final, preparatory breath he caught the faint but unmistakable scent of expensive wintergreen hair oil.

Betrayal seared through Hiro's mind like flame. Only one Iga shinobi used that scent, and until this moment Hiro had considered the man a brother.

Plunging a knife into Kazu's heart would hurt Hiro almost as much as suicide.

Almost, but not quite.

Hiro leaped from the beam as, below him, Kazu whispered, "Hiro? I need your help."

It was too late to arrest the fall. Hiro flung his arm to the side to stop the knife from striking a fatal blow.

Kazu jumped away, stumbled, and pitched forward onto the futon.

Hiro landed in a silent crouch, knife ready. He would give Kazu a chance to explain, but didn't let down his guard.

Kazu raised his empty hands. "Hiro, wait! It's me."

"I almost killed you," Hiro hissed. "What were you thinking, coming here unannounced and at this hour?"

Kazu pushed his cowl back onto his shoulders. His worried eyes reflected the moonlight.

"There's been a murder at the shogunate."

"The shogun?" Hiro's expression softened as he realized why Kazu had taken the risk.

Shogun Ashikaga supported the Jesuits' presence in Kyoto, despite his opponents' demands that he expel the Portuguese missionaries or execute them as spies. The shogun's death would threaten both Father Mateo's life and Hiro's assignment to protect the priest.

"Not the shogun," Kazu whispered, "his cousin, Saburo."

"Your supervisor?" Hiro's gratitude splintered into anger. He barely managed to keep his voice a whisper. "Have you lost your senses? You risk exposing us both by coming here."

"Please." The catch in Kazu's voice reminded Hiro that Kazu had only twenty years to Hiro's twenty-five, and although the younger shinobi had come to Kyoto first, Hiro had been an assassin for years before Kazu even received his first official orders—an assignment to spy within the Ashikaga shogunate.

"Someone murdered Saburo with my dagger," Kazu continued. "The shogun will think I killed him."

"That doesn't excuse your acting like a fool." Hiro inhaled slowly to calm his fury. It didn't work. "Have you forgotten your training completely? If something compromises your cover, you leave Kyoto. Even a novice knows not to put others at risk."

"I'm sorry." Remorse flooded Kazu's voice. "I panicked."

"Why come here?" Hiro asked. "Why not run?"

"I couldn't leave the city. No one passes the outer barricades at night without a travel pass and a good excuse." Kazu raised his hands, palms up. "I don't have either."

Kazu's fear didn't soothe Hiro's anger. Still, the damage was done, and further scolding would not undo it. The shinobi code required Hiro to help a clansman in need unless doing so would compromise his mission. Since Kazu's arrest might expose both men as shinobi, the choice seemed clear.

"Are you sure no one followed you?" Hiro asked.

Kazu nodded.

"Then tell me what happened, in detail—but first, get off my futon."

Chapter 2

Kazu knelt on the woven tatami that covered the floor. Hiro sheathed his knife.

"I was working late," Kazu said, "updating the schedule for the shogun's personal bodyguards."

"You work in the records bureau," Hiro said, "not shogunate defense."

"True, but a month ago Saburo persuaded the shogun to transfer the bodyguards away from military command and under Saburo's personal control. He said it wasn't wise to trust a man from another clan with the shogun's personal safety. The shogun agreed."

"The military officials aren't Ashikaga retainers?" Hiro asked.

"Not all of them," Kazu said, "and with Lord Oda eager to seize the capital and the shogunate, Saburo's concern makes sense. The shogun thought so, anyway."

"Is Lord Oda advancing on Kyoto?" Hiro felt a surge of concern.

"Not openly," Kazu said, "but he's sent an embassy to the city. Officially, it comes bearing gifts for the emperor and the shogun."

"And unofficially?" Hiro asked.

"Everyone knows Lord Oda's intentions. Saburo feared an assassin among the ambassadors."

"Apparently not without reason," Hiro said. "When did Lord Oda's men arrive?"

"They're not here yet," Kazu said.

"Then how did Saburo die?"

"I don't know exactly." Kazu shook his head. "I went to Ginjiro's brewery for a drink, and when I returned to the office I found Saburo dead."

"Killed with your dagger."

"But not by me," Kazu said. "I accidentally left the weapon on my desk. Anyone could have picked it up and used it."

"Did you alert the shogunate guards?"

"They would have killed me on the spot!"

"You had just returned from Ginjiro's," Hiro said. "The gate guards could have vouched for your innocence."

"I didn't use the gate." Kazu paused. "Saburo ordered me not to leave the compound until I finished my work, but that could have taken all night. I slipped out over the wall and returned the same way. I've done it before. No one's ever noticed."

Hiro shook his head. "You have to leave Kyoto at once."

"I can't," Kazu said. "I left my travel pass at the shogunate, and there's no way to get through the checkpoints at the city exits unnoticed. The shogun has every barricade guarded because of Lord Oda's embassy."

"Go back to the shogunate and retrieve the pass," Hiro said.

"Someone will have discovered the body by now. They'll have guards in the office." Kazu shook his head again. "I can't risk it. Not even over the wall."

Hiro thought for a moment. "Itinerant monks don't need papers to travel. I have a *komusō*'s robe and hat you can borrow. If you're careful, the disguise will get you all the way to Iga."

He opened his clothing cabinet and retrieved a dingy robe and a pair of fraying sandals, along with a woven basket-hat that smelled faintly of reeds and disuse.

Kazu gave Hiro a grateful smile. "I'm sorry I put you in danger."

"Don't mention it," Hiro said, "especially to Hanzo."

Hiro lifted the lid of his ironbound weapons chest and withdrew a bamboo shakuhachi flute. He offered it to Kazu. "There's a dagger hidden inside."

A loud knocking echoed through the house. Hiro froze. Someone was at the Jesuit's front door.

"You were followed!" Hiro hurried across the room and threw open the large wooden chest that sat on the floor beside the clothing cabinet. "Get in."

Kazu wrapped the monk's robe around his kimono and climbed into the chest. Hiro pulled the quilt off his futon and laid it over the younger man. It wasn't a great disguise, but they had no time for anything better.

"If anyone finds you," Hiro whispered, "you're on your own." He pulled the quilt over Kazu's face and closed the chest.

The knocking increased in volume.

Hiro shoved the basket-hat back into the cabinet, slipped on a long-sleeved tunic, and slid open the paneled shoji door separating his room from the *oe*, or common room, beyond.

Father Mateo had just emerged from the adjacent room. His shoulder-length hair stuck out at odd angles, mussed from sleep. He bit his lower lip in concentration as he tied an obi sash around his hurriedly donned kimono.

Even after three years in Kyoto, the Jesuit had trouble dressing quickly.

Father Mateo looked up as he tightened the sash. "Who could it be, at this hour?"

Hiro shrugged and forced a smile. He didn't want to guess.

A little over a year before, a predawn visit had summoned the men to a teahouse where an entertainer stood accused of murdering her samurai guest. When Father Mateo intervened to save the girl, the dead man's son had forced them to find his father's killer or share the condemned entertainer's fate.

Hiro hoped this visitor wouldn't make a similar demand.

He followed Father Mateo into the tiny foyer that opened off the southern side of the common room.

"Who is there?" the Jesuit called through the carved front door.

"God's peace be with you, Father Mateo," a voice called, "it is Izumo. Father Vilela sent me."

Hiro breathed a silent sigh of relief. Izumo was an acolyte at the official Jesuit mission in central Kyoto. Since Father Mateo's work among the commoners would alienate the samurai elite whose support was requisite for the Catholic Church's presence in the capital, the Jesuits kept their missions separated. Hiro had never met Gaspar Vilela, the senior Jesuit in Kyoto and Father Mateo's nominal superior. However, the shinobi knew Izumo, and he recognized the acolyte's voice and accent.

Hiro withdrew to his room as Father Mateo opened the door for Izumo. The shinobi left his shoji slightly ajar to ensure the Jesuits' words would carry clearly through the air.

Father Mateo considered eavesdropping sinful, but Hiro considered himself exempt from the priest's religious rules.

The shinobi shed his jacket and trousers in favor of a smoke-gray kimono cut in the latest samurai style. As he dressed, he listened to the conversation taking place in the common room.

"I apologize for waking you so early," Izumo said.

The acolyte sounded uneasy. Hiro knew why. The Japanese considered an unplanned predawn visit exceedingly rude.

"No need for apologies," Father Mateo said. "What's happened?"

"There has been a murder," Izumo said, "and the shogun requests your help in finding the killer."

Chapter 3

Hiro froze, stunned by Izumo's words.

"Hiro!" Father Mateo called.

The shinobi grabbed his swords from the weapon stand.

Although trained as assassins, Hiro's family descended from samurai, which gave Hiro the legal right to wear two swords—an exclusive privilege that also provided quite an effective disguise. He thrust the shorter *wakizashi* down the left side of his obi and pushed the katana's longer scabbard upward through the same side of the sash. Only then did he answer Father Mateo's call.

Hiro returned to the common room and bowed to Izumo, who seemed undisturbed by Father Mateo's voluble breach of manners. Either the other Jesuits also yelled like overexcited children or the Japanese convert had learned to ignore their rudeness. Hiro guessed the latter.

"There has been a murder," Father Mateo said.

Hiro feigned ignorance. "One of the foreign priests?" He caught a whiff of incense from the visitor's faded robe.

"No." Izumo shook his head. "A senior clerk at the shogunate—a man named Ashikaga Saburo. He was also a second cousin to the shogun."

"Most unfortunate," Hiro said.

"The shogun requested Father Mateo's assistance in solving the crime," Izumo added.

"I don't understand," Father Mateo said. "I've met the shogun only once, and that was years ago. I didn't think he even knew my name."

"When the body was discovered, the shogun summoned Father Vilela to pray for the dead man's soul," Izumo said.

"When did the shogun become a Christian?" Father Mateo asked.

"He isn't," Izumo said. "After the prayers, Shogun Ashikaga mentioned hearing that you had captured Akechi Hideyoshi's killer a year ago. Father Vilela was summoned so that the shogun could politely ask for you."

The acolyte's tone suggested that he—and, by implication, Father Vilela—was not entirely pleased with this turn of events.

Hiro wasn't either. "I am very sorry, but Father Mateo must decline."

"Hiro!" Father Mateo turned to Izumo. "We would be honored to assist the shogun."

"I apologize," Hiro said, "but I must insist. Father Mateo is a priest. I am a translator. We are not qualified to investigate murders."

Izumo smiled, but his shifting feet betrayed discomfort.

"My translator speaks out of turn," Father Mateo said in perfect Japanese. "Please tell Father Vilela that Hiro and I will obey the shogun's command."

Izumo smiled stiffly. "While I appreciate your willingness, the shogun requested you . . . and you alone."

"But I did not solve the Akechi murder alone," Father Mateo said. "I require Hiro's assistance."

Izumo looked from Father Mateo to Hiro as if wishing the shinobi would renew his objection. Hiro said nothing.

"If there is no alternative," Izumo said at last, "but please explain to the shogun that the Jesuit mission delivered his request without alteration." He bowed. "When you reach the shogunate, ask for Matsunaga Hisahide. He will supervise your investigation.

"Now, if you will excuse me, I must return to Father Vilela."

Father Mateo and Hiro escorted the visitor back to the door. Izumo stepped outside, slipped on his sandals, and hurried away.

The Jesuit closed the door and spun around quickly. Hiro jumped back to avoid a collision.

"Why did you refuse him?" Father Mateo demanded.

The Jesuit's rare but genuine frustration startled Hiro, and it took the shinobi a moment to recover.

"We are not in the business of solving murders," Hiro said at last. "The Akechi incident almost got us killed, and that was only a teahouse. The shogunate is infinitely more dangerous."

"The shogun requested our aid," Father Mateo said, "and Father Vilela seconded his request. Refusal is not an option."

"Father Vilela seconded it unwillingly," Hiro countered. "Not even you could have missed Izumo's discomfort—and neither Vilela nor Izumo understands the danger fully. I will not allow you to risk your life in this manner."

"Fortunately, your consent is not required." Father Mateo paused. "What makes you think my life is at risk?"

"Have you forgotten the details of the Akechi murder? The dead man's family tried to hold you responsible."

"That was different. My converts aren't involved this time." Father Mateo stepped backward warily. "Hiro, what haven't you told me?"

Before the shinobi could answer, a woman's scream echoed through the house.

Chapter 4

Hiro ran to his room with Father Mateo close behind. They paused in the doorway, seeking the source of the sound.

The Jesuit's aging housekeeper, Ana, stood beside Hiro's futon chest with her back to the door and her hands in the air. A rumpled quilt lay on the floor at her feet. She shrieked again and bent to pummel Kazu, who cowered inside the chest, eyes wide and arms raised in self-defense.

He noticed the other men in the doorway. "Hiro, please!" he called.

The housekeeper whirled. A scowl added even more lines to her wrinkled face. Her black eyes glittered with fury and uncomfortable surprise.

"Hiro," she said. "I should have known."

The shinobi opened his mouth to deny involvement, but changed his mind. "It's Kazu," he said, then added, "you know Kazu."

"I know he does not belong in the futon chest." Ana gave Hiro a sideways look and waggled her finger as if at a naughty child. "You put him there to scare me, didn't you?"

"He did not." Kazu stood up and straightened his robe. "He put me there so I wouldn't."

"Hm." Ana gathered up the fallen quilt and muttered, "Didn't work."

She started toward the door and paused directly in front of Hiro. "Your kimonos need airing too. Will I find a pair of dancing girls in your wardrobe?"

"Only if he's lucky," Kazu quipped.

Ana shot a glare over her shoulder and bustled from the room.

Father Mateo looked from the departing maid to Hiro. "Why was he hiding in the futon chest?"

"A foolish prank," Kazu said, "for which I apologize. I stopped by to see if Hiro had a message for his family in Iga. I am heading there this morning."

"You work at the shogunate." Father Mateo's gaze shifted from Kazu to Hiro. "This is why you don't want us involved."

Hiro nodded once in silent admission.

The Jesuit looked at Kazu. "Did you kill Ashikaga Saburo?"

"No," Kazu said.

"But the shogun thinks you did." It wasn't a question.

Hiro admired the priest's quick inference but hoped Mateo wouldn't ask why Kazu had chosen the Jesuit's house to run to. The priest didn't know that Kazu was also shinobi, and Hiro had no intention of explaining.

"The murderer used my dagger," Kazu said, "but I swear—by all the kami in Japan—my hand did not wield it."

"There is only one God," Father Mateo said, "in Japan or otherwise. But if you are innocent, as you claim, His truth will set you free."

Kazu laughed. "The shogun doesn't care about your god's truth."

Father Mateo bowed. "Forgive my rudeness. I would like to speak with Hiro—alone."

The Jesuit backed out the door. When Hiro followed, Father Mateo closed the shoji that separated Hiro's room from the common room and crossed to the central hearth. A smell of dead ashes rose from the sunken pit where the fire usually burned.

Father Mateo lowered his voice and switched to Portuguese. "God's house does not shelter murderers."

"Kazu claims innocence," Hiro replied in the Jesuit's native tongue, "and I didn't offer him shelter. He arrived unannounced and will leave the same way, at dawn."

"This is serious." Father Mateo raised his right hand but stopped just short of running it through his hair. He returned the hand to his side, refusing to give in to the nervous habit. "The shogun permits me to live in Kyoto and preach God's word because I abide by Japanese law. If he learns I harbored a fugitive he will banish me from the city, and probably banish Father Vilela as well."

"He won't banish you." Hiro switched back to Japanese. "He'll kill you."

Before the Jesuit could reply Hiro continued, "I understand the danger. I would not have consented, had Kazu asked, and I would have prevented him from coming here if I could."

"I didn't think you invited him," Father Mateo said, "but you let him stay. I begin to suspect he is more than merely a friend from the sake shop."

The door to Hiro's room slid open. Kazu emerged, still wearing the dingy robe and carrying a pair of fraying sandals. A wicker basket-hat covered his head and rested on his shoulders. The narrow slit at the front of the basket allowed him to see but completely obscured his features.

"Hiro," Father Mateo said, "your friend has a basket on his head."

"A hat," Hiro corrected. "The *komusō* monks of Fuke Zen wear such things to distance themselves from the world."

"Thank you for your hospitality," Kazu said, his perfect Kyoto accent slightly muffled by the basket. "I will not impose upon you again."

Father Mateo bowed.

Hiro escorted Kazu out. When they reached the front door Kazu said, "You should help the Jesuit solve this murder."

Hiro raised an eyebrow in surprise. "You really didn't kill Saburo?"

The basket shimmied as Kazu shook his head. "No, but Hanzo will want to know who did."

Hiro didn't answer. Kazu was right. The head of the Iga *ryu* demanded an explanation for everything that impacted an Iga shinobi's mission, and he wasn't known to suffer failures well.

"Besides," Kazu added, "you will need to solve the crime to prove you didn't help me escape."

Hiro had thought of that too. Samurai justice often condemned a guilty man's friends and family if the criminal escaped the grasp of justice. No one in Kyoto knew that Hiro and Kazu shared more than a casual friendship, but the two were well-known as friends and drinking companions. Since Kazu had no family in the capital, his friends would bear the brunt of the shogun's anger.

"Travel safely," Hiro said. "Give my regards to everyone at Iga."

Kazu paused as if wanting to say something more, but after a moment he set down the sandals, slipped them on, and headed for the street.

The sky had lightened, though clouds prevented a visible sunrise. A bird chirped in a nearby tree, and Kazu's sandals crunched an accompaniment on the gravel path. At the narrow earthen road the young shinobi turned east, away from Kyoto.

Angry barking erupted from the yard across the street.

On the narrow strip of grass beside the house, a huge akita strained at the end of a braided rope secured to a wooden stake. The dog weighed almost as much as a man and stood three feet high at the shoulder. It barked ferociously at Kazu, barely pausing to draw a breath.

Hiro found it odd that the dog was home. The woodsman who lived across the street usually left before dawn and always took the akita with him.

After watching long enough to ensure the dog would not break free, Hiro shifted his gaze to Kazu's retreating form. He hoped that Kazu hadn't killed Saburo. If the investigation proved otherwise, the shogun would execute both Hiro and Father Mateo the moment he learned that Kazu had slipped away.

Hiro didn't want to get involved in another murder, but no man could easily refuse a command from the shogun. Father Mateo had to find the killer, and Hiro—sworn to protect the priest—had no choice but to follow him into danger.

An unexpected rush of excitement struck the shinobi as he turned back into the house and closed the door. Although he wouldn't have chosen this assignment, solving a murder allowed him to use his special training in a way his bodyguard duties seldom offered. Hiro found himself looking forward to the challenge, even though accepting it went against his better judgment.

He returned to the common room as Father Mateo emerged from his bedroom wearing a formal kimono.

Before Hiro could speak the Jesuit said, "You might as well skip the protest. I'm solving this murder and you're going to help me do it."

Chapter 5

Hiro and Father Mateo walked west along Marutama-chi Road past Okazaki Shrine, the Shinto temple that marked Kyoto's official eastern boundary.

They crossed the wood and stone bridge that spanned the Kamo River. As they entered the elite residential ward on the opposite side, Father Mateo said, "I'm glad Luis is out of town. If he'd heard Ana scream . . ."

He didn't need to finish the sentence. The Portuguese merchant whose weapon sales financed Father Mateo's mission kept a secret about as well as a toddler—and not even that well if he saw an advantage in talking.

A few blocks past the river, Hiro and Father Mateo turned north onto the road that led to the shogunate. The shogun's compound lay a block ahead on the western side of the street.

Twenty-foot walls of wood and stone surrounded the shogun's compound. A roof of curved black tiles surmounted the walls, punctuated at intervals by surveillance towers that jutted into the air like curling fangs from the mouth of a boar. The massive perimeter wall stretched two city blocks on every side. At the base of the wall lay a water-filled moat too broad for most men to jump.

"Such a large compound for only one man," Father Mateo said.

"The shogun is the most powerful man in Japan," Hiro answered, "more powerful than the emperor in every way that matters. And the shogunate isn't large just for the sake of display. It also houses the *bakufu*—the government offices."

"Yes, in the mansion," Father Mateo said. "That's where the shogun received me when I first arrived in Kyoto. The grounds are spectacular, too."

"Shogun Ashikaga has an eye for beauty," Hiro said, "though some men worry it blunts his martial edge."

Hiro fell silent as as they reached the eastern entrance to the compound. A wooden bridge spanned the moat and a black tile roof arched high above the massive wooden gates that stood open for shogunate business from dawn until dusk.

Half a dozen armored samurai stood guard around the entrance. They snapped to attention as Hiro and Father Mateo approached.

The Jesuit paused at the eastern end of the bridge and bowed to the guards. They returned the greeting in kind. Hiro noted with approval that the guards bowed deeply, from the waist, a more respectful greeting than samurai usually offered foreigners.

"I am Father Mateo Ávila de Santos," the Jesuit said. "I have come to see Matsunaga Hisahide."

"Greetings, Father," the tallest guard said. "Please wait here. I will inform Matsunaga-*san* of your arrival."

He disappeared into the compound as Hiro and Father Mateo crossed the bridge. While they waited for the guard to return, Hiro looked at the shogunate compound—or at least, at the portion visible from the gate.

The entrance opened onto a graveled courtyard. To the north and south, the yard was lined with stands of delicate maple trees interspersed with taller pines and cedars. On the western side, opposite the gates, lay the entrance to the massive government mansion.

The building rose higher than a normal one-story structure, creating a dramatic appearance and also allowing room for the shogun's spies to move beneath the rafters. Heavy cedar beams supported the tile roof, while decorative carvings adorned the woodwork, much of which was painted blue and gold.

The trees surrounding the mansion were carefully trimmed. Hiro smiled grimly. Not even he could leap that distance onto tiles without making noise and raising an alarm.

The gate guard emerged from the mansion with a young samurai at his side. At the edge of the veranda they slipped on their sandals and started across the yard.

Father Mateo leaned toward Hiro and whispered, "Is that Matsunaga Hisahide?"

The samurai wore a stylish black kimono with a black and white mon on the upper left side of the chest. Hiro recognized the symbol. The small white diamond within a larger black one was the crest of the Miyoshi samurai clan.

"He's too young," Hiro replied in Portuguese, then added, "Most likely a son of Daimyo Miyoshi."

"The lord of Yamato Province?" Father Mateo asked.

Hiro nodded. "One of the shogun's strongest allies."

The young man stopped in front of Father Mateo and dismissed the guard with a nod. He let the priest bow first, but returned a deeper bow than Hiro expected and held it long enough to show sincere respect.

"I am Miyoshi Akira," he said as he straightened, "second cousin to Daimyo Miyoshi of Yamato. I am assisting Matsunaga Hisahide with the murder investigation."

As an afterthought he added, "Welcome to the shogunate."

"I am Father Mateo, from Portugal," the Jesuit said in Japanese, then added, "Although I speak your language a little, I often require assistance to understand the finer points. This is my translator, Matsui Hiro."

The simple introduction, which stated no clan or province of origin, implied that Hiro was ronin, a masterless samurai forced to adopt a trade. As such, Hiro could claim no rank or privilege in the company of other samurai.

The shinobi bowed as deeply as possible.

To Hiro's surprise, Akira nodded respectfully and without any visible disdain. "I am pleased to make your acquaintance, Matsui-*san*."

Akira's gaze returned to the priest. "Matsunaga Hisahide sends his apologies. He wished to greet you himself but was unavoidably detained. You will follow me?"

He turned and led them across the courtyard.

Hiro inhaled the musky scent of cedars and a dampness in the air that promised rain. The clouds that obscured the sunrise had gathered and darkened. Hiro doubted his kimono would get home dry and wondered whether Ana would decide to forego the airing of quilts and clothes.

The maid would be in a foul mood if showers spoiled her work.

"Hisahide mentioned your previous work on behalf of the Akechi clan." Akira stepped out of his sandals and onto the wooden veranda encircling the mansion. "The shogun requires similar assistance, though I trust you understand that this situation requires even greater discretion."

He looked from Hiro to Father Mateo, awaiting confirmation. They left their sandals beside the veranda and joined him.

"I give you my word," the Jesuit said. "I will reveal nothing, and my translator is entirely trustworthy."

Akira led them into the mansion and through the six-mat room where petitioners waited for an audience with the shogun or one of the government officials. At that early hour, the room was empty except for a pair of sleepy-looking guards, who let the three men pass without comment.

Hiro and Father Mateo followed Akira through a maze of tatami-floored rooms separated by sliding shoji doors. The larger spaces functioned as audience chambers and meeting rooms, while the smaller ones were little more than passages with sliding doors on either side leading to private offices beyond. Low slatted ceilings, intended to hamper the use of swords, made even the largest rooms feel oppressively small for Hiro's taste.

After several minutes they entered a ten-mat audience room with renovations in progress. The tatami flooring was stacked in the southeast corner and covered to protect the woven mats against damage and dust. An assortment of brooms and carpentry tools lay neatly against the western wall beside an elaborate but unfinished transom screen and a waist-high pile of wooden ceiling slats.

Nearby, wooden props supported a thick cedar beam. A

section of missing ceiling indicated the place where the beam would become a rafter.

Akira paused as if embarrassed. "I apologize for the mess. The shogun wants this work completed before . . . as soon as possible." He indicated a sliding door on the north side of the room. "Ashikaga Saburo's office is on the right, just through those doors."

"Did he work alone?" Father Mateo asked.

"He had one assistant, Ito Kazu." Akira looked at Hiro. "A friend of yours."

Chapter 6

I do know Ito Kazu," Hiro said, "but I consider him an acquaintance, not a friend."

Akira gave Hiro a look that neither accepted nor denied the shinobi's statement.

"Touch nothing in Ashikaga-*san*'s office," Akira said as he led them across the room and into a narrow hall with doors on either side. "His family has not arrived."

Akira drew open the right-hand door and waited for the other men to enter.

Hiro stepped back to let Father Mateo lead, but not before his sensitive nose caught the mingling odors of documents, jasmine, and blood. The Jesuit entered the room and moved aside, giving Hiro his first clear view of the murder scene.

The six-mat room had a built-in desk and cabinet on the southern wall, to the right of the entrance. Piles of parchments lay on the desk, some neatly stacked and others spread out as if for examination. A monochromatic landscape scroll adorned the tokonoma, or decorative alcove, on the wall beside the desk. The room was otherwise empty of furniture and adornments.

An oblong pool of congealing blood the size and shape of a fallen man spread across the center of the room. A trail of bloody spots and streaks led from the pool to an open shoji in the northern wall. Rusty drops and elongated bloody spatters marked the floor and wall to the left of the door.

Judging by the size and location of the stains, the killer surprised Saburo in or near that northern entrance.

Hiro looked at the pool on the floor. The edges were crisp and linear, with very little smudging. Saburo hadn't moved much after falling, though Hiro felt fairly certain the victim had bled to death on the floor.

A single set of bloody footprints led from the pool to a sliding door in the eastern wall of the office. Judging from the natural light that streamed through the paper panels, the door opened onto some kind of garden or courtyard.

Father Mateo pointed to the door. "Where does that lead?"

Hiro wished the Jesuit would remember that samurai considered pointing rude.

"Nowhere," Akira said. "That is, it leads outside, but nowhere in particular. There's a veranda and a garden with a path that leads across the grounds. We think that's how the murderer escaped."

"So it seems." Father Mateo eyed the smudges of rusty blood around the door. "Do the tracks continue outside?"

Akira shook his head. "The killer must have removed his *tabi*." He looked at Hiro. "The priest understands the word '*tabi*,' socks?"

Hiro nodded. "Were the *tabi* left behind?"

"Unfortunately, no."

Hiro glanced at the desk. The document on top of the pile was a handwritten list of names. Elaborate characters flowed down the page with a rare precision that Hiro recognized as Kazu's. He examined the desk and the floor around it but saw no sign of blood.

As he turned, he noticed something in the bloody pool. He crouched and squinted, trying to identify the object without touching it.

"What room is that?" Father Mateo indicated the open door at the northern end of the room. This time, to Hiro's relief, the priest remembered to gesture like a Japanese.

"Saburo's private office," Akira said.

Hiro returned his attention to the floor.

A hair pin lay near the center of the pool of congealing blood. The pin resembled a chopstick with a spray of delicate silver flowers attached to the thicker end. The wood appeared to be lacquered, and possibly inlaid, but the blackening blood obscured the finer details.

Hiro leaned in for a closer look.

Father Mateo joined him. "What is that?"

"A *kanzashi*," Hiro said, "a woman's hair pin."

"Don't touch it," Akira snapped. "We're not to move anything before the family arrives."

Except the body, Hiro thought.

"Was Ashikaga-*san* lying faceup or facedown?" Hiro asked. "Who found him here?"

The lack of a body made it hard to reconstruct the murder scene, though Hiro hadn't really expected to find the corpse in place. Murder dishonored the victim, and leaving Saburo where he fell would embarrass the shogun's clan.

"A maid discovered the body," Akira said. "I didn't see it before it was moved and didn't ask about the position."

"Didn't the shogun order the scene preserved?" Father Mateo looked confused.

"That wouldn't include the body," Hiro said. "Respect for the dead takes precedence."

"Where did they take him?" the Jesuit asked.

Hiro gestured toward the opposite side of the room. "To his private office."

"How did you know that?" Akira's eyes widened with surprise.

"A guess, but it seemed the logical place until his family arrives." Hiro stood up. "May we see the body?"

"If you wish."

Hiro crossed the room, taking care to avoid the rusty drops on the floor. He could only imagine Ana's wrath if he stained his socks with blood.

Saburo's inner office also measured six mats, large for a clerk of Saburo's rank but consistent with his relationship to the shogun. A free-standing wooden desk near the eastern wall meant Saburo could face the veranda or the inner door, depending on the weather and his mood. A wooden back rest sat on the far side of the desk, indicating Saburo had faced the inner office the night he died.

A bloody *tanto* lay on the near side of the desk. Dark smears encrusted the dagger's blade and stained the lacquered wooden handle.

Even at a distance, Hiro recognized the weapon as a perfect match to Kazu's custom swords.

Saburo lay on his back beside the desk with his arms at his sides and his feet toward the door. The front of his torn kimono was drenched in blood, while more blood crusted the right side of his face. His hair had come loose from its samurai knot, presumably during the struggle. The crusty strands clung to his face like leftover noodles inside a dirty bowl.

Someone had closed Saburo's eyes, but the gesture didn't do much to improve his appearance.

Hiro knelt beside the body to confirm the cause of death. The amount of blood suggested exsanguination, and the *tanto* appeared to confirm it. The shinobi saw no injuries to Saburo's head or neck, but the three wounds in the samurai's chest all could have proven fatal. At least one, and possibly two, had pierced his heart.

A heavy metallic odor rose from the corpse, along with a faint, sickly sweet smell that Hiro recognized as the scent of death.

He looked over his shoulder. "May I touch him?"

Akira blanched. "Why would you want to?"

Hiro laid his thumb on Saburo's left cheek. The mottled skin had cooled to match the surrounding air and the muscles resisted pressure. They felt tense and hard beneath Hiro's thumb. Several hours had passed since the samurai's death.

The flesh beneath the bloody side of Saburo's face looked purple, though not very dark. Hardly surprising, given the copious blood loss.

"How long do you think he's been dead?" Father Mateo asked.

Hiro looked up, surprised that the Jesuit guessed—correctly—what the shinobi was trying to discern. "At least nine hours, maybe more. I'd say he died after dark, but before midnight."

"You didn't have to touch him." Akira sounded disgusted. "We already know he was killed last night. Besides, how does a translator know so much about death?"

Hiro forced the bitter smile of a ronin. "I was not always as I am now." He indicated Saburo's ragged and bloody sleeve. "See the slash marks? He fought his killer."

"Why would a killer strike the arm?" Akira asked.

Hiro raised his hand to cover his face. "Ashikaga-*san* was protecting himself."

Father Mateo pointed to a sheath at Saburo's side. "Why didn't he draw his sword?"

"Because he had nothing to grip it with." Hiro reached across the body and raised the corpse's rigid arm. Three of the right-hand fingers were missing. The last one dangled from the hand like a fish on a line, attached by only a paper-thin flap of skin.

Father Mateo paled and ran a hand through his hair. "How did that happen?"

Hiro nodded to the desk. "I'm guessing the *tanto.*"

"That is the murder weapon," Akira confirmed. "It was lodged in Saburo's back."

Father Mateo closed his eyes and looked away. "Would you put that arm down please?"

Hiro shrugged and laid the arm at Saburo's side. "Did someone recover the fingers?"

Akira nodded. "The family will want them for the funeral."

Hiro took hold of Saburo's bloody kimono. "Let's turn him over."

"Stop," Akira protested, "You shouldn't—"

But the objection came too late.

Chapter 7

Hiro and Father Mateo rolled the corpse onto its stomach.

"Don't do that," Akira objected.

"Don't worry," Hiro said, "I'll turn him over again before anyone sees him. We need to know exactly how he died to determine who killed him."

Saburo's back looked cleaner than his chest. The single wound between his shoulders had barely bled enough to stain the surrounding fabric.

"That's where the dagger was found?" Hiro indicated the wound.

"I don't know," Akira said. "I wasn't there. Is that the wound that killed him?"

"No," Hiro said. "He was already dead when this happened, or very close."

"You can tell that?" Akira asked. "How?"

"Men don't bleed after death," Hiro said. "Blood drains from the wounds, but only for a little while and only in the direction of the ground."

"Which means Ashikaga-*san* died facedown," Akira said. He straightened as if remembering that death defiled everyone who came in contact with it. "How can you stand to touch him?"

Hiro smiled. "Fortunately, I live with a priest who can bless the defilement away."

Father Mateo gave the shinobi a sideways look. Hiro would rather receive a beating than a blessing.

They rolled the corpse back to its original position. Saburo's blood-drenched kimono left smudges on the pale floor, but Hiro doubted anyone would notice. With all the blood, some stains would be expected.

He had learned all he could from the body. He stood up and studied the room.

Neatly organized bookshelves covered the western wall. Bound volumes occupied the upper shelves while the lower ones held both books and scrolls. Spaces revealed where volumes had been removed, though Hiro didn't notice an obvious pattern.

Saburo's desk looked equally in order. An inkwell and a pitcher of water sat in the right-hand corner, alongside a round ceramic container of pasty vermilion ink. A cylindrical marble seal stood upright beside the container. The seal represented Saburo's official signature, and Hiro found it interesting that the murderer didn't steal it.

A tray of dirty dishes sat on the floor beside the door to the outer office.

"Did Saburo often eat here?" Hiro asked.

Akira followed his gaze. "I wouldn't know. I didn't have much contact with this office."

Hiro noticed some tiny particles on the floor between the desk and the doorway. He picked one up and rubbed it between his fingers as he raised it to his nose.

"What are you doing?" Akira asked.

Hiro inhaled, then lowered his hand and balanced the speck on his finger. "This is sawdust. Cedar, to be exact."

"Carpenters' dust," Akira said. "It gets everywhere from the construction."

Hiro remembered the spotless floor around the construction site. Before he decided whether to mention it, Father Mateo asked, "How often are these offices cleaned?"

"Every evening." Akira frowned. "Someone must have tracked that in last night, or this morning when they moved Saburo."

"We would like to speak with the carpenters," Hiro said, "and also with the maid who discovered the body."

"The carpenters should be here soon," Akira said, "but Hisahide sent the girl to spend a few days with her parents."

Hiro noted the use of Matsunaga Hisahide's given name. It surprised him. Most men would never refer to their superiors so casually, and until that moment Akira had seemed unusually polite by nature.

"Does the girl's family live far away?" Father Mateo asked.

"I believe they live in Kyoto," Akira said.

"Would it be possible to send a messenger for her?" Hiro asked. "I would like to know exactly what she saw."

"A wise request," said a voice from the outer office.

A samurai stepped into the room with the silent grace of a tiger. His graying hair was pulled back from a shaven forehead that crowned a handsome, emotionless face. He wore a black kimono adorned with the double-diamond Miyoshi mon, and his swords were sheathed in expensive scabbards. His confident posture and slender but muscular build suggested unusual fitness, especially in a man of middle age.

Hiro bowed. Father Mateo followed. The samurai merely nodded in return.

"Greetings, Matsunaga-*sama*," Akira said, using the higher honorific expected of an assistant addressing a master. "May I introduce the foreign priest, Father Mat-teo Avilo, and his translator, Matsui Hiro."

Hiro bowed again, an unnecessary gesture but one that obligated Hisahide to speak first.

"You are the man who captured Akechi Hideyoshi's murderer." Hisahide looked at Hiro as he spoke.

"Father Mateo solved the crime," the shinobi said. "I am merely his translator."

Hisahide smiled. "You are Matsui Hiro of Iga Province, second and only surviving son of Matsui Jiro. Your father served his daimyo with honor, though his early death forced you to come to Kyoto and seek employment as a scribe. Three years ago, this foreigner hired you as a translator—a most unfortunate turn of fate, though reports suggest you bear the burden honorably."

"Thank you, Matsunaga-*sama*," Hiro said with another bow.

The information was mostly wrong, but it accurately reflected the story Hiro had planted upon his arrival in Kyoto. He was glad to know his cover story had fooled the Miyoshi spies.

"The shogun expects me to find and punish the man who killed his cousin," Hisahide said, "and I expect both of you to help me do it."

"We would be honored to assist your investigation," Father Mateo said.

Hisahide turned to Akira. "You may leave us and send a messenger for the maid who found Saburo."

Frustration flickered across Akira's face, but the man bowed and left the room without a word.

When he had gone Hisahide said, "The shogun believes there is no real need for investigation. The dagger that killed Saburo belongs to a man named Ito Kazu." He looked at Hiro. "I also know that Ito-*san* is a friend of yours."

Hiro returned Hisahide's stare. He suspected the Akechi investigation was just a convenient excuse to get him to the shogunate. If Kazu couldn't be found and punished, a friend or family member would have to do.

"Ito Kazu is an acquaintance," Hiro said. "We met at Ginjiro's brewery shortly after I arrived in Kyoto. When we realized we were both from Iga, Kazu offered to help me find a job. Unfortunately, his efforts were unsuccessful."

"I am told you drink together often," Hisahide said.

"Sometimes," Hiro said. "We reminisce about Iga. All men miss their ancestral homes."

Hisahide's face revealed nothing. "Where is Kazu this morning?"

"If he murdered a man, he probably fled the city," Hiro said. "It's what I would have done in his place."

"Perhaps, but your response does not answer my question."

Chapter 8

Hiro admired Hisahide's resistance to distraction. "I do not know where Ito Kazu is this morning," he said.

It was technically true. He hadn't seen Kazu since dawn.

"Forgive my ignorance," Father Mateo said, "but if you know who committed the murder, why did you ask for our help?"

Hiro suspected the ignorance was feigned. Father Mateo knew enough about samurai justice to recognize the danger.

"The shogun requested you, not me," Hisahide said, "and I believe he wanted you more for your connection to Kazu than anything else. But since you are here, I see no reason not to utilize your skills."

Hisahide glanced toward the outer office. "Many people—Akira included—agree that the evidence leaves no room for doubt, but I am not completely convinced of Ito-*san*'s guilt. He is known for competence, yet no competent man would leave his weapon behind. This troubles me, even though I cannot question the shogun's interpretation of the evidence without proof to the contrary."

"I understand," Hiro said. A seed of doubt about Kazu's innocence sprouted in his mind. A shinobi assassin might leave his weapon as a distraction, precisely because no samurai would do so. Hiro might have chosen to do the same in Kazu's place—assuming Kazu was the killer, which suddenly seemed more likely than Hiro wanted to admit.

"The shogun wants me to question Ito-*san*," Hisahide said, "and I will do so when he arrives for work this morning. In the meantime, you will make no assumptions about his guilt or innocence. Can you do this, despite your familiarity?"

"We can and we will," Father Mateo said.

Hisahide's gaze fell on Hiro.

"We will uncover the truth, however unpleasant," Hiro said, though he wouldn't promise what he would do with the information once he had it.

"You have three days to identify the killer," Hisahide said.

"Three days?" Hiro repeated.

"It was sufficient to find Akechi Hideyoshi's killer," Hisahide said, "or so I am told."

That crime had taken place a year before. The investigation hadn't been public, but the Akechi clan had ties to the shogun and information traveled well in Kyoto.

"Three days is a very short time to catch a murderer," Father Mateo said.

"Then you will work quickly," Hisahide replied. "Daimyo Oda has sent an embassy to Kyoto. His men will arrive by the eighteenth day of the month—four days from now—and Saburo's killer must be caught and punished before they arrive. The shogunate cannot seem vulnerable to attack."

"What if we cannot solve the crime so quickly?" Father Mateo asked.

"A murderer will die before Lord Oda's men arrive," Hisahide said. "One way or another."

Hiro understood the threat. Innocence wouldn't save Kazu if the guilty party escaped. Unfortunately, with Kazu gone, Hiro and Father Mateo were next in line and equally viable candidates for punishment. The law would hold Hiro liable because he was Kazu's friend. But the chain of responsibility extended upward too, and Father Mateo was Hiro's official employer. If anyone suspected Hiro of helping Kazu escape, or decided to punish him in Kazu's absence, the Jesuit would share the shinobi's penalty.

Father Mateo frowned. "We will not help you kill an innocent man."

Hiro glanced at the priest in surprise. He hadn't expected Father Mateo to catch Hisahide's meaning.

The samurai looked equally startled, though the surprise left his face as quickly as it appeared.

"Foreigners do not set conditions for obedience," Hisahide said. "I will forgive your ignorance once, but you will not repeat this mistake."

Hiro hoped the priest would apologize, or at least retract his objection, but he doubted Father Mateo would do either. The Jesuit had a dangerous dedication to moral truth.

The shinobi had almost decided to make an apology on Father Mateo's behalf when the priest bowed deeply and said, "I apologize for my lack of discretion."

Hiro's momentary relief disappeared as the Jesuit continued, "I mistakenly believed the Bushido code required a samurai to seek justice rather than executing an innocent man merely to ensure that a crime is punished."

Father Mateo held Hisahide's gaze without faltering.

Hisahide smiled but his eyes were cold. "If I wanted empty justice, Ito Kazu would already be dead. That said, I will keep the shogunate out of Lord Oda's hands at any price. One innocent life means nothing when compared with the cost of war."

Hiro spoke up to keep the Jesuit silent. "We will find the real killer in three days' time, provided you place no restrictions on our movement."

"Impossible," Hisahide said. "The shogun cannot be disturbed, and this murder must not be made a public spectacle."

"We will use discretion," Hiro said, "but we must have sufficient freedom to investigate."

He hoped Hisahide would deny his demands and relieve them of the duty to solve the crime.

Instead, the samurai nodded. "I understand. You may investigate the *bakufu* mansion and grounds, but the shogun's personal quarters remain off limits. You may speak with servants and guards without restriction. I will schedule interviews with officials upon request.

"Will that suffice?"

"Yes," Father Mateo said. "We will abide by those constraints."

Hiro still wished Hisahide had sent them away.

Akira appeared in the doorway and bowed. "A messenger has gone to fetch the girl."

"Thank you, Akira," Hisahide said. "You will assist Father Mateo and Matsui-*san* with their investigation."

And report to Hisahide on our progress, Hiro thought.

Akira struggled to hide his dismay. Hiro didn't blame him. A daimyo's cousin was not a servant, but the order effectively made him one, at least for the next three days.

"If you will excuse me," Hisahide said, "I have business to attend to." He departed without awaiting a response.

Akira forced a smile. "Where would you like to begin?"

"Could we speak with the carpenters while we wait for the maid?" Hiro asked.

"The carpenters?" Akira sounded surprised. "Not Ito Kazu?"

"Matsunaga-*san* intends to conduct that interview himself," Hiro said. "He did not ask us to join him."

"What could a carpenter know?" Akira shook his head, suggesting typical samurai disdain for the lower classes.

"There is sawdust on the floor," Hiro said. "A samurai might have tracked it here but the carpenters may have seen or heard something useful."

Akira's mouth opened slightly in surprise. It apparently hadn't occurred to him that workers might listen to samurai conversations. He led Hiro and Father Mateo back through the outer office and into the audience room beyond.

A carpenter stood beside the sawhorses, plane in hand, surveying the cedar beam. He wore baggy trousers instead of the usual loincloth, doubtless a concession to shogunate formality.

When Akira entered the room the workman knelt and pressed his forehead to the floor.

On the opposite side of the room a second carpenter stood high on a ladder, measuring the transom space above the southern entrance. He had his back to Akira and didn't notice the samurai right away. Like the other workman, he wore trousers and a long-sleeved tunic. He had his voluminous sleeves pulled high on his arms and tied out of the way with a strip of cloth.

Akira had barely started across the room when the second carpenter lowered his measuring stick and descended the ladder. When he reached the ground he turned and bowed. He did not kneel or lay his head on the floor.

As he straightened, his face became an expectant mask, though Hiro noted unusual intelligence in his eyes. The shinobi had little doubt this man noticed everything that went on around him.

The only question was whether he would reveal it.

Chapter 9

Samurai owed no courtesy to commoners, and Akira wasted no time on greetings. "Introduce yourself."

The carpenter bowed again. "I am Master Carpenter Ozuru." He gestured to the kneeling man on the other side of the room. "My assistant is called Goro."

"This is Father Mateo of Portugal," Hiro said. "I am his translator, Matsui Hiro."

"These men are investigating a murder," Akira said. "You will answer their questions honestly and tell the entire truth. The foreigner has captured many criminals. He can recognize a lie before you speak it."

Ozuru's face remained a mask.

Akira bristled at the carpenter's lack of reaction, but before he could threaten the man again Father Mateo said, "Thank you for speaking with us."

Ozuru glanced at Goro.

"We do not require your assistant at this time," Hiro said.

Ozuru gestured to the kneeling man. "Up. I want the beam ready to hang when the others arrive."

Goro stood up, bowed, and retrieved his plane. He tried

not to stare at the foreigner, but his eyes kept darting to Father Mateo's face, reminding Hiro how strange the Jesuit's pale skin and Western features appeared to Japanese eyes.

Akira's lips twitched in an unwilling smile. "Please excuse me. I must check on the messenger's progress."

He disappeared through the southern door before anyone could respond.

Hiro turned his attention to Ozuru. The lines around the carpenter's eyes were caused by sun, not time. His wiry, muscled arms revealed strength, and although his hands were gnarled by work they lacked the darkened spots of advancing age.

A samurai would see only a peasant in stained and dusty trousers, but Hiro understood that carpentry demanded precision, artistic talent, and physical prowess at least as great as those required for swordplay. Only men with impeccable skills would achieve a master's title, and few of them would achieve it by middle age.

The shinobi knew, if Akira did not, that Ozuru deserved respect.

He was still deciding how to approach the interview when Father Mateo said, "Please tell us anything you know about Ashikaga-*san*'s murder."

Hiro looked at the priest in disbelief. Directness was anathema to the Japanese.

"I know only that he was killed," Ozuru said, "and learned that only when I arrived for work this morning."

"Did you work yesterday?" Hiro asked.

"Yes, from dawn until two hours after sunset. I stayed late to work on the transom carving." He pointed to the wooden screen that rested against the wall. When complete, the elaborate transom panel would cover the gap between the top of the doors and the ceiling while also allowing air flow between the rooms.

"You are skilled," Father Mateo said.

Ozuru bowed his head humbly. "Thank you, Father-Mateo-*sama*." He pronounced the name and honorific as a single word. "My father was a carpenter, my grandfather a master carver. They trained me in both disciplines."

He spoke carefully, and with simple words, to ensure the priest understood.

"Would you like to see the screens more closely?" he offered.

Father Mateo seemed inclined to agree, but Hiro had no intention of letting the carpenter distract them from their objective.

"Do you work late often?" Hiro asked.

Ozuru paused before answering, as if he no longer remembered the previous topic. At last he nodded in understanding. "Yes, quite often. My assistants leave at sundown and I stay to work in silence."

"Most artisans have a workshop," Hiro said.

"As do I," Ozuru replied, "but the shogun demands that I do my work on the premises. He believes it leads to faster completion, and I am in no position to argue with samurai."

"The shogun wants the work finished quickly?" Father Mateo asked.

"Yes," Ozuru glanced at the ceiling, "because of the rats."

"Rats?" the Jesuit looked up quickly.

"They live above the ceilings, under the roof," Ozuru said. "It would be most inconvenient for a rat to jump down on a passing samurai."

"Does that happen?" Father Mateo's eyes widened.

Ozuru shrugged. "It depends how long the roof goes un-repaired."

Once again the conversation had drifted away from the murder.

"Where did you go when you left last night?" Hiro asked.

"Home, as always."

"Did you stop on the way?"

"No," Ozuru said, "and I live alone, so no one can tell you what time I arrived or confirm that I went directly to sleep, though I did."

Hiro heard no defensiveness in the carpenter's voice. If anything, Ozuru seemed amused.

"How long have you worked here?" Hiro asked.

"For the shogun? Or in this room?"

Hiro didn't answer.

"This project began a month ago," Ozuru said, "but I've worked in this compound off and on for several years. I succeeded the previous master when he retired."

"Do you know why someone would want to kill Ashikaga Saburo?" Father Mateo asked.

"Walls have ears," Ozuru said with a smile, "but intelligent workmen have none."

"What about you?" Hiro asked. "Did you argue with Ashikaga-*san*?"

Ozuru's smile faded. "What makes you ask?"

The question had been instinctive, but it seemed to have hit a mark.

Hiro hazarded a version of the truth. "I understand Ashikaga-*san* did not appreciate independent men, particularly those who fail to grovel."

Ozuru gave Hiro an appraising look. "You have guessed correctly. I will not hide the truth. Last night Ashikaga-*san* complained about the noise of my chisel and ordered me to leave. I refused, and he grew angry."

"You refused?" Father Mateo started to raise a hand to his hair, but lowered it. Hiro took the averted gesture as a sign of the priest's surprise.

"The shogun imposed strict deadlines on this work." Ozuru indicated the open ceiling. "My job depends on completing this room within the next three days.

"I have never missed a deadline. I won't miss this one, despite the shortened time. The shogun gave me permission to work as many hours as necessary. Ashikaga-*san* had no right to countermand that order."

"Did you tell Ashikaga-*san* about the shogun's instructions?" Hiro asked.

Ozuru's lips raised in a humorless smile. "Ashikaga-*san* was not a man to whom carpenters explain anything."

Akira strode into the room. "The maid has arrived. She is waiting for you in the kitchen."

Chapter 10

"Thank you for speaking with us," Father Mateo said to Ozuru.

The carpenter bowed and returned to work as Akira gave the Jesuit a disapproving look.

Hiro and Father Mateo followed the samurai back into the passage that passed Saburo's office and several other shoji, though the doors were shut, obscuring the rooms beyond.

At the opposite end of the passage from where they entered, they emerged from the mansion onto a covered veranda abutting a graveled courtyard. A covered walkway led to a one-story kitchen.

Hiro looked down and saw his geta, and Father Mateo's, waiting at the edge of the veranda, along with a third pair of about Akira's size.

Akira followed the shinobi's gaze. "I had a servant bring our sandals."

Hiro nodded and stepped down into his shoes. Akira and Father Mateo did the same.

The air carried a smoky odor of grilling meat. Hiro's stomach growled as he followed Akira across the yard and up the two wooden steps to the kitchen entrance. The samurai pushed open the swinging doors, revealing a servants' chamber.

The six-mat room provided a place for maids and other servants to wait between duties. A kettle hung from a chain above the central hearth, as it would in the common room of a home. Tatami covered the floor, though the mats were of lower quality than the ones in the *bakufu* mansion. The paneled wooden walls did little to muffle the chopping and clattering from the adjacent kitchen.

A woman knelt by the hearth. She wore a blue kimono and orange obi, and Hiro placed her age at almost twenty. She had an unusual face, the features attractive individually but mismatched as a whole. Full lips overwhelmed her almond eyes and her hair, though glossy, was far too unruly for beauty.

She saw Akira and bowed her face to the mat. As she straightened, she noticed Father Mateo. She smiled and clasped her hands in supplication.

"Do not stare!" Akira ordered.

"I apologize." She ducked her chin and looked at the floor.

"These men have questions about Ashikaga-*san*'s murder," Akira said. "They want to hear about how you discovered the body."

The woman nodded. Her nose turned red. Pink blotches appeared on her cheeks.

Hiro knew Father Mateo could persuade the girl to speak, but only if Akira left the room. Few maids had the courage to speak in front of highly ranked samurai, and the girl's initial reaction wasn't encouraging.

Hiro bowed to Akira. "Miyoshi-*san*, may I beg a favor? I

have heard that the *bakufu* keeps detailed records of visitors. Could you obtain a list of the people who entered the shogunate yesterday?"

"Every one?" Akira asked.

"Every one who did not leave by sunset," Hiro said. "I regret the inconvenience, but we would be grateful if you obtained this information before we leave."

Akira frowned.

"We understand if you cannot do it," Father Mateo said. "Please let us know who else to ask."

The Jesuit seemed unaware of the insult in his words. No samurai could accuse another of weakness or incompetence without consequence. Fortunately, in a foreigner's mouth the comment seemed only an ignorant oversight.

Still, Hiro wondered whether Akira would take offense.

After a moment, the samurai nodded curtly. "I can obtain the information."

Father Mateo bowed. "We are in your debt."

"Do not leave this room until I return." Akira turned on his heel and left the building.

As Hiro hoped, the maid relaxed the moment Akira departed. She unfolded her hands and laid them in her lap. A quavering smile flickered over her face.

"May I offer you tea?" She raised her face to Father Mateo.

"No, thank you." The Jesuit knelt opposite the maid. "May I ask your name?"

Hiro noted with approval that Father Mateo did not introduce himself. No samurai would offer his name to a woman of lesser rank. Few enough would bother to ask a servant's name at all, though Hiro knew the Jesuit always would.

"I am called Jun," she said.

"You serve the shogun?" Father Mateo asked.

"I am a maid at the shogunate." Her gaze fell to the floor. "I have never seen the shogun. This is because I am not beautiful. My father says I look more like the pit than the peach."

"Yet when the peach falls away the pit remains constant," Father Mateo said.

Hiro doubted any woman would fall for such awkward and obvious flattery, but Jun blushed and covered her smile with her hands.

"My translator and I are trying to learn who killed Ashikaga Saburo," Father Mateo said. "We would appreciate any help you can give us."

Jun's eyes widened. She shook her head. "I didn't see the murder. I don't know."

She bit her lip.

"Don't be frightened," Father Mateo said. "Just tell me what you saw."

She swallowed hard and took a deep breath to calm herself. "Last night I took a tray of food to Ashikaga-*san* in his office. He often ate meals there when working late.

"Early this morning, I went to retrieve the tray. Ashikaga-*san* does not like dirty dishes in his office when he arrives." She paused. "He was there, on the floor. There was blood . . ."

She raised her hands to her mouth. Tears welled up in her reddening eyes. Her shoulders heaved with her efforts to keep from crying.

Father Mateo waited while she regained control.

At last she lowered her hands and continued, "I screamed. Someone came and pushed me out of the room."

"Who was it?" Father Mateo asked.

"I don't remember. I was crying. Ashikaga-*san* was dead

when I found him. I don't know who did it. May his ghost haunt me forever if I lie." Jun's breathing grew rapid. The pink spots on her cheeks flushed crimson.

Her tears looked real, but Hiro thought her story sounded rehearsed.

Father Mateo waited in silence as Jun regained her composure yet again.

Hiro became impatient. The interview wasn't proceeding as effectively as he hoped. In fact, he believed the girl was playing a role. Before he figured out how to prove it, Father Mateo asked, "Can you think of anyone who wanted to kill Ashikaga-*san*?"

The girl looked horrified. "No."

"Did you ever hear anyone argue with him?"

Jun's eyes widened. She shook her head. "No. He was a good man."

And you are a liar, Hiro thought, but he had no chance to say so.

The door slid open behind him. Akira had returned.

Chapter 11

The shogun's guards report no visitors yesterday evening," Akira said. "All business was concluded and all petitioners left the compound more than an hour before they closed the gates for the night."

He narrowed his eyes at the maid. "Did she tell you everything you need to know?"

Jun looked at the floor.

"She was most helpful." Father Mateo stood up and straightened his kimono. "We have no further questions. She was not involved in the crime."

"I could have told you that," Akira said. "If you are finished I will escort you to the gates."

Akira led them out of the kitchen and through the well-groomed gardens surrounding the *bakufu* mansion. The clouds had darkened and the smell of rain increased.

As they passed a koi pond Hiro asked, "Can the guards confirm that no strangers entered the compound after dark last night?"

"Of course," Akira said. "I interviewed most of them personally this morning. No one entered the compound after they closed the gates at sunset."

"What time did Ozuru leave?" Hiro asked.

Akira's forehead wrinkled as he tried to place the name. "The carpenter? The guards wouldn't know that. Workmen use the stable gate, which is locked at sundown. Anyone leaving later would have to see the stable master."

"Did you speak with him this morning?" Hiro asked.

"There was no need."

"May we speak with the stable master now?" Father Mateo asked.

Akira altered his course to the west and led them onto an earthen path wide enough for two horsemen to ride abreast.

To their right, the shogun's private mansion sat behind high walls at the center of an artificial lake. Unlike the *bakufu* mansion, where government business and audiences took place, the shogun's palace was strictly off limits except to the shogun, his women, and his guards.

Past the palace, the path curved right and continued along the inner side of the compound's southern and western walls until it reached the stable yard, an open area large enough to saddle and exercise the shogun's horses.

At the western side of the yard, a pair of massive wooden gates stood open to the street. Beyond them, Hiro caught a glimpse of a wooden bridge and half a dozen armored samurai guards.

Just past the gates, but inside the compound, a long, low stable huddled against the western wall.

"Does the shogun always have guards at this gate?" Father Mateo asked.

"In the daytime," Akira said, "but only four. He ordered extra guards this morning because of the murder."

Hiro looked at the stable as he listened. The wide doors

on the building's southern end stood open, allowing a view of the dim interior. Windows along the eastern wall were covered with angled wooden slats to allow the passage of air and a little light.

A muscular man emerged from the stable. Silver hair stood up on his head like the bristles of an ancient boar. His crooked nose had broken and healed more than once. He wore a faded surcoat and baggy trousers that flared as he bowed to Hiro and the others.

"Good morning, Miyoshi-*san*," the stableman said to Akira. He smiled in greeting, revealing a missing upper tooth.

Akira did not return the greeting. Instead he told Father Mateo, "Masao is the shogun's stable master. He can tell you what time the carpenters left yesterday."

"I apologize," Masao said, "but I fear I cannot. I was not here when they left."

Akira's eyes narrowed. His lips turned down. "Where were you?"

"My cousin came to Kyoto yesterday, on business. We ate dinner together near Sanjō Bridge. I left before sunset and returned about an hour after midnight."

"Is your cousin still in Kyoto?" Hiro asked, "To confirm your story?"

"Unfortunately, no. He finished his business yesterday and planned to leave the city at dawn this morning."

"Where was he going?" Father Mateo asked.

"He owns an apothecary shop at Ōtsu, on the Tōkaidō Road. He comes to Kyoto once a month for supplies."

"Tōkaidō," Father Mateo repeated. "The travelers' road between Kyoto and Edo?"

"Yes. Ōtsu is the first station outside Kyoto."

"Who watched the stable in your absence?" Hiro asked.

"The guards would have locked the gates at sunset," Masao said. "After that, no one. The horses don't need care through the evening."

"What about Den?" Akira asked.

Masao glanced at the gates. "He's away, seeing relatives in the country."

Hiro suspected a lie. "Who is Den?"

"My apprentice," Masao said. "He lives here with me."

"He must miss his family," Father Mateo said. "Does he visit them often?"

"Not often." Masao said. "His parents are farmers . . . poor."

He spoke the last word quietly. Hiro understood. Many farmers could barely afford to feed themselves, let alone their children.

"When did Den leave?" Hiro asked.

"Yesterday afternoon," Masao said. "He wanted to pass the checkpoints before sunset."

"Then no one watched the gate after dark," Hiro said.

"That is correct."

Hiro opened his mouth, but before he could speak Akira asked, "Then who let the carpenter out?"

Masao looked confused. "The carpenters leave at sunset. The guards would have let them out."

"The master carpenter, Ozuru, worked late last night," Hiro said.

"He must have left by the other gate," Masao said. "This one was locked when I returned. I came back through the eastern gate myself."

Akira frowned. "The guards didn't tell me that."

"Do you know that a man was murdered here last night?" Father Mateo asked.

Masao nodded. "I saw Jun as she left this morning."

"You know the maid by name?" Hiro asked.

"Of course," Masao said. "She brings us leftovers from the kitchen, though I suspect she intends them more for Den than for me." He smiled fondly, but the smile faded as he noticed Akira's frown. "Their relationship is appropriate and properly supervised."

Hiro changed the subject. "Did you see Ashikaga-*san* yesterday?"

"I must have." Masao glanced upward, thinking. "He always arrives after dawn, on horseback. I stable his horse. I don't remember yesterday being different."

"Is his horse in the stable?" Hiro asked.

"No. The messenger who carried the news to Ashikaga-*san*'s family took it with him."

"Very considerate," Father Mateo said. "Do you know who would want to kill Ashikaga-*san*?"

Masao shook his head. "I'm sorry. The news was a surprise to me."

"If you remember anything else, or hear anything of interest, please let us know," Hiro said.

"My house is on Marutamachi Road," Father Mateo added, "just past Okazaki Shrine. You are welcome there any time and for any reason."

Akira narrowed his eyes at the priest.

Masao bowed. "Thank you." He bowed even more deeply to Akira.

Hooves thumped on the drawbridge. A child's voice shouted, "Master Masao!"

Hiro turned as a bay horse trotted into the yard. On its back sat a boy of about ten years. His unshaven forehead marked him as a child, not yet an adult samurai, but his hair was long and tied back in a warrior's knot. He wore a gray kimono emblazoned with the Ashikaga mon—a black-edged circle with five horizontal bars, alternating black and white.

The boy's handsome features looked eerily familiar.

Hiro had seen them not an hour before, on a dead man's face.

Chapter 12

Father Mateo leaned toward Hiro but fixed his eyes on the boy. "Do you think that's Saburo's son?" he whispered in Portuguese.

"I've never seen a stronger family resemblance," Hiro said.

A second rider entered the yard, a samurai woman whose face bore a strong and unfortunate resemblance to her aging mare. Her gray-streaked hair was pulled back without adornment, though she wore an expensive gray kimono cut in the latest style.

Masao approached the woman's horse, bowed low, and held the animal steady as she dismounted.

The boy didn't wait for assistance. He slipped off his horse with practiced ease and pulled the reins over its head. He patted the animal's neck and turned to Akira.

The samurai ignored the child but bowed to the woman. "Good morning, Ashikaga-*dono*. I am sorry for your loss."

Father Mateo stepped closer to Hiro and whispered, "-*Dono*? Not -*san*?"

Hiro switched to Portuguese. "-*San* implies the speaker's inferiority to the person addressed. Polite self-deprecation, if you will. -*Dono* implies equal rank—it's less polite, though permitted when a samurai speaks to a woman."

The boy took a step toward Akira.

"What about me?" he asked. "I have lost my father. The least you can do is bow."

Hiro hid his surprise as Akira complied with the child's demand. "My condolences, young master Ashikaga."

The boy watched Akira's bow with a critical eye. He seemed disinclined to return it, but Saburo's wife gave her son a look and the boy bent forward gracefully.

As he straightened, he noticed Father Mateo. His mouth fell open in surprise and he hurried toward the foreign priest. When he reached a comfortable speaking distance he stopped, pulled his hands to his sides, and bowed.

"*Bun dia*," he said in strongly accented Portuguese. "You are not Father Virera, though you are from his country, I think."

The boy's pronunciation needed work, and he mangled Father Vilela's name, but few Japanese spoke Portuguese at all.

"*Bom dia*," Father Mateo said.

The boy cocked his head to the side like a bird inspecting an interesting seed.

"*Bom dia*," he repeated. This time he pronounced it perfectly.

"And to you." The Jesuit bowed low and switched to Japanese. "My name is Father Mateo."

"I am Ashikaga Ichiro, only son of Ashikaga Saburo. This is my mother, Lady Netsuko." After a pause he added, "I have not seen you here before."

"I work in another part of Kyoto," Father Mateo said, "near Okazaki Shrine."

The boy's eyes widened. "There are two Christian temples in Kyoto?" He looked at Akira. "Did you know this?"

"There is only one of consequence." Akira gave the Jesuit a hostile look. "These men are helping us find your father's killer."

Ichiro looked at Hiro. "And you? What is your name?"

Hiro bowed. "I am Matsui Hiro, Father Mateo's translator and scribe."

The boy looked from Hiro to the priest. "He seems to speak our language well enough."

"Simple phrases, yes." Hiro offered the standard explanation. "But he often misses the finer implications of Japanese speech."

Ichiro considered this. After a moment he nodded once and continued, "Your speech has the accent of Iga Province. Do you know Ito Kazu?" The boy frowned. "Kazu did not kill my father."

Hiro regarded Ichiro with surprise. "Does someone say he did?"

Before the boy could answer, his mother laid a restraining hand on his shoulder.

"My son must have overheard the messenger," she said, "the one who delivered the news of my husband's death. He claimed Saburo was killed with Kazu's dagger."

"Kazu did not do this." Ichiro looked and sounded like a tiny samurai.

Hiro decided to treat him as one. "Why do you think he is innocent?"

Netsuko spoke first. "Kazu was Ichiro's tutor."

"He remains my tutor, and I am not a child who needs a woman to speak in his place." Ichiro shook off his mother's arm. "You do not know Kazu as I do. He is an honorable man."

Ichiro's hands clenched at his sides. He looked at each man in turn, as if daring them to contradict his words.

"Indeed?" Hiro found the boy's reaction interesting. Except for his size, Ichiro didn't seem like a child.

"You do not believe me." Ichiro squared his shoulders. "I am fourteen and ready for *genpuku*."

He paused. His fists clenched tighter. His lips pressed into a line as he took a deep, slow breath. "That is, I would have been, had my father lived to approve Kazu's recommendation."

"I am very sorry," Hiro said. "Please accept my condolences." He found the boy's restraint impressive, especially under the circumstances.

"Thank you," Ichiro said. "I am pleased to have this chance to speak with the men investigating my father's death. I will not have Kazu wrongfully accused. I know him better than any of you, and I know he did not do this."

Hiro found the boy's loyalty surprising, particularly since Kazu had never mentioned Ichiro. Then again, Kazu didn't discuss his work in detail. No shinobi would.

Hiro felt a flash of regret for encouraging Kazu's flight. An innocent man should have stayed to defend himself. In the predawn confusion, an execution seemed inescapable. Now Hiro wasn't so certain. But then, he no longer felt sure of Kazu's innocence either.

Father Mateo bowed to Akira. "Thank you for your assistance this morning. We will leave you to escort Ashikaga-*san*'s family and return to continue our work in the afternoon."

The men exchanged bows, and Hiro and Father Mateo left the compound.

They walked as far as the Kamo River in silence. As they crossed the bridge Father Mateo asked, "What do you think? Is the boy correct about Kazu?"

That very question had bothered Hiro since leaving the shogunate. "Kazu claims he did not kill Saburo. As yet, I have no reason to think he lied. I am more concerned about finding the killer before Lord Oda's embassy arrives."

"Three days," Father Mateo said. "Perhaps the shogun would grant an extension?"

"No chance of that," Hiro said, "and if we fail to find the true murderer, Hisahide will probably execute me instead."

And perhaps you also.

"You?" Father Mateo raised his hands in surprise. "He didn't say that."

"Not openly, but he made his meaning clear. The shogun wants a dead murderer to impress Lord Oda's retainers, and an innocent corpse looks very much like a guilty one."

"But why you?" Father Mateo asked. "I know the law permits execution of relatives in a criminal's place, on the theory that the clan should pay for the crime, but you and Kazu are not related."

"We are both from Iga Province, and we are friends. That will suffice."

"You assumed all that from Hisahide's comments?" Father Mateo asked.

"I don't make assumptions and didn't need to. He made himself perfectly clear."

"To a samurai, maybe." Father Mateo shook his head in frustration. "A man should say what he means directly."

Hiro shrugged. It was not the Japanese way.

"If that's the case," the priest continued, "Kazu had better have told the truth."

Father Mateo said no more, but Hiro had the same thought himself.

"Indeed," the shinobi said, "I will find it most inconvenient if Kazu killed Saburo and left me to bear the punishment in his stead."

Chapter 13

Hiro and Father Mateo found Ana on the front porch of the Jesuit's house, wielding a broom like a warrior monk. She flung up clouds of dust with a force that made the shinobi wonder what new irritation caused the fit of pique.

She noticed the men approaching and laid one hand on her hip in a manner that boded ill for someone. Hiro didn't have to wonder who. In Ana's eyes, the Jesuit did no wrong.

The shinobi ran through the usual list of complaints, but came up empty. He hadn't brought sake home since Ana dumped the last flask in the koi pond to demonstrate her disapproval of alcohol, and she didn't know that Hiro was shinobi.

Still, she watched him approach like a mother preparing to paddle a naughty child.

"Hm," she sniffed as he reached the veranda. "You said your friend was leaving."

"He did leave." Hiro paused. "He came back?"

Relief flooded through him. If Kazu hadn't left Kyoto, they might still preserve the illusion of his innocence.

"Well, I don't mean Gato," Ana said.

"When did Kazu return?" Father Mateo asked.

"A few minutes after you left," she said. "I mistook him for a monk in that crazy outfit. He walked right into the house without even knocking. When I told him to leave, he took off his hat and said he would wait for you instead."

"And you let him?" Hiro hoped she let Kazu stay. He needed to talk with the younger shinobi before Hisahide did.

Ana's frown deepened the wrinkles around her eyes. "I didn't want to. But he threatened to tell the neighbors Father Mateo refused a meal to a monk in need. I couldn't let him say a thing like that!"

Hiro stifled a smile. Ana's loyalty made her easy to manipulate.

"I told him to wait by the hearth," she said, then added, "I didn't give him anything to eat."

She sounded triumphant. To Ana, withholding food was a serious punishment.

"Has Luis returned?" Father Mateo tried to sound conversational, but Hiro caught a hint of concern in his voice. The merchant could not be trusted to keep Kazu's visit secret.

"Not yet," Ana said.

Hiro stepped out of his sandals and onto the veranda. "I'll talk to Kazu. He won't stay long."

"Hm," Ana said, "he better not. You cause enough trouble. I don't need your vagrant friends underfoot." She raised the broom and resumed her vigorous sweeping.

Hiro found Kazu by the hearth. The basket-hat sat on the floor beside him.

"I'm sorry, Hiro." Kazu stood up and bowed. "The shogun has guards on all the roads. They're checking everyone, even monks."

"I'm glad you couldn't get through," Hiro said. "You need to get back to the shogunate."

"For my execution?" Kazu shook his head. "No thank you."

Ana's voice carried in from the porch. "Welcome back, Luis-*san*!"

Hiro appreciated the warning. "My room. Now."

Kazu scooped up the basket-hat and hurried across the *oe*. He slid open Hiro's door and disappeared through it. Hiro followed. He had just reached the doorway when Luis entered the common room.

The merchant's face looked even more flushed than usual, as if his doublet and puff-sleeved shirt conspired to strangle him. A pair of tight wool breeches did no favors for Luis's portly legs.

As always, Hiro found the merchant's Portuguese clothing foolish and inconvenient.

Luis glared at Hiro. "You people and your impossible demands," he fumed. "Why can't you understand simple logic?"

Hiro raised an eyebrow at the merchant.

Luis thumped across the tatami and flung himself down by the hearth with a heavy sigh. As usual, he took the host's position opposite the entrance.

"Ana!" he yelled. "Tea!"

Hiro heard the vehement swish of a broom against the veranda. Ana had no intention of responding to Luis's call.

Father Mateo tested the pot that hung above the hearth. "There's water here. You have tea in your room, don't you?"

"Assuming someone didn't steal it all." Luis stood up and pulled his green doublet down over his bulging stomach. His girth and the unfortunate color made Hiro think of a giant *sudachi*, though Luis's face looked even sourer than the bitter little citrus fruit.

Hiro started to enter his room, but Luis's next complaint made him pause.

"How on earth can he expect me to find two hundred arquebuses in three days' time?"

"Two hundred?" Father Mateo repeated.

"Yes," Luis grumbled. "An impossible number of fire-arms on an equally irrational timeline."

"Who wants them?" the Jesuit asked.

Luis hadn't stopped talking. "I told him it was impossible, but of course he wouldn't listen. Samurai are all alike. Demand, insist, threaten—that's all they know. If the profits didn't run so high, I'd have left this godforsaken island years ago."

"God has not forsaken Japan." Father Mateo spoke with unusual sharpness.

Luis snorted.

Hiro could see the priest preparing to argue and jumped in to keep the conversation going. "Why does this samurai need the weapons so quickly?"

Luis turned, eager to continue his litany of complaints. "A show of force, to keep some uppity lord from attacking Kyoto. I told him the shogun could hold his compound with half that many firearms, but he insisted. No less than two hundred will do."

"So the shogun wants them?" Hiro asked.

"No." Luis shook his head. "One of his retainers. Matsu-something."

"Matsunaga Hisahide," Hiro said.

"That's the one."

"What will happen if the weapons don't arrive in time?" Hiro asked.

Luis looked smug. "Of course they'll get here in time. Most merchants couldn't have managed it, but I have special connections. Where do you think I've been? I rode to Osaka to check the warehouse there. They hadn't enough, but they expect a shipment today or tomorrow and said they would send them on immediately."

"Dispatch is no guarantee of arrival," Hiro said.

Luis sniffed. "This sale will fund Mateo's work for a year, and my own share is nothing to sneer at. I'll see that the arquebuses arrive on time."

The merchant turned back to Father Mateo, dismissing Hiro from the conversation. The shinobi didn't mind. He stepped into his room and closed the door behind him.

The room looked empty, but Hiro knew better. He crossed to the futon chest and rapped softly on the lid.

"Kazu, it's safe to come out."

Chapter 14

The wooden chest opened, revealing Kazu's face. "How did you know where I was?"

"Because I put you there earlier," Hiro said, "and you've never been good at hiding."

"Not everyone can turn to smoke at will." Kazu stood up and stepped out of the chest. "Which reminds me. Why did Hanzo send the best shinobi in Iga to guard a priest?"

Hiro regarded the younger man evenly. "Should he have sent a novice, doomed to fail?"

Kazu could wonder about the assignment all he wished. Hiro would never reveal the truth—even if he had known it.

Instead, he changed the subject.

"Who killed Saburo?"

"I don't know," Kazu said. "If I did I would have turned him in myself."

"Ask around when you return to work. You might learn something."

Kazu's eyes widened. "I can't go back."

"You must. Hisahide doubts your guilt, and Saburo's son proclaims your innocence. Miyoshi Akira believes you're guilty, but I think we can persuade him otherwise."

"Persuade him?" Kazu shook his head. "I can't even explain where I was without looking guilty."

"I have a plan," Hiro said. "Is there somewhere you can hide for a few more hours?"

Kazu gestured. "What's wrong with here?"

"I won't risk Father Mateo's safety." Hiro indicated the woven hat. "Put your disguise back on and go into the city. Keep moving, and stay by the river—it's less busy in the rain. Don't talk if you can avoid it. And meet me at Ginjiro's three hours from now."

"How will staying away excuse my absence?" Kazu asked.

"Because you weren't absent," Hiro said. "You were drunk."

"Drunk?"

"Exceedingly drunk. You left Ginjiro's after midnight, already intoxicated. From there you went to a teahouse and drank yourself senseless. You woke up this afternoon under a bridge, with no idea how you got there."

"But I got hungry," Kazu said, picking up on the story, "and returned to Ginjiro's to eat." He nodded slowly. "You know, that might actually work."

"Only if we find the real killer in time." Hiro explained about the shogun's command and Hisahide's intent to fulfill it by any means necessary. When he finished, he added, "I need you to tell me everything you remember about Saburo. Someone wanted to kill him. The question is who?"

"Everyone wanted him dead," Kazu said, "but no one would dare to do it."

"Someone dared," Hiro said. "What do you mean by 'everyone wanted him dead'?"

"He never used a gentle word when harshness would suffice, and he thought himself the most important person in any room. No one likes a man like that."

In Hiro's mind dislike didn't translate to wishing for someone's death, but he let the comment pass. "Did Saburo have any arguments recently?"

"No more than usual." Kazu raised a hand, remembering. "Wait—he did have an argument yesterday evening.

"The carpenters finish their work at dusk, but we heard hammering into the evening hours. Saburo stormed out to see what was going on. I heard him yelling, but couldn't make out the words. He returned to the office angrier than he left."

"Did he explain why?"

"No, and I didn't ask, though I wondered what Ozuru said to provoke him."

"What makes you blame Ozuru?" Hiro noted that Kazu referred to the man by name.

"The other carpenters leave at sundown."

"Ozuru stays late?"

"Most evenings, yes. The shogun wants the work completed quickly, and the delicate carvings have to be finished on-site." Kazu shook his head slowly. "I don't think Ozuru did this. He's an artisan, not a killer."

"They're mutually exclusive?" Hiro asked.

"I'm more suspicious of Lady Netsuko." Kazu glanced at the door and lowered his voice to a whisper. "Saburo was not a faithful husband. Ichiro didn't know, but Netsuko did. Saburo claimed she didn't mind, but recently he complained that she grew intolerant of his mistress."

"But would she stab him to death?" Hiro wished he had looked more closely at Lady Netsuko. From what he remembered, she didn't seem physically capable of killing her husband in hand-to-hand combat.

"I don't know her well," Kazu said, "but she's an unusual woman and stronger than average."

"Physically or emotionally?"

"Both."

"Why kill him at the shogunate, risking witnesses?" Hiro asked. "That doesn't make sense."

"If she killed him at home, Ichiro might have seen her. She loves the boy. She wouldn't have wanted that."

"It's worth looking into," Hiro said, though he had no intention of doing so. "What did you actually do last night?"

Kazu gave him an innocent look. "I was passed out under a bridge, remember?"

Hiro frowned.

"I told you," Kazu said. "I left the shogunate and went to Ginjiro's, hoping Saburo would take his temper home and leave me in peace. When I returned to the office Saburo was dead."

"How did you leave the shogunate after you found him?"

"Back over the wall, so I wouldn't alert the guards. No one saw me enter or leave."

"All right," Hiro said, "wait ten minutes and leave by the veranda door. If Luis sees you, don't tell him your name. You're a wandering monk that Father Mateo allowed to spend the night in the garden."

"He won't question that?" Kazu asked.

"He'll find it foolish, but no, he won't ask questions."

Hiro left Kazu and returned to the common room. Father Mateo sat alone by the hearth.

"Where's Luis?" Hiro asked.

The Jesuit pointed to a door on the opposite side of the room. It led to Luis's chamber. "Sleeping, or so he said. Did you finish your business?"

"Yes, and now we need to return to the shogun's

compound. I want to talk with Ozuru. After that, we're going to Ginjiro's."

"The sake shop? Why?" Father Mateo looked confused.

"To witness Kazu's miraculous reappearance."

Chapter 15

Hiro and Father Mateo waited at the shogunate gates while the guards sent a runner for Akira.

One of the samurai guards regarded Father Mateo with interest, though social convention prevented him from addressing a higher-ranked man without invitation.

The Jesuit noticed and bowed.

Hiro stifled a disapproving sigh. Only foreigners and children ignored etiquette so bluntly. The shinobi cared little for social norms himself but recognized the importance of disappearing into a crowd. Then again, Father Mateo could hardly avoid attracting attention.

"Good morning," the Jesuit said.

The guard gave an awkward smile and bowed.

"Good morning, Father-*san*," he said as he straightened. "Please forgive my forwardness, but I am also a follower of the Jesus God, and yet I have never seen you in church. Are you new to Kyoto?"

"I have lived here almost three years," Father Mateo said, "but my work rarely brings me to Father Vilela's mission. I spread the Word among the merchants."

At least he didn't mention the entertainers and prostitutes, Hiro thought.

The guard looked curious rather than offended. "Does God hear commoners' prayers?"

"Our Lord was born a commoner," Father Mateo said.

The guard squinted as if trying to understand. "I never thought of that."

"Indeed," Father Mateo said. "God loves all men equally, regardless of status or birth."

Hiro turned and bowed as Akira arrived.

The young samurai ignored the shinobi's greeting. He narrowed his eyes at the guard. "The shogun does not pay you to gossip about your foreign religion."

"I apologize, Miyoshi-*san*." The guard returned to his post with a guilty expression.

"Please do not blame him," Father Mateo said. "The fault is mine."

"You are here to investigate a murder." Akira paused and brought his temper under control, as if remembering that the priest was the shogun's guest. He turned to Hiro. "I notice you have not found Ito Kazu."

"Not yet," Father Mateo said. "We returned to gather more evidence."

Hiro stole a glance at the priest. He hadn't expected the Jesuit to lie.

"We would like to speak with the carpenter Ozuru," Hiro said.

"Why do you care about carpenters?" Akira's eyebrows gathered like angry clouds. "Ito Kazu is to blame."

"I am not so sure," Hiro said.

"The evidence points to his guilt."

"I will explain on the way to Saburo's office," Hiro said. "We also wish to review the scene of the crime."

Akira frowned but led them toward the mansion. At the entrance he stopped and asked again, "What makes you think Kazu is innocent?"

"A murderer wouldn't leave his own dagger behind," Hiro said.

"Especially such a distinctive one," Father Mateo added.

"The murderer could not hide the cause of death." Akira led them into the mansion and through the maze of wood-paneled rooms. "Only a dagger could have caused Saburo's injuries."

"True," Hiro said, "but knowing the type of weapon is very different from identifying its owner. The killer may have left the dagger behind because he intended us to draw a false conclusion."

"Or else he was frightened," Akira said. "Or maybe Kazu left it behind as a distraction, expecting us to believe he would not do so."

Hiro hadn't ruled that out, despite his hope that Kazu would prove truthful.

"That suggestion seems brought back from a distance," Father Mateo said.

Akira stopped walking. "Pardon me?"

"He means that it seems unlikely," Hiro said. "The Portuguese idiom doesn't translate well. It's closer to 'fetched from afar.'"

Akira shook his head and resumed his pace. "It's a miracle we can understand him at all."

"Despite his awkwardness, he makes a point," Hiro said.

"A dagger is simple to conceal. Only a fool would leave it behind."

"Then how did someone else get Kazu's dagger?" Akira led them into the room where the carpenters worked.

A trio of workmen bent over the unfinished beam. Their planes rasped in a rhythmic chorus. The scent of cedar shavings filled the air. The carpenters had made significant progress since the morning, and it looked as though they might finish the beam that day.

But Ozuru wasn't there.

Akira continued across the room, still talking, oblivious to the master carpenter's absence. "Maybe Saburo caught Kazu stealing, and Kazu killed him to keep the matter quiet."

"What would Kazu have stolen?" Father Mateo asked. "Did Saburo keep gold or valuables in his office?"

They had reached the opposite side of the room. Hiro decided not to mention the missing carpenter. Ozuru might simply have gone to the latrine.

Akira slid open the door to the room where Saburo died. "He had access to secret documents. Maybe Kazu is a spy."

That touched too close to the truth for Hiro's comfort, but it would only increase suspicion to deny it.

"How long has Kazu worked for the shogun?" Father Mateo asked.

"He was here when I arrived a year ago," Akira said, "and he didn't seem new."

"Then your suggestion stretches imagination," Father Mateo said. "The shogun's guards would have caught a spy long ago."

"More importantly," Hiro said, "there is a simpler explanation."

Akira stepped into the office and moved aside to let the other men enter behind him. "Which is?"

"Ozuru admitted to arguing with Saburo yesterday evening. Did the guards remember what time the carpenter left the compound?"

Akira shook his head. "I spoke with them after you left this morning. No one remembers seeing the carpenter leave."

"So he just disappeared?" Hiro paused. "If Saburo was killed by a spy—and I'm far from convinced he was—Ozuru's guilt seems far more likely than Kazu's."

Akira hung his head. "I was sure Kazu did it, but now . . ." His head jerked upward. His hand flew to his sword. "We must seize Ozuru!"

"Wait," Hiro said. "A guilty man may escape if arrested too quickly. We can't explain how the killer acquired Kazu's dagger or why he chose Saburo as the victim. If you arrest Ozuru without sufficient evidence, you will give him time to construct a persuasive lie."

Akira hesitated, torn between slow justice and immediate vengeance. Slowly, he lowered his hand. "Very well, but be quick about it. Someone must pay for this crime, and the shogun is not a patient man."

Chapter 16

Hiro turned his attention to the office and tried to reconstruct the murder.

He already knew the attack occurred in the doorway between the outer room and Saburo's inner office. The bloody spatters on the wall to the left of the door suggested the victim lost his fingers early, possibly as he stepped into the room.

"Can you tell what happened?" Father Mateo asked.

Akira seemed curious too.

"We know Saburo didn't draw his sword," Hiro said, "which means he either knew his killer or didn't see the attack in time.

"The killer severed Saburo's fingers near that door." Hiro gestured toward the inner office. "The blood that spurted from his hand left all those streaks on the wall."

"How do you know?" Akira asked.

"Have you never noticed that flying blood makes patterns? It's harder to see in battle, but still visible if you know what you're looking for."

Akira glanced away, embarrassed. "I've never fought in battle."

"That's something to be proud of," Father Mateo said.

Akira seemed relieved, though he tried to hide it.

Hiro continued his explanation. "The stains grow denser and more frequent approaching the place where Saburo fell. He was bleeding harder, both from injuries and exertion. We see most of the blood on the west side of the room, which means Saburo was facing the outer door throughout the struggle."

"There was a struggle?" Akira asked.

Hiro looked at the floor. "I see two sets of bloody footprints—one facing Saburo's office, the other facing away. Neither moves in a standard linear pattern. That suggests a struggle to me."

"So Saburo fought with his killer," Akira said. "What else do you see?"

"I think he knew the murderer," Father Mateo said, "because he didn't shout or raise an alarm."

Hiro agreed, though he didn't like it. That fact implicated Kazu.

"Of course he knew the killer," Akira said. "Strangers can't enter the shogun's compound at night."

Hiro knew better, but didn't say so.

He dropped his gaze to the blackening pool where Saburo's body fell. The tatami had absorbed more blood since morning, making the hair pin's presence more distinct.

Hiro wondered again who it belonged to.

"Who else worked here last night?" Father Mateo asked.

"No one," Akira said. "The maids stay late, and the guards of course, but most officials leave at sunset, or very soon thereafter. Only Saburo and Ito Kazu were in this office after the gates were closed."

"Do guards patrol the mansion after dark?" Hiro asked.

"No," Akira said. "We have guards at the gates and on the towers. A few patrol the grounds, and of course the shogun has warriors posted around his personal quarters, but there's no need for guards inside at night."

"So Saburo might have called for help," Father Mateo said, "but no one heard him."

Akira's lip curled. "No samurai cries for help."

Hiro walked to the door of Saburo's inner office. The coppery scent of blood increased as he crossed the floor.

The corpse was gone, leaving only brownish stains on the white tatami and a fading smell of blood and death in the air, along with an undertone of aging food.

Hiro looked down. The dinner tray remained by the door.

The bloody dagger still sat on the desk beside the ink and inkwells, but Saburo's marble seal had disappeared.

"Who moved Saburo's *inkan*?" Hiro asked.

Akira and Father Mateo joined him in Saburo's office.

"Hisahide took it," Akira said, "to keep it safe."

Father Mateo walked to the bookcase nearest Saburo's desk. He pointed at a shelf near the top. "There were six ledgers here earlier. Now there are five."

"Are you certain?" Akira asked.

Father Mateo looked at Hiro. "Absolutely."

Akira joined the Jesuit by the bookcase. He took down a ledger and opened it, keeping the contents hidden. After a brief examination he closed the book and returned it to the shelf.

"These are the secret duty schedules of the shogun's personal guards."

"Secret?" Father Mateo asked. "Anyone could walk in here and read them. You just did."

"These aren't the current schedules," Akira said. "These are records from previous months."

"The current schedule seems to be missing," Hiro said.

"How do you know that?" Akira demanded, suddenly suspicious.

Hiro nodded toward the ledgers. "The spines are numbered one through five, for the first five months of the year. I haven't seen this month's ledger anywhere in this room or the outer office, and if it was here this morning someone must have taken it since we left."

Akira's eyes widened. A look of horror spread across his face. "I must report this to Hisahide immediately."

Hiro nodded. "We will speak with Ozuru while we wait."

"Come with me," Akira said, "I will escort you there."

When they reached the nearby audience chamber, Ozuru had not returned. Akira walked halfway across the room but stopped far enough from the workers to avoid getting dust on his kimono.

"Where is the master carpenter?" he demanded.

The workmen dropped to their knees and laid their heads on the floor. After a moment, one of them raised his head just enough to prevent the floorboards from muffling his words.

"The master's favorite chisel broke. He went to buy another."

Akira looked suspicious. "When did he leave?"

The workman didn't look up. "Just over an hour ago. We expect him back very soon."

"I didn't ask when he would return," Akira said.

Hiro thought the reaction unfair. The carpenter's answer

was reasonable and probably anticipated exactly what the samurai would have asked.

"I know you are in a hurry," Hiro told Akira. "We can talk with the apprentices and wait for Ozuru while you speak with Matsunaga-*san*."

"As you wish," Akira said, "but do not leave this room until I return."

He gave the construction site a wide berth and left through the southern door.

Father Mateo approached the carpenters. "Please stand up. You don't have to kneel for us."

The workmen slowly got to their feet but continued to watch the floor. The youngest man fidgeted nervously. The other two stood straight and still.

"We are investigating Ashikaga Saburo's murder," Father Mateo said.

The oldest carpenter nodded. His bushy gray eyebrows sported more hair than the rest of his head put together. Hiro remembered the carpenter's name was Goro.

"Master Carpenter Ozuru helped us greatly earlier," Father Mateo said. "He told us you left work at sunset yesterday and returned this morning at the usual time."

Hiro stifled a sigh. The priest had an excellent intellect and passable social skills, but he still hadn't learned that questions should not reveal the desired answer.

As Hiro expected, Goro nodded. "Yes, we left and re-turned at the usual time."

"Have you worked with Ozuru long?" Hiro asked.

"Several years," Goro said without looking up.

"Is he a difficult master?"

Goro bit the inside of his lip.

"We will not tell him what you say," Father Mateo added.

All three carpenters shook their heads, though only Goro answered. "Stern, perhaps, but artisans always are. He is fair when we work hard and do not complain."

"And when you do complain?" Father Mateo asked. "What then?"

The carpenter looked up. "Complaints, like failures, have consequences. But this, too, is always so."

"Did Ozuru leave work with you last night?" Hiro asked.

The carpenter tilted his head to the side. "You already know he didn't." He straightened as if realizing his slip into familiarity. "Ozuru remained to work on the transom carvings."

"Do you know what time he left?" Hiro asked.

Goro shook his head. "We report to Ozuru, not the other way around."

"Thank you for your assistance," Hiro said. "You may return to work."

The carpenters bowed. As they picked up their planes, Hiro turned away and walked toward Saburo's office.

Father Mateo hurried after him. "Akira told us to stay in that room."

"And Hisahide gave us permission to investigate without interference."

Hiro stopped in the doorway of Saburo's outer office.

A woman knelt beside the bloody pool with her back to the door. As Hiro watched, she slipped something into the sleeve of her kimono.

Chapter 17

Is that your hair pin?" Hiro asked.

The woman startled. She jumped to her feet and whirled to face the door.

"Jun, isn't it?" Hiro asked, though he already knew the answer.

She bowed, "Yes, sir."

"Was it your *kanzashi*?"

Her gaze shifted from Hiro to Father Mateo and then to the floor.

The shinobi expected her to lie, but she nodded and said, "Yes. It must have fallen out when I found Ashikaga-*san*. I noticed it when I came to retrieve the dinner tray."

She started to point to the inner office but returned her hand to her side.

"Do you remember anything else about last night?" Hiro asked. "Anything you forgot to tell us earlier?"

"No." She forced a smile. "I am very sorry. If you will excuse me . . . the cook wants me to return the tray immediately."

"Of course," Hiro said. "You may go."

Jun bowed and walked to Saburo's office with mincing steps that avoided the bloody stains on the floor. She knelt in the doorway, retrieved the tray, and hurried out without another word.

When Hiro was sure she had gone he said, "I wonder why she lied."

"What do you mean?" Father Mateo asked.

"Had the hairpin fallen out when she discovered Saburo's body, it would have landed on the corpse or possibly beside it. Either way, the pin would have been on top of the blood. But Jun's *kanzashi* was thoroughly coated—that pin was on the floor when Saburo died."

"Perhaps it rolled through the blood when the body was moved," Father Mateo said.

Hiro shook his head. "The pin lay in the center of the pool, where the blood was thick and largely undisturbed.

"Also—did you notice how many hair pins Jun is wearing?"

Father Mateo thought for a moment. "Two."

"The normal number for the way her hair is styled," Hiro said. "Had she lost one this morning and only now discovered it missing, she wouldn't have two clean ones in her hair."

"She did go home," Father Mateo said. "She might have replaced it then."

"Too distraught to work, but aware enough to replace a missing hair pin?" Hiro shook his head. "I don't believe it."

"Perhaps her parents noticed?"

"Possible . . ." Hiro heard footsteps approaching. He turned to face the door.

Hisahide stepped into the room with Akira behind him.

"Ito Kazu did not come to work this morning," Hisahide said, "a fact which does little to persuade me of his innocence."

"The carpenter, Ozuru, is also missing," Akira said.

"Is this true?" Hisahide asked.

"The workmen said he went to replace a chisel," Father Mateo said.

"Nonetheless," Akira continued, "he hasn't returned, and, as Hiro pointed out, a guilty man would not leave his own weapon behind."

Hiro found the young samurai's shifting opinion entertaining. It seemed Akira was willing to blame whoever seemed most likely at the moment—a common trait among men whose rank exceeded their intelligence.

"You no longer believe Kazu left the dagger by accident?" Hiro asked.

"A samurai does not forget his blades," Akira said.

"Then why has Kazu not come to work today?" Hisahide asked.

Akira looked to Hiro for support, or perhaps an explanation.

"Daggers can be stolen," Hiro said, "and we can inquire about Kazu's tardiness when we find him."

"We checked his home," Hisahide said. "He wasn't there."

Hiro raised an eyebrow. "Unmarried men do not always sleep at home."

Akira's lip curled with distaste. "A samurai should not consort with prostitutes. I thought Kazu was an honorable man."

"Even saints can sin," Father Mateo said.

"What?" Akira asked.

"He means that all men commit errors in judgment," Hiro said.

"He could have said so directly."

"Irrelevant." Hisahide waved a hand to dismiss Akira's comment. "Find Ito Kazu—and also Ozuru, if he has disappeared . . . though I hope the artisan didn't commit this crime."

"Why?" Father Mateo asked.

Hisahide's lips twitched. "The shogun is fond of Ozuru," he said. "It would be inconvenient and embarrassing to execute the carpenter for this crime."

"Embarrassing?" Father Mateo asked.

"To admit that a commoner killed a samurai inside the shogun's compound," Hiro said.

Hisahide nodded. "Lord Oda's spies must not learn that such a thing is possible. It makes the shogun's security seem dangerously weak."

"But Ozuru was already here," Father Mateo said. "He didn't breach the walls."

"Any successful murder demonstrates a security weakness," Hisahide said. "If a workman can kill the shogun's cousin, assassins may believe they too can infiltrate the shogunate, and belief is the first step toward success.

"Your suspicions about the carpenter must not become widely known."

"We will not speak of this to anyone," Father Mateo said.

"No, you won't," Hisahide replied, "particularly if the evidence proves you correct."

Hiro heard the unspoken threat. Hisahide would rather kill them both than risk their revealing the shogunate's vulnerability. That fact concerned him even more than finding the killer in time.

The shinobi changed the subject. "Did Akira tell you about the missing ledger?"

"It isn't missing," Hisahide said. "The shogun asked me to bring him the ledger, and also Saburo's seal. Is anything else missing from this office?"

"Not that we've discovered," Hiro said.

"Then I suggest you turn your attention to finding Kazu—and also our missing artisan."

"Precisely my intention," Hiro said. "Kazu spends his evenings at Ginjiro's, drinking sake. The brewer may know where Kazu spent last night."

"And the carpenter?" Akira asked.

"It's possible that he really did just go to replace a chisel," Hiro said.

"Very well," Hisahide said, "you may start with Kazu. Akira, go with them and report to me as soon as you return."

Chapter 18

Hiro stepped out of the *bakufu* mansion into a fine-misted drizzle that hung in the air as if a cloud had settled onto the courtyard. After the death-scented air of Saburo's office, the gentle drops felt pleasant and refreshing, though Hiro knew the rain would soon increase.

The earthen road outside the shogun's compound already sported a sticky layer of mud. The three men had barely left the gates when Akira said, "We should have taken horses. Didn't you ride here?"

Hiro smiled. "Father Mateo does not own a horse."

"Why not?" Akira asked. "Only poor men and commoners walk."

"God walked, when he was on the earth," Father Mateo said.

"Your foreign god wins no arguments with me," Akira sneered. "No man of worth would walk when he could ride."

Father Mateo did not reply.

In Hiro's experience, value seldom equated to social standing, though he sensed the younger man's frustration went beyond religion and muddy sandals. Only samurai had the legal right to ride horses, and only the wealthiest samurai could afford them.

The young Miyoshi wanted his status symbol.

They reached Ginjiro's brewery at midafternoon, late enough for the shop to be open but early enough to avoid the evening crowd.

As they approached the raised floor that stretched the length of the open brewery storefront, the rain increased from a misty drizzle to heavy drops. Hiro paused at the edge of the elevated floor just long enough to draw his katana and lay it safely on the tatami inside the shop. Gathering his kimono, he knelt up onto the brewery floor.

Akira and Father Mateo followed.

No customers sat by the low wooden counter that ran along the left side of the shop. The long, tatami-covered floor was empty except for a pile of stained brown cloth in the right front corner of the brewery. It looked like a heap of rags set out to await a passing beggar, but Hiro noticed the pile rose and fell in the gentle rhythm of sleep.

Hiro shifted his gaze to Ginjiro, the brewer, who stood in the lowered space behind the wooden counter and wiped the honey-colored wood with a cloth while he waited for customers. Behind Ginjiro, a doorway led to the kitchen where the brewer's wife and daughter cooked food for the patrons. The brewery and storage rooms lay beyond the kitchen, though Hiro had never seen them. A *noren* of indigo cloth hung in the narrow doorway, blocking the view of the private rooms beyond.

Ginjiro looked up as Hiro approached the counter. He smiled and bowed but didn't call out his usual greeting.

Hiro returned the bow in silence. He knew Ginjiro didn't want to wake the mendicant monk asleep in the opposite corner of the shop.

Akira and Father Mateo joined Hiro at the counter. All three knelt and offered their swords across the wooden countertop.

"Good afternoon, Matsui-*san*." Ginjiro accepted Hiro's katana and placed it in a wooden rack designed to hold patrons' swords. As he turned back to the counter he caught Hiro's eye and raised his eyebrows a fraction in silent inquiry.

The shinobi glanced at Akira. Hiro held Father Mateo in higher regard, but Akira would take offense if the brewer greeted the Jesuit first.

Ginjiro bowed to the samurai and took his sword with a respectful greeting. A moment later he did the same for Father Mateo.

With all three swords placed safely on the rack, Ginjiro asked, "May I offer you sake and snacks?"

Father Mateo opened his mouth to respond, but Akira cut him off. "No, thank you. We are here on the shogun's business."

All emotion drained from Ginjiro's face. He bowed again, more deeply. "How may I assist the shogunate?"

"Where is Ito Kazu?" Akira asked.

Ginjiro's gaze flickered to Hiro. The shinobi gave an almost imperceptible nod, though he wondered what the brewer knew that made him seek approval to answer the question. Ginjiro didn't know Hiro's real identity, or Kazu's. He knew them only as regular patrons.

"I'm afraid I don't know," Ginjiro said, "but if you wish to wait, he should arrive within an hour or two."

The response made Hiro certain that Ginjiro knew more than he would reveal with Akira present.

"How do you know?" the samurai asked. "Do you have a meeting with him?"

Ginjiro smiled and shook his head. "We have no appointment. Ito-*san* often drinks here in the evenings. I expect him every night, though truthfully he doesn't always come."

"What about last night?" Akira asked. "Was he here?"

"Ito-*san* was here last night." Ginjiro used rigidly formal language and did not take his eyes from Akira's face, though as custom demanded he made no direct eye contact.

The brewer played the role of polite subordinate perfectly, suggesting he had experience using etiquette to conceal a spoken lie. Hiro doubted Akira noticed, but the shinobi had used the trick too often to miss it.

"What time did he arrive?" Akira asked. "How late did he stay?"

The questions clattered through the silent shop like a horse's hooves on stone.

Hiro heard a rustle of cloth behind him. The sleeping monk had awakened.

Ginjiro smiled politely. "He arrived after dark. I apologize, but I did not note the time. I don't always hear the temple bells when the shop is busy."

"How late did he stay?" Akira repeated.

Before Ginjiro could respond, Hiro heard a muffled thump and a yelp of pain.

Akira whirled toward the sound, reaching for the *wakizashi* at his side. Father Mateo startled too, but Hiro turned more slowly. He already knew what had happened. The monk had rolled off the platform and fallen into the street.

A balding head appeared above the edge of the brewery floor.

"Sir, are you hurt?" Father Mateo called.

The monk blinked like a sun-dazzled owl. He looked up and touched his forehead as if to confirm the existence of falling rain. When he looked back into the shop, his mouth split open in a nearly toothless grin.

"Hiro-*san!*" He waved a skinny arm and wobbled on his feet.

Akira looked down his nose at Hiro. "He knows you?"

"His name is Suke," Hiro said, "and he knows all of Ginjiro's customers."

Hiro followed Father Mateo across the shop and helped the priest lift Suke back into the brewery.

"I was sleeping." Suke's eyebrows shot up as if trying to escape his hairless forehead. "An *oni* must have pushed me!"

"I doubt the demons are bored enough to shove old men out of breweries." Hiro knelt and looked the monk in the eye. "Are you hurt?"

Suke's gaze darted to the counter. "Nothing a little sake wouldn't cure."

Ginjiro glared at the monk and shook his head. The brewer considered Suke a nuisance, but wouldn't risk the monastery's displeasure, or that of the kami, by forcing the ancient monk into the street.

"Shall I buy you a cup?" Hiro already knew the answer, but the question was part of the game, and Suke's response would prove the monk hadn't injured himself in the fall.

"A cup might help a little," Suke said, "but a flask would earn you a thousand blessings."

Hiro nodded. The monk was fine.

"Ginjiro," the shinobi called, "draw a flask for Suke, and bring a bowl of rice with meat."

The brewer sighed and disappeared into the kitchen.

Father Mateo returned to the counter without a word.

Hiro turned to follow, but Suke laid a restraining hand on his arm. The monk's wiry fingers had surprising strength.

"If there's trouble," Suke whispered, "I will swear that Ito Kazu was here all night."

Chapter 19

Hiro doubted Suke's oath would persuade a child, let alone the shogun, but he appreciated the offer. He returned to the counter as Suke settled cross-legged on the floor.

"Do you buy him food often?" Father Mateo asked.

Hiro shrugged. "It keeps him from drooling into mine."

Ginjiro returned and set a pair of bowls on the countertop. One held a generous mound of steaming rice. The other held pickled vegetables and five thick slices of fatty pork.

The brewer didn't like Suke, but he never shorted a paying customer.

Hiro looked from the bowls to Ginjiro and waited.

The brewer sighed and bent below the counter. When he straightened, he set a ceramic flask and an egg-sized sake cup beside the bowls. Hiro nodded approval and carried the food and drink to the waiting monk.

Suke clapped his hands in delight. "A thousand blessings upon you, Hiro-*san*."

The monk swallowed two cups of sake in quick succession, wiped his mouth, and removed a pair of wooden chopsticks from his filthy robe.

Hiro returned to the counter as Suke shoveled vegetables into his mouth.

Akira had already resumed his questioning. "Can you confirm how late Ito Kazu stayed?"

Ginjiro's smile froze. "Some time after midnight."

"Was he drinking all evening?" Hiro asked. "If so, he would have been very drunk when he left."

Father Mateo gave the shinobi a sidelong look, but Hiro ignored him. The wording was neither careless nor accidental.

Ginjiro nodded and gave the desired answer. "More so than I'd ever seen him. I'd be surprised if he made it home in that condition."

Hiro made a mental note to tip Ginjiro handsomely.

"Did Kazu tell you where he was going?" Akira asked.

"My patrons don't usually ask permission to leave." Ginjiro looked at Hiro with concern. "Is Ito-*san* injured?"

"We don't know," Hiro said. "No one has seen him since last night."

The *noren* fluttered in the kitchen doorway, giving Hiro a glimpse of a purple kimono behind the fabric panels. Ginjiro's daughter, Tomiko, had a crush on Kazu as well as a tendency to eavesdrop.

"Does Kazu have a woman in Pontocho?" Akira asked.

Ginjiro pressed his lips together. "I don't know. If he does, he's never mentioned her and never brought her here. I certainly never asked. It is not my place to inquire about a customer's business in the pleasure district."

The brewer's comments revealed his disapproval. Akira's question overstepped the bounds of polite inquiry.

Akira turned to Hiro, ignoring the brewer's tactful reprimand. "You were wrong. He doesn't know anything useful."

"On the contrary," Hiro said, "we know that Kazu spent the evening here and left in a drunken stupor."

Akira thrust an expectant hand across the counter. Ginjiro retrieved the samurai's sword and also Father Mateo's. When the brewer returned Hiro's katana, the shinobi accepted the weapon with both hands, an unnecessary courtesy intended to show respect. Ginjiro had tried to keep Kazu out of trouble, and Hiro appreciated the brewer's loyalty.

The shinobi sheathed his katana and handed Ginjiro a silver coin for Suke's meal and a second one to express his thanks for the brewer's cooperation.

After joining Akira and Father Mateo in the street, Hiro stepped to the edge of the floor where Suke squatted and asked, "Did you notice which way Kazu went when he left last night?"

The monk paused, mouth full of rice. After a moment he nodded and mumbled, "River."

Several grains of rice popped out from between his lips. He pushed them back into his mouth with a grubby finger.

Akira's nostrils flared in disgust.

Father Mateo bowed. "Thank you, Suke-*san*."

Suke nodded and returned his attention to his rice.

The rain had slowed to a mist again while the men were inside the brewery, but the brief downpour left puddles in the road. The shinobi took care to avoid them.

As the men walked east toward the Kamo River, Hiro wondered why Kazu failed to meet them at the brewery as planned. He didn't like doubting a fellow shinobi, but Kazu's conduct didn't inspire confidence.

Just outside the winding alley that housed the pleasure district of Pontocho, a pair of young women huddled beneath an oiled paper umbrella. They wore expensive kimonos patterned with summer scenes. Red linings peeked from the neck of their robes, marking the girls as *maiko*, or apprentice entertainers. Hiro knew them for novices even before he saw the collars. Water ruined time-consuming makeup and costly hairstyles. Experienced entertainers stayed inside on a rainy day.

The girls scooted up against a building, gaping with astonishment at the sight of the foreign priest. Father Mateo bowed without slowing. Akira ignored the girls and Hiro looked away. He refused to acknowledge women who lacked the sense to get out of the rain.

When they reached the river, Hiro paused to watch the raindrops fall on the flowing water. They dimpled the surface and disappeared, consumed by the thirsty river.

"Perhaps we should go back," Akira said, "and search Pontocho?"

"If you like." Hiro hoped the samurai wouldn't insist. The shinobi hated Pontocho.

"I'd rather not." Akira glanced over his shoulder. "It's hardly an appropriate place to be seen."

In daytime, anyway, Hiro thought.

Samurai flooded Pontocho at night, despite the ethical prohibition on nobles consorting with prostitutes. No one paid attention, and, for the most part, no one cared.

By daylight, however, a man in Pontocho attracted considerable notice.

Akira started north along the road that followed the river bank. "I'm not risking my reputation. If Kazu's alive, he'll turn up sooner or later."

"And if he's not alive?" Father Mateo matched Akira's pace.

The samurai turned. "Do you think the murderer killed him too?"

"He has disappeared," Father Mateo said.

"But why would the killer hide the second victim?" Akira asked.

"He wouldn't, without a reason." Hiro said.

The shinobi walked on Akira's right, closest to the river.

"Why do you think the murderer killed Saburo?" Akira asked.

"The evidence makes robbery unlikely," Hiro said.

"Vengeance, maybe?" Akira offered.

"Perhaps," Hiro said. "Did anyone have a grudge against Saburo?"

Akira's momentary silence suggested unwillingness to speak, but eventually he said, "Saburo was not popular. He thought his name entitled him to privileges above his rank."

"He demanded unusual deference?" Father Mateo asked.

Akira gave an awkward smile. "Yes, but also . . . with the maids."

Hiro understood at once. "Do any of the girls he approached still work at the shogunate?"

"I don't know," Akira said. "It is a delicate situation."

"Perhaps Saburo's wife knows more about it," Hiro said.

Akira's eyes widened. His cheeks flushed. "I would rather you didn't . . ."

Before he could finish the sentence, Father Mateo made a startled sound.

Just ahead, a male figure emerged from beneath a bridge. His blue kimono was streaked with mud. Dead grass and broken reeds poked out of the ragged samurai knot atop his head, and his face was bruised and battered. The man raised a hand to his temple as if to soothe its aching, but the effort seemed to increase his pain and he lowered his hand to his side.

Shock forced a name from Hiro's lips.

"Kazu?" he asked. "What are you doing here?"

Chapter 20

Mud and grass clung to Kazu's kimono as if he had rolled on the river bank. Bruises marked his cheek and temple. His right eye was purple and swollen nearly shut.

Kazu opened his mouth, winced, and raised a hand to a blackening, bloody scab on his lower lip. He touched the injury gingerly and glanced at his fingers to see if the wound was bleeding.

Hiro could tell the pain was real.

Father Mateo rushed forward. "Ito-*san*, what happened?"

Kazu blinked at the sky. "What time is it?"

"Late afternoon," Akira said. "Where have you been all morning?"

Kazu looked over his shoulder at the river. "Under the bridge, I think." He blinked and looked up. "It's raining."

"You slept under a bridge?" Akira's forehead wrinkled, caught between concern and disgust.

Hiro wanted to hear the answer, even though he knew Kazu would lie.

"Thieves attacked me." Kazu sounded disoriented, as if remembering a dream. "I was walking home from Ginjiro's and saw shadows near the bridge. I fought back, but there were too many. The next thing I remember, I woke up—just now—and saw you on the path.

"They must have left me under the bridge."

Talking had cracked the scab on Kazu's lip. He dabbed at the drop of blood that oozed from the wound.

His eyes widened. He searched through his kimono. "My purse is gone! Fifty silver *chogin!*"

Akira's mouth fell open in dismay. "Fifty?"

The sum was more than some samurai made in a year, though well within the range a wealthy man might carry in Kyoto. Hiro didn't know the size of Kazu's stipend from the Iga *ryu*, but money was vital to Kazu's cover story. The wealthy eldest son of an Iga nobleman would have plenty of coins to spend.

"Were they samurai?" Father Mateo asked. "The thieves, I mean."

Akira looked down his nose at the priest—a difficult task, given the Jesuit's eight-inch height advantage. "Samurai do not become thieves."

Once again, Hiro knew better, but as before he let the inaccurate statement pass without comment.

"No," Kazu said, "just common brigands."

"Did you see their faces?" Akira asked. "We should report this to the police."

Kazu started to shake his head but stopped, as if the motion made him dizzy. "They wore hoods and covered their faces. I wouldn't recognize them if I saw them."

"Insolent thugs," Akira said, "most likely wasting your money as we speak. The police are paid to patrol this river at night. I'll have Hisahide speak to the ward commander."

"Matsunaga-*san* obeys your commands?" Hiro asked.

Akira flushed. "I meant I would ask him." After an awkward pause he continued, "Hisahide will want to know. This attack might be connected to the one at the shogunate."

"Attack at the shogunate?" Kazu repeated. "Was the shogun also robbed?"

Akira shook his head. "I am sorry to bear bad news. Ashikaga Saburo has been murdered."

Hiro caught a whiff of something terrible, like sake mixed with urine.

"Murdered?" Kazu stepped toward Akira. "What happened?"

The smell increased. It was coming from Kazu's robe. The scents of the rain and the river had covered the unpleasant odor initially, but the longer they stood on the bank, the more it permeated the air.

Hiro wrinkled his nose. Kazu had overdone it.

"He was killed last night, in his office at the shogunate." Akira seemed to notice the smell. He stepped away from Kazu but covered the movement by gesturing to Hiro and Father Mateo. "The shogun asked these men to help Hisahide find the killer."

"Hiro?" Kazu squinted in confusion. "Why?"

"He has solved murders before," Akira said. Hiro could see the samurai trying not to inhale too deeply. The smell lingered unpleasantly on the air. Etiquette forbade Akira from mentioning it, but no one could have missed the pungent odor.

"Saburo was stabbed to death with your dagger," Hiro said. "If you killed him, confess it now."

"Me?" Kazu stepped backward. The fear in his eyes looked real.

"You were missing," Father Mateo said. "Matsunaga Hisahide asked us to find you."

"I didn't . . ." Kazu paused. "Who would kill Saburo?" He looked up the road to the north. "I need to get to the shogunate. I can search the office, identify things out of place."

"You need a physician," Father Mateo said.

"Only my pride is injured."

"Under the circumstances, I think you should rest—and possibly change," Akira said. "I will explain to Hisahide, and he will inform the shogun of your whereabouts."

"With respect, I must refuse. Saburo's confidential papers must be protected and delivered to the shogun." Kazu's face fell. "Also, I should pay my respects to Ichiro."

The catch in Kazu's voice sounded genuine. Hiro studied the younger shinobi with a concern that had nothing to do with Kazu's injuries. A shinobi must always remain detached from his mission. Real emotion was dangerous and forbidden.

Hiro's friendship with Father Mateo violated the rule too, but Hiro pardoned his own transgression because his assignment was permanent and tied his own life to the priest's. Kazu's assignment was neither lifelong nor dependent upon anyone's survival but his own.

"Ichiro seemed fine this morning," Hiro said. "He accompanied his mother to the shogunate."

"I should pay my respects," Kazu repeated. "As his tutor, it is my duty."

Hiro hoped Kazu's attachment to the child was merely a pretense.

"Lady Ashikaga will not welcome you today," Father Mateo said. "She believes you killed her husband."

Kazu raised his chin and squared his shoulders. "Then I must convince her otherwise."

"It will help if I accompany you," Akira said.

Hiro hadn't expected that offer, especially given the way Kazu looked and smelled. It raised his estimate of Akira considerably.

"Would you?" Kazu asked. "Could we go now?"

Akira nodded. "I will explain that you were indisposed and could not have killed Saburo." He paused. "But perhaps you would like to change your kimono first?"

Hiro's frustration with Kazu hadn't faded. The younger man should not have altered the cover story. His failure to meet them at Ginjiro's ruined Hiro's original plan. Still, Akira seemed to believe Kazu's alternate claims, so maybe the changes hadn't done any harm.

Hiro just hoped the police wouldn't investigate the alleged assault too closely.

"If you will pardon my presumption," Father Mateo said, "we should all get out of the rain."

They walked together as far as the bridge at Marutamachi Road. There, Akira and Kazu turned into the wealthy residential district that housed the imperial palace and the shogunate, while Hiro and Father Mateo crossed the bridge and headed home.

As they passed Okazaki Shrine Father Mateo asked, "Do you think Kazu is safe? Akira seemed to believe him, but samurai often hide their thoughts."

"Kazu can take care of himself," Hiro said.

"Speaking of which, where did his bruises come from? And that smell . . ."

"Sake," Hiro said, "mixed with what it becomes a few hours later."

"And the injuries?"

Hiro shrugged. Every shinobi knew about self-inflicted wounds and how to cause them, but Hiro couldn't explain that without also revealing that Kazu was more than just a man from Iga Province.

Moreover, Kazu's wounds didn't look entirely self-inflicted. Few men could strike themselves hard enough to split a lip and blacken an eye that badly. Kazu must have enlisted help, but Hiro didn't know who the younger man would trust to do him harm.

Suddenly, a name sprang to mind. It seemed absurd, but Hiro knew it had to be the right one. He shook his head and smiled, though the expression faded quickly at the sight of the stranger standing in the road in front of Father Mateo's home.

Chapter 21

The stranger wore a dark brown robe and woven sandals. Graying stubble covered his balding head. He stood in the street, holding the reins of a skinny chestnut gelding and a glossy black stallion that stomped the muddy ground as if impatient with the rain.

The brown horse wore a simple wooden saddle and a bridle made of rope, but the stallion had expensive leather trappings and a foreign bridle set with silver rings. It towered over the chestnut like a samurai beside a farmer's child.

Father Mateo slowed his pace for a moment and then hurried toward the house.

"Samurai do not run," Hiro murmured. He increased the length of his strides to match the priest's.

Father Mateo slowed to a walk and made a nervous gesture toward the stallion. "That's Father Vilela's horse."

"The black one?" As Hiro said the words, he realized his perception of priests had changed. Two years ago he would have assumed the nicer horse belonged to the wealthy foreigner, but Father Mateo's ascetic nature had altered Hiro's expectations. He now found it odd that a Jesuit priest would ride an expensive stallion.

Father Mateo didn't miss the surprise in Hiro's voice. "It was a gift from the shogun."

"Interesting." Hiro masked concern behind a casual tone. Father Vilela had never visited Father Mateo before.

Father Mateo ran a hand through his dark brown hair. "He must have news from Portugal."

The brown-robed servant bowed as they passed but kept his eyes on the road. Father Mateo returned the bow, though for once he didn't stop to address the stranger.

Ordinarily, the Jesuit's adherence to Japanese etiquette would have drawn an approving nod from Hiro, but the fear on Father Mateo's face deprived the shinobi of any satisfaction. Father Mateo had family and friends in Portugal. News arrived infrequently, and only tragic news would merit a personal visit from Father Vilela.

Father Mateo slipped out of his sandals and hurried across the veranda into the house. Hiro followed, alert but apprehensive. Father Mateo had not mastered the Japanese art of stifling emotion in difficult circumstances, and emotional moments made Hiro uncomfortable.

The shinobi had seen Gaspar Vilela only once, and at a distance, but he recognized the kimono-clad Jesuit instantly.

Except for his foreign features and the wooden cross that hung around his neck, Father Vilela could have passed for a samurai. His hair was so dark that not even a Japanese would call it brown, and he wore it in the samurai style, with a shaven pate and neatly tied *chonmage* atop his head. A hooked nose perched between his deep brown eyes, and beneath it Vilela's mouth fell naturally into stern but neutral lines.

Hiro wished Father Mateo looked as much like a samurai.

Father Vilela bowed from a seated position but did not rise. Hiro and Father Mateo returned the gesture and joined the senior Jesuit at the hearth.

"Mateo," Father Vilela said, "I hope you don't mind my waiting."

He spoke Japanese, doubtless in recognition of Hiro's presence. The shinobi found that courtesy intriguing.

"Of course not," Father Mateo said. "I am honored by your visit."

"And no doubt, confused." Father Vilela's sternness melted away in the warmth of his smile. "Are you comfortable here? Now that I see it, the house looks rather small."

"I have everything I need," Father Mateo said, "and my parishioners appreciate humble houses."

Father Vilela nodded. "If it pleases you, then it pleases me also."

Watching the senior Jesuit, Hiro wondered—not for the first time—why a samurai client had hired the Iga *ryu* to protect Mateo instead of Gaspar Vilela. Both men came from Portugal, and Vilela was undoubtedly more important to the Church.

Hiro didn't know the client's identity and couldn't guess at his motives, but the choice of Father Mateo suggested the unknown client's motivations went beyond an appreciation of the Catholic faith.

As always, Hiro dismissed the question as soon as he found himself asking. So long as the client paid his bill, a shinobi would follow instructions, and the man who insisted on Father Mateo's safety paid very often and very well indeed.

"May I offer you tea or cakes?" Father Mateo looked for Ana.

"Your maidservant offered when I arrived," Father Vilela said, as if reading the other Jesuit's thoughts, "but unfortunately I cannot stay long enough to enjoy your hospitality."

"Is there news from Portugal?" Father Mateo ran his hand through his hair again, but this time flushed with embarrassment as he lowered the hand to his lap.

Hiro noted the flush with satisfaction. At least the priest remembered that in Japan, a nervous gesture was considered a sign of weakness.

"Not lately." Father Vilela shook his head as if confused by the question. Almost at once, his eyes widened with understanding. "Did you think I brought bad news from home? That's not why I have come."

Father Mateo looked relieved, but the tone of Father Vilela's final words mimicked samurai disapproval too closely for coincidence. Hiro prepared himself for unpleasant news.

"Miyoshi Akira sent me a message this morning," Father Vilela said.

"Akira is a Christian?" Father Mateo drew back in surprise.

"He is not," Father Vilela said, "though several high-ranked members of his clan have accepted the faith. Akira wrote to express displeasure with your treatment of the shogun's servants."

Father Mateo's mouth fell open. "I assure you, we mistreated no one." He looked to Hiro for support.

"On the contrary." Vilela sounded more like a samurai than ever. "You treated everyone far too well. In addition, Miyoshi-*san* expressed displeasure with your statements that Christianity is available to commoners."

The hint of a smile passed over Vilela's face, then disappeared. "He accuses you of believing all men are equal."

"All men are equal in God's sight," Father Mateo said. "Should I treat them otherwise?"

"The Japanese are a complex people, with intricate social rules. We have made great progress here, but that progress must come on Japanese terms. Father Xavier left very specific instructions—we argue with the Japanese only on vital points of doctrine."

"Equality before God is a vital point of doctrine." Father Mateo's voice rose in pitch.

Father Vilela raised a hand like a parent calming an angry child. "It is your manner that offended. You must learn to speak the truth another way. Samurai do not want to hear that servants are the same as noble men."

"I will not exchange the truth for samurai rudeness." Father Mateo kept a civil tone, but barely. Hiro had seldom, if ever, seen the priest so angry. "No man deserves ill treatment just because of common birth."

"I have not asked for any man's mistreatment," Father Vilela said, his voice as calm as a midnight pond, "merely that you remember you do not speak for yourself alone."

"I speak for men who cannot speak for themselves."

"Do you help their cause by making their lords resent us?"

Hiro watched, impressed, as Father Mateo's expression changed from anger to chastened realization and then regret. Few men had the strength to acknowledge errors that flowed from a commitment to moral values.

"I apologize," Father Mateo said. "It would be wrong for me to tear down what you and others have built."

"To be clear," Father Vilela said, "I am not asking you to change your message, merely to remember that words have appropriate times and places."

"I will apologize to Miyoshi-*san*," Father Mateo said.

"Unnecessary," Father Vilela said, "and impossible, since you will not return to the shogunate."

Chapter 22

Father Mateo's eyes widened. "Are you ordering us to abandon the investigation?"

"Not both of you." Father Vilela indicated Hiro. "I believe you said Matsui-*san* helped you solve the previous murder. I am sure he can solve this one in your absence."

The shinobi shook his head. "We worked together to find the Akechi killer."

"You will find this one alone." Father Vilela's tone permitted no argument, which naturally made Hiro inclined to argue.

"Did Miyoshi Akira demand this?" Hiro asked.

"No," Father Vilela said, "but Akira made his meaning clear. His message complained of Mateo's behavior and said that the shogun didn't want to trouble the foreign mission with further investigation of Japanese crimes."

"What of me?" Hiro asked.

"The message indicated that your help is still desired," Father Vilela said. "You are not a common servant, to be commanded, but I would consider it a favor—to Mateo and to me—if you would do as Miyoshi Akira requests."

"And Father Mateo?" Hiro asked.

"Has nothing more to do with this investigation." Father Vilela's mind was made up.

Hiro disagreed, but even a samurai servant lacked the status to contradict a priest, and as far as Father Vilela knew the shinobi was merely a translator.

Father Mateo nodded once. "I understand. I will not return to the shogunate."

"Thank you," Father Vilela said. "We are making progress in Kyoto. Sometimes it comes at substantial cost, but the end result will be worth it—for commoners as well as for samurai."

He rose and bowed, first to Father Mateo and then to Hiro. "Thank you for your hospitality. *Pax vobiscum.*"

"Peace be with you also." Father Mateo stood and escorted the senior Jesuit to the door.

When he returned, alone, Hiro asked, "Do you really intend to abandon the search for Saburo's killer?"

"Father Vilela told me to, and Akira demanded it."

Hiro frowned. "You surrendered too quickly. You claim to believe in truth at any cost, yet you resigned without argument. Akira will think he was right and you were wrong, not only about equality, but about everything else as well."

Father Mateo met Hiro's gaze with calm determination. "I made the right decision. Akira is mistaken, but he was born and raised to believe himself superior to commoners. To him, that too is truth, not opinion. Arguing with his beliefs will never change them.

"Father Vilela is correct—I must find another way."

"There is an important reason for you to continue," Hiro said. "If Lord Oda's men are spies, their arrival could lead to violence—and not just at the shogunate. I cannot protect you adequately if you quit the investigation and I do not."

Father Mateo smiled. "I never agreed to abandon the investigation. If you remember, I merely said I would not return to the shogunate."

Hiro considered the priest. Father Vilela might look more like a samurai, but Father Mateo thought like a shinobi.

Ana entered the *oe* through the kitchen door on the north side of the room. Hiro's kitten, Gato, pranced along in her wake. The maid crossed to the hearth and removed the teapot from its chain. Lost in thought, Father Mateo didn't seem to notice.

Hiro looked at Ana. "Did the broom handle split Kazu's lip right away or did you have to hit him more than once?"

"Hm." She straightened, kettle in hand. "You think I can't split a lip in one blow?"

"You beat Kazu?" Father Mateo sounded horrified.

"He said if I didn't the shogun would think you hid him." Ana glared at Hiro. "Why did you let that drunken pig sleep off his sake here? You know we don't allow alcohol in this house!"

"He didn't bring any with him." Hiro remembered the smell of Kazu's robe and wished he hadn't mentioned it.

"But . . . you beat him?" Father Mateo repeated.

Ana set her free hand on her hip. "I will not let Hiro's lazy friends bring trouble on this house. Staying out to all hours, coming here drunk, hiding from responsibility! That lazy good-for-nothing deserved far worse than I gave him! Good sons stay home and take care of their parents. Shameful drunken carousing . . ."

She disappeared into the kitchen, still muttering about inconsiderate children who abandoned their aging parents to live debauched and useless lives in the city.

Hiro heard the front door open. He turned, surprised

and a bit relieved, as Luis entered the common room. Until that moment, Hiro thought the merchant was still sleeping.

"Good evening, Luis." Father Mateo bowed.

"Not really." Luis waved a hand in the air. "Nasty rain and insufferable samurai." He crossed to the hearth without returning the Jesuit's bow. As he lowered himself to the floor in the host's position, he shouted, "Ana! Food! And tea!"

He looked at Father Mateo. "I have to ride back to Ōtsu to fetch the shipment. The shogunate won't issue a pass for shippers to bring the firearms into the city, even though the weapons are for the shogun."

"Why not?" Father Mateo asked.

"Some hot-headed samurai murdered a clerk at the shogunate, and the *bakufu* office won't issue new passes until the killer is caught."

"The magistrates normally issue travel passes, not the shogun," Hiro said.

"Not for firearms," Luis snapped.

"I thought so," Hiro said. "The shogun wouldn't shut down Kyoto's supply lines over a killing."

Luis hadn't stopped fuming. "The ban is on new permits only, and only for weapons. It doesn't apply to other merchants or to food, as far as I can tell. I can bring the weapons into the city myself, I just can't hire a Japanese merchant to cart them here from Ōtsu.

"Typical samurai nonsense."

"A murder didn't cause this." Hiro explained about Lord Oda's approaching embassy. "The shogun doesn't want Oda's warriors sneaking weapons into Kyoto."

The explanation only made Luis angrier.

"Ridiculous waste of time," he grumbled. "These are the

shogun's weapons, in marked containers! But now I have to close the warehouse, ride to Ōtsu, and bring the shipment back myself—and with the price already set, I can't even charge him extra for my trouble."

Hiro suspected that was the real problem. Luis just wanted more money for the job.

"But you can bring the weapons into the city?" Father Mateo asked.

Luis nodded. "Police had better not try to seize them. Murder investigation or no, I'm getting paid for these firearms."

"I wouldn't worry about that," Hiro said. "The Kyoto police aren't investigating this murder."

Luis turned to Father Mateo. "How does he know that?"

"Hiro and I spent most of the day at the shogunate," Father Mateo said.

"You're investigating this murder?" Luis turned purple. "What are you thinking? The last one nearly got you killed."

Chapter 23

"Father Vilela asked us to help the shogun," Father Mateo said. "I couldn't refuse."

"But now he has instructed Father Mateo to quit the investigation," Hiro added.

Luis shook his head. "Jesuits—almost as inscrutable as Japanese."

Ana carried a tray of soup and pickled vegetables into the room. She set it down in front of Luis and asked, "Father Mateo, would you like to eat now too?"

"Please." The Jesuit knelt beside Luis. Unlike the merchant, Father Mateo had trained himself to sit in the Japanese style. "Hiro? Will you join us?"

"No thank you." The shinobi slid open the door to his room. Gato raced through the opening the moment the gap was large enough to admit her narrow frame.

Hiro shook his head and followed the kitten into the room. As he slid the door shut behind him he heard Luis tell Father Mateo, "I'm heading for Ōtsu tomorrow morning. I'll be gone overnight and back on the sixteenth, hopefully by midday. . . ."

The door closed and Hiro stopped listening. The merchant's words held no further interest.

Gato ran halfway across the room and flopped down on her side. She stretched herself in a backward arc, legs splayed out and claws extended. She finished the stretch, rolled upright, and looked at Hiro.

He snapped his fingers. The kitten jumped up and trotted toward him with a trill. Hiro stroked her fur as she padded back and forth, purring in a low but constant rumble reminiscent of a temblor. Hiro smiled. At least her rumbling wouldn't set the room to shaking.

When Gato wandered off, the shinobi exchanged his gray kimono for a dark blue surcoat and black *hakama* trousers. He slipped a *shuriken* into the tunic's inner pocket and tied an obi around his waist. As he passed a hand over his hair, he decided to retie his *chonmage*. The morning's hurried dressing had pulled the knot out of place, and the leather tie pinched when he turned his head.

Hiro removed the outer tie that secured the knot but left the second, inner band in place. Retying the outer knot was hard enough without assistance.

He ran a comb through his hair until the well-oiled tail hung smoothly to his waist. He set down the comb and twisted the hair in his hands, preparing to double it over the top of his head. Most samurai used a hairdresser, and Hiro preferred that option too, but necessity had forced him to learn to tie a passable knot on his own.

The attack came from behind and without warning.

A dozen tiny daggers punctured Hiro's shoulder and upper back. He grunted with surprise and pain and tried to twist away, but the effort made Gato sink her claws even deeper into his flesh. Her free paw batted his hand and grabbed at the swaying tail of hair.

"Ow!" Hiro grabbed for Gato, determined to pry the kitten away before her efforts ruined his hair completely. He felt her claws release as the kitten slithered away through the oiled strands, clawing furiously as she slid to the floor.

He whirled to prevent a second attack, but the kitten moved even faster. She sprang for his back, and once again he felt her needle-sharp claws dig into his skin.

When he finally managed to grab the kitten, she purred at him through a mouthful of oiled hair.

"Stop it!" Hiro maneuvered Gato's paws into one hand and used the other to extract the overexcited kitten from his hair. As he finished, Gato wrapped her paws around his wrist and sank her tiny teeth into his thumb. Her green eyes glowed with excitement. She kicked his sleeve with her legs. Her purr crescendoed.

"No!" Hiro dislodged the kitten from his wrist and set her on the floor. She fell to her side, paws extended, eager to continue the wrestling match.

Hiro looked for something to distract her.

A piece of rumpled parchment sat in the discard pail beside the desk. He grabbed the paper and crumpled it into a ball.

Gato mewed and jumped to her feet.

Hiro tossed the paper across the floor. Gato sprang after it, purring loudly, and tackled the target as it hit the ground. Kitten and parchment somersaulted across the floor and rolled to a stop. Gato clutched the paper between her paws and kicked contentedly at her captured prey.

Hiro took advantage of her distraction to fix his *chon-*

mage. By the time he finished, Gato had shredded the parchment and started to eat it.

The shinobi scooped up the scraps and dropped them into the discard pail, imagining Ana's fury if Gato threw up parchment on the clean tatami floor. The maid wouldn't blame the cat. Ana believed that Gato, like Father Mateo, could do no wrong. Hiro would bear the brunt of her wrath for feeding the kitten paper in the first place.

He tucked his swords through his obi and left the room as Gato curled up for a nap.

As Hiro passed through the common room, Father Mateo asked, "Will you join us?"

The Jesuit and Luis sat by the hearth enjoying a cup of tea. It smelled expensive, almost certainly *ichibancha* from Luis's personal supply.

"No thank you," Hiro said. "I need something stronger than tea."

Father Mateo's smile faded. "You're going to Ginjiro's?"

Hiro ignored the obvious, and familiar, disapproval. "Care to join me?"

"I have a worship service here in an hour. Why don't you stay?"

"Another time." Hiro avoided the Jesuit's preaching as diligently as the priest avoided sake.

Hiro walked up Marutamachi Road as the darkening sky turned the clouds from gray to black. The evening air smelled of earth and smoldering fires, and though the rain had stopped for the moment the rainy season had definitely arrived.

The torii gate at the entrance to Okazaki Shrine glowed red, reflecting the charcoal fires in the braziers at its base. A whiff of acrid smoke from the coals made Hiro think of hell. He wasn't sure he believed in the flaming pit of the Christian god or the multilayered Buddhist hells where evil met a variety of peculiarly twisted punishments. He was more concerned with avoiding the torments inflicted upon the living—and ensuring that Father Mateo did the same.

Hiro crossed the Kamo River and continued south along the river road. As he walked, he considered what he knew of Saburo's murder.

The body's condition indicated that Saburo died around midnight. By that hour, all visitors would have left the shogunate grounds. Kazu and Ozuru, as well as Jun, admitted to staying after the gates were closed, though each of them claimed no knowledge of the murder.

Saburo hadn't drawn his sword, which suggested the dead man knew the killer and didn't question his appearance in the office so late at night.

All of which looked increasingly bad for Kazu.

Hiro hoped Ginjiro, and possibly Suke, could fill in some of the gaps in Kazu's evening. If not, the shinobi might have to depend upon Kazu's word and inferences drawn from the younger man's story, and though Hiro trusted Kazu more than almost anyone else in the world, the shinobi's distrust of assumptions ran even deeper than his faith in friends.

Chapter 24

As Hiro approached Ginjiro's brewery, the hum of masculine voices told him the evening crowd had arrived. Most of the regulars knew one another on sight and Hiro was no exception. A samurai patron called a greeting, echoed by several others, and the shinobi acknowledged the welcome with a polite if not heartfelt smile.

Suke sat in his usual corner farthest from the counter, but the monk seemed too absorbed in a flask of sake to notice Hiro's approach.

The shinobi noted Kazu's absence with relief. Ginjiro might talk more openly without the younger man present.

Unfortunately, the brewer was absent too.

Ginjiro's daughter, Tomiko, stood alone behind the counter waiting on patrons. She wore a purple kimono with a repeating pattern of bamboo and paulownia leaves. Its trailing sleeves revealed her unmarried status, unusual in a girl of twenty years, and though Tomiko's face would not stop a man in the street, she had an understated beauty that appealed to those who preferred a real flower to an artificial bloom.

Tomiko looked up as Hiro approached. Her eyes lit and

she smiled in recognition, though the shinobi noticed her gaze flicker over his shoulder. He didn't have to guess who she hoped to see. To her credit, the girl's smile didn't waver much when she saw that Hiro arrived alone.

The shinobi handed his sword across the counter. Tomiko accepted it with both hands. She bowed. "Good evening, Matsui-*san*. May I draw you a flask?"

"Thank you," Hiro said, "but not this evening. I hoped to speak with your father."

She bowed again, this time in assent. "Please wait. I will get him for you."

Hiro remembered the *noren* fluttering during his visit that afternoon. He glanced along the counter. The other patrons had already turned back to their conversations.

"Before you go," he said softly, "perhaps you will answer a question for me. Did you see Ito Kazu last night?"

The girl looked down at the countertop as a blush darkened her cheeks. "Yes, Ito-*san* was here."

"What time did he arrive?" Hiro hoped Tomiko's feelings for Kazu would make her helpful rather than deceptive.

She looked up before answering. "After sunset. I don't remember the time exactly. It was already dark. First he was not here, and then he was. I am sorry I can't be more specific."

Her answer matched her father's, as well as Kazu's. More importantly, she looked the shinobi in the eye and showed no discomfort as she answered the question.

"Do you remember what time he left?" Hiro asked.

She glanced at the counter. "He was here when I left the shop for the night." She bit her lower lip. "Is he well?"

"He is fine," Hiro said. "I am sure he would appreciate your concern."

Tomiko nodded. The blush returned.

Hiro couldn't help but feel sorry for the girl. She wasn't the first to fall for the dashing Kazu, and she would fare no better than the others, though the shinobi suspected Tomiko knew her crush was a hopeless cause. No samurai ever married a brewer's daughter. As far as Tomiko knew, Ito Kazu lay beyond her reach.

The *noren* ruffled as Ginjiro entered the shop from the kitchen. He bowed to Hiro and straightened with a smile.

"Thank you, Tomiko," he said. "You may join your mother."

The girl gave Hiro a look that suggested she wanted to say something more. She changed her mind and departed with a bow.

As Tomiko disappeared through the *noren* Ginjiro lowered his voice and asked, "Does Ito-*san* need help?"

Ginjiro had dealt in sake, and with its drinkers, long enough to develop a nose for trouble.

"I don't think so," Hiro said, "but I do need to know what time he really left last night."

"Half an hour before the temple bells rang midnight."

"Before midnight," Hiro repeated.

"Should I have said so earlier?" Ginjiro asked. "I didn't like your samurai companion. He looked like a man in search of someone to blame. I heard about the murder at the shogunate and didn't want to cause trouble for Kazu. Was he involved?"

"How did you hear about the killing?" Hiro asked.

The brewer shook his head. "I'd no more betray my sources to you than I'd turn Ito-*san* over to that preening shogunate monkey.

"Before you ask," Ginjiro continued, "I don't know who

killed the shogun's clerk, and I have no intention of getting involved. What Ito-*san* does—or doesn't do—outside my shop is none of my concern."

"Why tell me this?" Hiro asked. "I can make trouble for Kazu as easily as the shogun's men."

A knowing smile curled the brewer's lips. "You won't. I know men as well as I know my flasks, and your flaws don't run to betrayal."

Hiro raised an eyebrow but changed the subject. "Are you positive Kazu left before midnight?"

"My wife goes to sleep when the bells ring the midnight hour," Ginjiro said. "I make the last call for snacks half an hour before that. Kazu left the shop as I made the announcement. I'm certain about the time."

"One last question," Hiro said.

Ginjiro didn't even need to hear it. "Kazu wasn't drunk."

The brewer's words fell on Hiro like stones. Kazu had left the brewery in time to kill Saburo, and he hadn't told Hiro the truth about his actions.

The shinobi clenched his jaw to fight the anger that rose, unbidden and unexpected, in his chest. He didn't care about killing Saburo—assassination was a shinobi's trade—but Kazu's lies endangered a fellow shinobi's mission, a serious offense against both Hiro and the *ryu*.

"Have my answers upset you?" Ginjiro looked across the counter, concerned by Hiro's silence.

The shinobi forced a smile. "No. I appreciate your assistance and discretion. You need not worry about Kazu. He was robbed last night, by the river, but he's unharmed."

Ginjiro frowned and swiped the counter with a towel. "The police should patrol that river at night. The thieves are getting bold."

"Desperate men are always bold." As he spoke the words, Hiro felt his anger evaporate, replaced by a sudden chill. If Kazu had murdered Saburo on Hattori Hanzo's orders, the *ryu* would also condone the death of everyone who knew or suspected that Kazu committed the crime. Kazu knew that Hiro and Father Mateo had solved the Akechi murder and could have suspected the shogun would ask for their help with this one. His plea for assistance might have been a ruse to throw them off the track.

But Hiro hadn't fallen for it, and if his persistence threatened to expose Kazu as the killer . . . a trained shinobi would have to counter that threat with lethal force. Hiro fought better than Kazu did, but Kazu also knew that Hiro's greatest weakness lay with the Jesuit priest.

Hiro wanted to believe that kinship—and friendship—would stay Kazu's hand, but the master shinobi was too well-trained to fool himself with hopes. Kazu would kill Father Mateo if he thought his mission required it.

And Hiro had left the Jesuit unguarded.

He hurried home, barely restraining his pace enough to avoid undue attention. He wanted to run but held himself to a rapid walk. Stopping to answer a curious policeman's questions would only delay him more.

He let himself break into a run as he passed Okazaki Shrine. His geta squished in the gummy street and spattered his robe with mud, but at that moment he didn't care about cleanliness.

Only once before in his life had Hiro wished so desperately to be wrong. To his regret, he hadn't been—and this time the life at risk was more important than Hiro's own.

Chapter 25

As Hiro approached the Jesuit's home, he heard voices wailing. He froze, stomach cold and churning like the muddy street beneath his wooden sandals.

In the silence the wailing took on a familiar sound—voices singing a hymn in Japanese. As always, Hiro found the music mournful though the lyrics spoke of praise.

The shinobi bent forward, weak with relief. His breathing slowed and his thoughts grew clear. He berated himself for falling prey to ill-founded worries. Illogical thinking guaranteed failure as surely as an assassin's blade.

He slipped through the gate in the garden wall and entered his room through the veranda door. He decided not to tell Father Mateo that Kazu had lied. Not until he knew why and whether the Jesuit was in danger. Fortunately, the worship service made the priest unavailable anyway.

A few minutes later Hiro emerged from the house wearing special trousers that tied at the ankles, a midnight-colored surcoat, and a cloth that obscured his face.

He pulled himself onto the damp veranda roof and climbed the sloping thatch all the way to the heavy wooden beam at the peak of the house. Mumbling prayers and off-key singing wafted up from the rooms below, covering even the minimal noise of his movements. As he straddled the beam, Hiro glanced at the cloudy sky and hoped the rain had finished for the night.

Inside the house the silent mumble increased to a babble. The front door opened, discharging the chattering congregants into the street. Their lanterns bobbed like fireflies in the gathering darkness.

Hiro bent over the beam. In the cloudy twilight, and without the moon to betray him, only an owl's eyes would see the shinobi perched on the roof, but Hiro didn't believe in taking chances. Not unnecessary chances, anyway.

Angry barking burst from the yard across the street, startling the parishioners. A group of women clustered together as if their numbers might deter attack. A child cried out in fear. The barking increased, and Hiro half expected to see the neighbor's massive akita run into the road. The vicious beast had escaped before, but the owner had always recaptured the dog before it caused any harm.

This time the dog did not appear.

After a moment, the women giggled nervously and dispersed. The barking slowed as the street grew still. Eventually the akita gave a final peevish bark and then fell silent.

Hiro allowed himself a moment of envy for the dog. The akita's world held only friends and enemies, and the lines between the two remained distinct.

Dawn found Hiro still on the roof, damp from the rain that emptied the clouds and allowed the rising sun to send golden streamers through the sky. He yawned and stretched his muscles, stiff from exhaustion but satisfied. Even if guilty, Kazu would go back to work to keep up appearances, which meant that Father Mateo was safe until nightfall.

Hiro slipped down from his perch and into the house. He shed his wet clothes and lay down on his futon for a nap. Gato joined him almost at once, and the shinobi fell asleep to the kitten's rumbling purr.

An hour later, Father Mateo's morning prayers woke Hiro from a sleep that diminished exhaustion but not concern. Foregoing both breakfast and explanations, Hiro put on his gray kimono and left the house by the veranda door.

When the shogunate gates swung open for the day, Hiro was there and waiting. But before the guards could ask his business, he saw a familiar figure in the road.

"Please excuse me," Hiro said to the puzzled guards, "I have already found the man I need to see."

He turned away and walked toward Kazu at a pace designed to ensure that he would meet the younger man far enough from the gates to prevent the guards from hearing their conversation.

Kazu saw him approaching and stopped to bow.

"Have you eaten?" Hiro asked. "I know a good noodle cart nearby."

"Is there one in Kyoto you don't know?" Kazu smiled. "I can't. I'll be late for work."

"Not as late as you will be when I accuse you of killing Saburo."

Kazu's eyes widened, then narrowed. "I told you I didn't do it."

"You lied."

Kazu's face revealed nothing.

"You left Ginjiro's before midnight," Hiro said. "You had plenty of time to kill Saburo."

BLADE OF THE SAMURAI   133

"You checked my story?" Kazu's left hand balled into a fist. "You didn't trust me."

"With good reason," Hiro said. "You didn't tell the truth."

He started walking away from the shogunate gates. As he expected, Kazu followed. Hiro watched the younger man carefully. He doubted Kazu would risk an attack within sight of the guards, but a wise man made no assumptions.

When they had almost reached the end of the block Hiro asked, "Did you think I wouldn't reveal you as the murderer? Or did you just think yourself too smart to be caught?"

"I did not kill Saburo," Kazu muttered through clenched teeth. "I swear it on my honor."

Hiro bit back a snide remark about liars' honor. Some things no man could hear without a fight. "Where were you two nights ago?"

"At Ginjiro's, as I told you," Kazu said. "Ask Den, the stable boy. He was in the garden outside the mansion when I returned."

"You claimed no one saw you return," Hiro said. "Besides, Den was out of town."

"He wasn't out of town," Kazu said. "When I slipped back over the wall I saw him in the garden northeast of the kitchen, near the *bakufu* mansion. He saw me too, and bowed, so I pretended I was merely out for a stroll.

"And I told you that no one saw me come over the wall."

Kazu sounded truthful, but his words didn't match the stable master's story.

Hiro considered the scars on his own shoulder and inner thigh, the price of another misplaced trust.

"The stable is on the opposite side of the compound," Hiro said. "If Den was in Kyoto, which Masao disputes, what was he doing so far from his proper place?"

"He seemed to be crying," Kazu said.

Male servants did not cry.

Hiro shook his head. "Masao said Den left the city."

They had reached the southeast corner of the compound. Kazu looked to his right, along the road that paralleled the southern wall of the shogunate. "We should ask Masao why he lied."

"I intend to," Hiro said, "but there is no 'we.'"

"You don't trust me."

Hiro looked at Kazu without emotion. "Your presence could frighten him into a different lie. Besides, I need your help another way."

"So now you want the help of a murdering liar?" Kazu asked.

Hiro heard himself in the younger man's tone but tried to ignore it. "A schedule book disappeared from Saburo's office after the murder. Hisahide says the shogun asked him to retrieve it. I need to know if that's true, and whether anything else was taken."

It was risky to ask for the younger man's help, but Hiro knew no other way to monitor Kazu's movements without offending.

"I don't believe Hisahide's story," Kazu said. "The shogun would have retrieved the ledger personally. He wouldn't have trusted anyone else to handle it—especially Matsunaga Hisahide." Kazu glanced over his shoulder and lowered his voice. "Do you know why Hisahide came to Kyoto?"

Hiro shook his head. His assignment hadn't required a detailed study of provincial politics.

"When Daimyo Miyoshi Chokei died last year, most people expected his childhood friend—Matsunaga Hisahide—to succeed him as the lord of Yamato Province."

"The daimyo had no relatives?" Hiro asked.

"He had three brothers, and a son, all of whom prede-
ceased him under suspicious circumstances."

"Hisahide killed them?"

"No one dared suggest it," Kazu said, "and with good
reason. Hisahide is a dangerous man.

"After Miyoshi Chokei died, his will revealed that he had
adopted his nephew in secret and named the boy his heir.
But the new daimyo is only a child. His regents—trusted
Miyoshi clansmen—sent Hisahide to Kyoto immediately."

"And the shogun knows this?" Hiro asked, though he
guessed the answer before he saw Kazu's nod of confirmation.

"I'll find out about the ledger," Kazu said.

"I'll come to your office after I speak with Masao."

Chapter 26

Kazu turned back toward the compound entrance, but Hiro headed west along the southern wall of the shogunate compound. The shinobi refused to deny his growling stomach a bowl of noodles just because Kazu didn't want to be late for work.

Half an hour and one large breakfast later, Hiro entered the shogunate through the stable gate in the western wall. He found Masao sweeping the earthen yard.

"Good morning," Hiro said. "Have you remembered anything more about the night Ashikaga-*san* died?"

The stable master feigned a smile that would have fooled most men. "There is nothing to remember. I wasn't here and Den was visiting relatives out of town."

"Curious," Hiro said. "A samurai claims to have seen Den here that evening."

Masao's smile faded. "Please come with me."

Hiro followed him into the stable. The long wooden structure had double doors on either end for easy access to the stalls that lined the interior. A hay-strewn corridor ran up the center of the building, and a raised wooden platform at one end provided a living space for Masao and Den.

The air inside the stable was fresh but heavily scented with horses, hay, and the underlying odors of wood and leather.

Masao leaned his broom against the wall and turned to Hiro, face grim, like a man owning up to a crime. "Den left Kyoto the night Ashikaga-*san* died."

"Why did you say otherwise?" Hiro asked.

"Why does any man lie? I was afraid. But Den did not kill Ashikaga Saburo." Masao gestured to the platform. "Please sit, if you wish. I'm sorry I have no better place to offer."

Ths shinobi didn't move.

Masao nodded, accepting Hiro's decision to stand. "When I returned from dinner I thought I would find Den sleeping, but he was awake and terrified. He said he had argued with Ashikaga-*san* about a girl. I've felt the brunt of Ashikaga-*san*'s temper more than once, and I thought it wise to send the boy out of town to let the samurai's anger cool."

"Would the girl be Jun, the maid?" Hiro asked.

Masao raised his hands defensively. "I promise you, the relationship is entirely innocent. Den hopes to marry Jun, in time, though he hasn't mentioned it to her. It wouldn't be appropriate before he finishes his apprenticeship."

Hiro found Masao's concern understandable but irrelevant. "Did Den describe the argument?"

Masao indicated the stable door. "He said that Jun ran in, out of breath, and claimed that Ashikaga-*san* was chasing her. Den hid the girl in an empty stall. When Ashikaga-*san* arrived Den claimed he hadn't seen her."

"Which Ashikaga-*san* disputed."

Masao nodded. "Den wouldn't change his story, so Ashikaga-*san* left in a rage. Jun hid here a while longer, and afterward Den walked her back to the kitchen."

Assuming the timing matched, which it could, Masao's

new story put Den outside the shogunate kitchen exactly as Kazu claimed. That didn't prove Kazu's innocence, but it told Hiro what to investigate next.

"I need to speak with Den," he said.

"Why?" Masao asked. "I've told you everything."

Hiro knew concern for the boy was the key to obtaining the stable master's assistance. "I need to speak with him personally in order to persuade the shogun that Den did not kill Saburo."

A genuine smile relaxed Masao's face. "He is staying with my cousin, the apothecary, at Ōtsu. But, if you please . . . would you speak to Den there, rather than bringing him back to Kyoto? I am worried about his safety."

"Ashikaga Saburo is dead," Hiro said. "His anger is no longer cause for concern."

When Masao's smile faltered, Hiro added, "I have no intention of blaming an innocent boy for this crime or allowing anyone else to do so either."

Hiro left the compound and retraced his route to the shogunate's east entrance along the public roads. The shinobi could have reached Kazu's office faster by crossing the shogun's compound, but he decided not to risk it without an escort. Heightened security gave the guards a motive to detain and interrogate strangers, and Hiro wanted to finish his business and leave for Ōtsu as quickly as possible.

The shogun's guards escorted Hiro into the waiting room of the *bakufu* mansion and sent a runner for Kazu. The six-mat room overflowed with samurai waiting for an audience. The musty odor of sweat-dampened silk overpowered the sandalwood incense smoking wanly in a brazier near the entrance.

A pair of richly dressed samurai stood by the door. When Hiro entered, one of them leaned toward the other and whispered, "Ronin." Both men sneered as if smelling something foul.

Hiro ignored them and waited.

Minutes passed. One of the well-dressed samurai sneezed, presumably from standing too close to the incense.

Eventually Kazu arrived and led Hiro back through the mansion's many tatami-floored chambers.

"You were right," Kazu said as they passed through an empty room, "this month's guard schedule is missing from the office."

"Does the shogun have it?" Hiro asked.

"I don't know." Kazu looked uncomfortable. "I can't approach him directly, and asking questions might raise suspicions."

Hiro decided not to mention that Kazu's refusal to ask was suspicious too.

When they reached the final audience chamber before Saburo's office, Hiro noticed Ozuru at work on the transom carving. The master carpenter had his back to the entrance. His chisel and hammer tapped a steady accompaniment to the other men's scraping planes.

Hiro leaned toward Kazu. "I need to speak with the carpenter for a moment."

Ozuru turned, surprising Hiro, who didn't think he spoke loudly enough to be heard.

The master carpenter bowed. His subordinates noticed the samurai and knelt.

"Get up and get back to work," Kazu said.

The assistants stood and resumed their planing. Ozuru waited, inaction confirming he heard the shinobi's words.

"I'll wait for you in the office." Kazu continued across the room.

"May I help you?" Ozuru asked.

Hiro wasted no time on pleasantries. "Two nights ago, which gate did you use to leave the shogunate compound?"

Ozuru smiled. "Servants and artisans always use the stable gate."

"What time did you leave?"

"Just before midnight," Ozuru said. "The bells rang as I reached the gates of my ward."

"Who let you out of the compound?"

The carpenter glanced at the transom carving as if he longed to return to work. "The stable boy. I'm afraid I don't know his name."

"I have one more question," Hiro said. "Why did you leave work yesterday?"

"I broke a chisel. I went to buy another."

Ozuru's polite but conversational tone struck Hiro as unusual. Few commoners exhibited such composure when speaking with samurai. Then again, Ozuru had worked at the shogunate long enough to become accustomed to conversing with men of higher rank.

"Thank you," Hiro said. "I will not keep you from your work."

Ozuru bowed and returned to his carving as Hiro left the room.

The shinobi paused in the doorway to Saburo's outer office. The grassy scent of fresh tatami permeated the air, along with the sharper odor of Kazu's wintergreen hair oil.

Someone had replaced the ruined mats and scrubbed the bloodstains from the floor. New paper panels set the wall aglow.

Kazu knelt before the desk to the right of the entrance. He gestured for Hiro to enter and close the shoji. As the paneled door slid closed Kazu opened a lacquered box that sat on the desk before him. He removed a folded parchment and extended it toward Hiro.

"You'll want to see this. It was hidden in Saburo's letter box."

Chapter 27

Hiro unfolded the parchment. "It's unsigned."

"Read it," Kazu said. "Would you have signed it?"

The writer wasted no space on idle words. Even the salutation had been omitted.

Our friends will arrive on the eighteenth, as planned. Make sure they gain access and find the proper men on duty. Full payment is expected upon completion

Hiro looked up. "Completion of what?"

"I don't know," Kazu said. "The sentence looks unfinished, but I suspect that's intentional. The writer didn't want anyone but Saburo to understand."

After a pause he added, "Lord Oda's emissaries are expected on the eighteenth."

"Two days from now." Hiro turned the letter over. The back was blank. "You found this in Saburo's letter box? Strange that no one found it yesterday."

"Hisahide wouldn't have known to look," Kazu said. "Saburo kept the box a secret—even from me, or so he thought. I'm bothered by the letter, though. I'm not sure it's genuine. The parchment shows no signs of handling, suggesting it didn't travel far. But if the writer was in Kyoto he would have delivered that kind of message in person."

Hiro agreed. Only fools put things in writing unnecessarily.

"Also," Kazu continued, "the letter, combined with the missing ledger, implies a plot against the shogun—but I don't think Saburo would do that. He was greedy but never disloyal."

"Perhaps someone made him a better offer," Hiro said.

"Would you trust Lord Oda to keep his word?" Kazu shook his head. "Saburo was a selfish man, but he knew where his power came from."

"Did Saburo receive private correspondence often?" Hiro asked.

"Daily," Kazu said, "but most of it wasn't really confidential. I think he kept it private just for show."

Without warning, the door slid open. Hisahide entered the office, followed by Akira.

"What's that?" Hisahide frowned at the letter in Hiro's hands.

The shinobi handed over the parchment.

"Where did you find this?" Hisahide demanded. "Who was it sent to?"

"I found it this morning, in Ashikaga-*san*'s private letter box," Kazu said.

Hisahide glanced at Akira. "Why didn't you find this yesterday?"

Akira glared at Kazu. "What letter box?"

"A hidden box for private correspondence," Kazu said. "I was the only other person who knew about it."

Akira looked at Hiro. "You showed it to him?" He sounded offended.

"I apologize if I erred," Kazu said. "You told me Matsui Hiro was investigating the murder. The letter seemed relevant to his inquiry."

"Is this a good enough excuse to stop Lord Oda's men from entering Kyoto?" Hiro asked.

"Not without offending Lord Oda and risking war." Hisahide turned to Akira. "I need the new firearms immediately. Find the merchant and get the weapons now."

"If you mean the Portuguese merchant, Luis," Hiro said, "he left for Ōtsu this morning."

Hisahide looked surprised, but the emotion faded almost at once. Hiro suspected the samurai knew not only where Hiro lived but also who shared the house.

"When will he return?" Hisahide asked.

"Tomorrow," Hiro said, "and he will have your weapons with him."

"Leaving less than a day to equip the men," Hisahide said. "Akira, ride to Ōtsu and tell the merchant I need those weapons immediately. Use your shogunate pass and leave word with the guards to ensure there are no delays at the barricades."

"I'll go with you," Hiro said. "I have business at Ōtsu."

"You have no business outside Kyoto until Saburo's killer is found," Hisahide said.

"I need to interview Den, the stable boy," Hiro said, "and Den is currently at Ōtsu."

"He wasn't here when Saburo was killed. What could he possibly know?" Akira asked.

"He was here," Hiro said. "Two witnesses saw him here the night of the murder."

"I will let you leave the city on one condition," Hisahide said. "You will ride with Akira and will not leave his side. If you try to flee, I will kill the foreign priest."

Hiro had no intention of leaving Father Mateo behind as a hostage, but before he could object, Hisahide continued, "Please excuse me. The shogun will want to see this immediately."

He turned on his heel and left the room.

"Let's go," Akira said, "we should ride at once."

Hiro needed a minute to think. "It's a long ride to Ōtsu. I need to visit the latrine."

Akira tried not to show his distaste but failed. "Kazu can escort you and bring you to the stable when you finish. I'll meet you there."

As they approached the narrow building that housed the latrine Kazu asked, "Was that an excuse or do you really need . . . ?"

Hiro gestured for Kazu to follow him inside. The sharp scent of ammonia—and worse—rose from the oval slots in the floor, suggesting the collection pots beneath were in need of cleaning. Some air seeped in through the slatted windows, but barely enough to make the atmosphere bearable.

"Where did you go after leaving Ginjiro's the night Saburo died?" Hiro asked.

Kazu raised a hand to his nose. "That's what you needed me here to ask? Did you think the smell would make me change my story?"

"Diversion works only on those not trained to use it." Hiro turned to face the latrine. He heard Kazu leave the building but didn't worry. The younger man would wait.

When he left the latrine, Hiro took a deep breath of rain-scented air to flush the less pleasant odors from his lungs. He fell in step beside Kazu, who started walking the moment Hiro appeared.

"Where did you go between Ginjiro's and coming back to the shogunate?" Hiro asked.

For a moment, Kazu didn't answer. He gave Hiro a side-long glance. "I cannot tell you."

"You know what that implies."

"It implies exactly nothing." Kazu said. "I did not murder Saburo."

"So you claim, but that doesn't prove it."

Kazu turned on Hiro. "You question my word?"

"You are trained to lie." Hiro felt his anger rising to answer Kazu's.

"Not to you."

"To everyone," Hiro snapped, "unless your training failed."

The shinobi held Kazu's gaze but watched peripherally for movement. He stood as still as possible so as not to provoke a fight.

Kazu scowled. "It is brotherhood that has failed." He turned on his heel and stalked away down the path.

Hiro followed in a silence that lasted all the way to the stable. The shinobi wanted to mend the breach, but his mouth refused to form a single conciliatory word. His current mistrust of Kazu ran too deep. He also objected deeply to Kazu risking Father Mateo's safety—and Hiro's own—without offering the courtesy of the truth.

Hiro loathed feeling used, and at that moment he felt very ill used indeed.

When they reached the edge of the stable yard, Kazu

paused for only a moment and then departed without a word. Hiro noticed Akira waiting outside the stable and decided to obtain permission for Father Mateo to join their ride to Ōtsu. The shinobi had no intention of leaving the Jesuit alone in Kyoto with Kazu and Hisahide.

Hooves pounded on the bridge as Ichiro rode into the yard on his tall bay horse.

The boy leaned back in his saddle, brought the horse to a stop, and dismounted.

"Masao," he called, "take my horse, I'm late!"

Masao emerged from the stable, bowed, and took the horse's reins.

Ichiro noticed Hiro. "Good morning, Matsui-*san*," he said with a bow. "Have you captured my father's killer?"

Hiro bowed as if addressing an adult. "Not yet, Ashikaga-*san*, but I will."

"Kazu called on us last night. Thank you for proving that he was not to blame."

Hiro decided not to mention his reconsideration of Kazu's guilt. "Thank you for speaking on his behalf. Your opinion was very helpful."

"It was not an opinion." Ichiro straightened his shoulders and raised his chin. "I know that Kazu is not guilty."

"My apologies," Hiro said. "Thank you for sharing your knowledge."

Ichiro nodded. "Please excuse me. A samurai should never be late for his lessons. Tardiness shows disrespect for the tutor."

He strode off toward the mansion, head high and pace unhurried, looking more noble than most men twice his age.

The boy had barely left the yard when Akira asked, "Do

you have to obtain the priest's permission before you can leave Kyoto?"

"I am free to come and go as I please," Hiro said, "but—"

"You serve the wrong priest, you know," Akira said. "Father Vilela's mission is large and honorable. Your Father Mateo makes serious mistakes."

"Does he?" Hiro asked.

"All men are not equal. It is nonsense to suggest it and unacceptable even to mention such a thing to peasants. Commoners' ignorance leads them to folly quickly enough without the intervention of foreign priests."

"I assure you," Hiro said, "he intends no harm."

"And I assure you, his intentions are irrelevant. Persisting in this error will bring worse trouble than expulsion from the shogunate."

Masao emerged from the stable a second time, leading a pair of horses.

Akira took the larger horse's reins and swung into the saddle. He looked down his nose at Hiro. "You would do well to find employment elsewhere."

The guards at the gate cried out in surprise. A little boy raced past them into the yard.

Two samurai in lacquered armor ran after the child, but the boy eluded their grasp. He started for Hiro but froze at the sight of Akira and the horses.

The child's thin hands clutched at his faded kimono as if the fabric might protect him from samurai rage. His bare feet shuffled on the ground. He didn't seem to notice the mud that squelched between his toes.

A chill spread over Hiro as if he had plunged headfirst into an icy lake. The child was the only son of Father Mateo's neighbor across the street.

"Wait!" The shinobi raised a hand to the guards. "I know him. Let him speak."

The armored samurai paused and exchanged an awkward look.

The boy bent forward, struggling to catch his breath.

At last he straightened. "Hiro, come quickly! Father Mateo is dying!"

Chapter 28

D ying?" Hiro couldn't believe it. "How?"
    "*Otosan's* dog got loose." The boy sounded desperate.
"It went after Ana. Father Mateo tried to help but the dog
attacked him instead."

Questions swirled in Hiro's mind: how the akita escaped its tether, what it was doing at home again, and why
the owner hadn't noticed the dog's escape in time to prevent the attack.

He didn't stop to ask.

"I need this horse." Hiro took the reins from Masao and
swung into the saddle.

As the shinobi reined the horse in a circle Akira said,
"You may take it."

Hiro glanced over his shoulder, surprised by the samurai's consent.

"I may not like your Jesuit," Akira said, "but no honorable man would withhold assistance." He nodded. "Go."

Hiro pulled the neighbor's child up behind him on the
saddle. As soon as he felt the boy's hands on his waist, the
shinobi put his heels to the horse's sides.

"I'll go to Ōtsu," Akira called, "and bring Den back to Kyoto later tonight."

Hiro barely heard him over the sound of the horse's hooves on the wooden bridge.

He held the beast at a gallop the whole way home, scattering pedestrians and spattering the slower ones with mud from the stallion's hooves. For once, he didn't try to avoid attention. If Father Mateo died, it wouldn't matter who saw Hiro on the road.

When they reached the Jesuit's house the shinobi lowered the boy to the ground, dismounted, and handed the child the reins.

"Walk the horse to Okazaki Shrine, and ask a priest to return it to the shogunate."

A splash of crimson stained the grass by the veranda. Bloody droplets formed a trail across the porch, and a single bloody footprint smeared the threshold.

As he followed the trail inside, Hiro tried to calculate how much blood the priest had lost. Not enough to have bled to death immediately, but enough that Hiro worried he might still have come too late.

The trail continued through the foyer, across the *oe*, and under the door of Father Mateo's room. The wooden shoji frame and paper panels showed no bloody stains. Someone, probably Ana, had helped the Jesuit to his room.

Hiro laid a hand on the door, wanting and yet not wanting to see what lay on the other side. He took a breath and entered.

Darkening bloodstains spattered the tatami from the doorway to the center of the room. There, Father Mateo lay on a hastily opened futon. His eyes were closed. His misshapen, bloody hands lay folded across his stomach. Crimson stains covered his neck and the front of his brown kimono.

His face was pale. He wasn't moving.

"Mateo!" Hiro rushed to the Jesuit's side.

Father Mateo opened his eyes. "I stopped the dog." He tried to smile but failed. A bloody wound at the base of his throat sent a crimson trickle down his neck.

"You got here quickly," Ana bustled into the room with a steaming pot in one hand and strips of cream-colored silk in the other. "Taro must have found you at the shogunate."

She thrust the silk into Hiro's hands and set the pot on the floor beside Father Mateo.

The Jesuit's bloody neck and ruined hands told Hiro that water alone would not suffice.

"Boil another kettle," he said. "Add a handful of salt. And when you bring it, please get the medicine box from the shelf beside my desk."

Ana nodded, controlled as always, but Hiro saw the worry in her eyes.

When she left the room he knelt and turned his attention to the wounds.

The gash on the left side of Father Mateo's neck had bled heavily. Fortunately, the bleeding had slowed, though the skin of the Jesuit's throat looked badly torn.

Father Mateo's left hand bore a series of deep red punctures that oozed a mixture of blood and pinkish fluid. The surrounding flesh was ripped and swollen, indicating broken bones, probably crushed by the force of the bite. Blood covered the hand, some still red and the rest already dark and clotting.

The priest's right hand looked better, but only by comparison. The punctures were fewer in number and without the ragged gashes. The swelling seemed less prominent, too, but until the wounds were clean the shinobi couldn't tell how much damage the hand had suffered.

Hiro started to reach for the priest's left hand. He paused. Father Mateo's bloody sleeves and chest suggested additional injuries.

"Where else were you bitten?" Hiro asked.

Father Mateo started to raise his hands but stopped with a jerking motion and a grimace. He inhaled sharply against the pain. After a slow but not quite shuddering breath he said, "My hands, my left arm—and my neck. It could have been worse."

Hiro nodded. "It's important to clean them properly. This will hurt."

"It already hurts." The Jesuit closed his eyes. "Do what you need to."

Hiro drew back Father Mateo's sleeve, exposing deep bloody gashes on the Jesuit's left arm. The punctures were not as numerous as the ones on the hands, but they looked deep and the muscles seriously torn. Fortunately, the Jesuit's bones appeared intact.

"I don't think your arm is broken," Hiro said. "Can you move your fingers?"

Father Mateo opened his eyes. "Not easily, and I'd rather not even try. I asked Ana to send for a surgeon, but she insisted we wait for you."

"She was right," Hiro said. "I can treat wounds better than any Kyoto surgeon. It was part of my training."

"How would Ana know that? Did you tell her . . . ?"

Hiro shook his head. "She thinks I'm ronin, like everyone else does, but she's seen my medicine box and she recognized some of the healing herbs. She probably thinks since I own them I know how to use them."

"Do you?"

Hiro raised an eyebrow at the priest. "Most men in your position would worry more about the bites than about the treatment."

"Begging your pardon, but if you poison me the bites become less important."

The shinobi laughed despite his concern. "I know how to use the herbs."

Hiro found the Jesuit's fortitude impressive. Few samurai would endure the pain so well.

He glanced at the door and wished Ana would hurry. He needed salted water and medicines to clean the wounds before an infection started. The bleeding had stopped for the moment, but only time would tell if the Jesuit had lost too much blood to recover.

"Can you tell me about the attack?" Hiro asked.

Blood loss could cloud a victim's perception. Hiro hoped the answers would help him evaluate the priest's condition.

"Ana was outside, sweeping the steps. I heard her speak to the neighbor's son and went out to invite his family to church on Sunday."

"Why do you keep inviting them?" Hiro asked. "They never come."

"They are my neighbors," Father Mateo said. "I am treating them the way I would want to be treated."

Hiro bit his tongue. This wasn't the time to ask if the priest liked being harassed with unwanted invitations.

"As I opened the door I heard Taro shout a warning," Father Mateo said. "The dog ran into the yard with a frayed rope trailing behind it. It started for Ana. I yelled to distract it and jumped off the porch to protect her."

"You yelled at the dog?" Hiro asked.

"I did. A Portuguese dog would have fled."

Hiro shook his head. "Akitas attack when threatened."

"Now you tell me."

Hiro found the sarcasm encouraging.

Dying men didn't usually display a functional grasp of irony.

Chapter 29

D id you kill the dog?" Hiro asked.
"He did not." Ana entered the room with a steaming pot and a lacquered box retrieved from Hiro's room.
She set both on the floor and continued, "Taro's father pulled
the dog away."

"He's home today?" Hiro asked.

"His wife is ill." Ana looked at Father Mateo. "Good thing
I bought a fish this morning. The broth will help him."

"I agree," Hiro said.

Ana looked surprised, then nodded. "I'll cook it now.
Let me know if you need my help."

She hurried out and closed the door behind her.

Hiro dipped a strip of silk in the salted water. Based on
the saline odor that rose from the pot and the scalding heat
on his fingertips, Ana had done exactly as he requested. He
wrung the extra water from the silk and dabbed at the
Jesuit's neck.

Father Mateo drew a hissing breath.

"It's going to get worse," Hiro said. "Do you want a cloth
to bite on?"

Father Mateo opened his eyes. "I can manage without."

Blood saturated the first cloth almost immediately. Hiro dropped it into the pot of unsalted water and dipped another strip in the steaming brine. He cleaned the Jesuit's wounds, wiping firmly but carefully around each rip and puncture. The priest flinched only a little and didn't cry out at all.

Hiro remembered the painful salt-water cleansing of the wounds that scarred his own inner thigh and shoulder. Despite the years, the memory remained as vibrant—and as excruciating—as if it had happened only yesterday.

He forced his thoughts back to the present, unwilling to dwell on his injuries and even less willing to think of how he received them.

By the time Hiro finished cleaning the Jesuit's wounds, the bleeding had stopped. The deepest punctures still oozed a little fluid, but Hiro knew even that would stop very soon.

The shinobi dropped the last used piece of silk in the bloody water and raised the lid of the medicine box. He flipped through the rows of folded paper packets until he found the one he wanted.

Hiro removed the packet and broke the seal, revealing a crystalline powder within. A pungent odor filled the air.

"What is that?" Father Mateo opened his eyes.

"Camphor." Hiro tilted the envelope slightly so the priest could see the contents. He tried to ignore the unpleasant tingling the powder always caused in his sensitive nose. "In small doses it fights infection."

"Does it sting?"

"Some, but not for long, and it will numb the pain a little." Hiro decided not to explain that, in larger doses, camphor was also toxic.

He sprinkled the powder on Father Mateo's wounds. As before, the priest endured the process without protest.

"I don't suppose you have something else for the pain?" Father Mateo asked.

Hiro folded the camphor closed and returned it to the box. "Sake helps."

Father Mateo frowned.

The shinobi stifled a smile. On matters of morality, the Jesuit was nothing if not predictable.

When he finished bandaging the wounds. Hiro thumbed through his box and removed a twist of paper wrapped around an object about the size and shape of a soybean. "This will help. I'll ask Ana to make you some tea."

Father Mateo nodded and closed his eyes. His face relaxed and his lips began to move in silent prayer.

Knocking echoed through the house. Someone was at the door.

Father Mateo opened his eyes and raised his head but Hiro laid a restraining hand on the Jesuit's chest. "Ana will answer. If it's important, I'll handle it. You need rest."

Father Mateo closed his eyes without arguing.

The shinobi picked up his medicine box and turned to the door. The shoji slid open as he approached. Ana stood in the doorway and bowed, an unusual courtesy.

"You have a visitor, Matsui-*san*," the housekeeper said.

Hiro walked to the door and almost dropped his medicine box in surprise.

Ashikaga Netsuko—Saburo's wife—knelt by the hearth.

"Good afternoon, Lady Ashikaga." Hiro tucked the twist of paper into his sleeve and handed the medicine box to Ana.

The housekeeper bowed and scurried from the room.

"Is the priest away?" Netsuko asked as Hiro joined her at the hearth.

"I apologize, but he is unable to see you today."

She looked at a spot of blood on the floor and then raised her eyes to Hiro with a directness women usually avoided. The unspoken question was clear.

Hiro nodded. "There was an accident."

"Most unfortunate." Netsuko nodded politely. "I trust he will recover."

"Yes."

Etiquette prevented Netsuko from asking questions about the details, but Hiro sensed she didn't want them anyway. He also suspected it wasn't Father Mateo she came to see.

"May I offer you tea?" he asked.

As if on cue, Ana appeared with a plate of sweetened rice balls, a pair of porcelain cups and an expensive teapot reserved for Father Mateo's most important guests. In the years since he joined the Jesuit's household, Hiro had never seen the teapot used.

Ana knelt and placed the plate before the lady. She filled the pot with water from the kettle above the hearth, bowed low, and departed without a word.

Delicate steam rose from the teapot, perfuming the air with the sweetly grassy scent of expensive tea. Hiro tried to hide his surprise. The housekeeper must have recognized the shogun's family crest on Netsuko's kimono and raided Luis's personal stash of highest quality *ichibancha*.

Ana disapproved of Hiro, but she would never show it in front of guests.

Netsuko leaned forward and inhaled the steam. "*Gyokuro* tea?" She sounded impressed. "And, unless I'm mistaken, *ichibancha*?"

Recognizing teas by scent was a popular game among wealthy samurai. Hiro silently thanked Ana for making a good impression on his behalf.

"The Portuguese appreciate our ways," Hiro said, deliberately blending Father Mateo's cultural interest with Luis's taste for expensive delicacies.

"Really?" Netsuko gave Hiro a smile that no recent widow should give an unmarried man. "But no foreigner would know that first-picked leaves make the finest tea unless someone competent taught him. You, perhaps?"

Hiro poured a cup of tea for Netsuko and one for himself, thereby avoiding the need to respond to her comment. Netsuko's eyes widened. Hosts normally poured a visitor's tea, but samurai men rarely extended such courtesy to women.

She raised her teacup with a nod of thanks and inhaled the aromatic steam.

Hiro raised his own cup and examined the pale green liquid. He drank in tiny sips, enjoying the delicate sweetness and the heat of the tea on his tongue.

Netsuko also savored her tea in silence. After several minutes she set the empty cup on the mat.

Hiro reached for the pot to refill it.

As the steaming liquid flowed from the teapot into the porcelain cup, Netsuko said, "My husband was not faithful, but he did not deserve to die."

She spoke quietly and without emotion, as though discussing the weather or the tea.

As Hiro set the teapot down, Netsuko studied his face.

"It doesn't surprise you that I knew about his infidelity?" She tilted her head slightly and waited for a response.

Hiro kept his expression blank. "I try not to make assumptions about other men's wives."

"Then perhaps it will not shock you to learn that I approved of his affairs."

Chapter 30

Hiro waited for Netsuko to explain.

Once again she seemed surprised by his lack of reaction. "You don't condemn me for approving of my husband's infidelity?"

This time her pause required a response.

"You doubtless had your reasons." Hiro decided not to offer an excuse that she might substitute for truth.

"I married young," Netsuko said, "but old enough to understand my husband's parents did not choose me for my looks." She stared at Hiro as if daring him to deny her lack of beauty.

He said nothing.

She nodded once, as if confirming he had passed a test. "My husband had status, and a handsome face, but no one would ever call him a brilliant man. His family overlooked my appearance because I had the intelligence and social skills Saburo lacked. He complained at first, as any young man deprived of a beauty will do, but when he realized how much I could help him we reached an understanding.

"We agreed that once I gave birth to a son who survived to the age of three, Saburo could take a mistress, or more than one if he wished. I imposed only two conditions. First, deniability. He would never parade his women in public, discuss them with friends, or act in any way that might bring shame on me or on our son. Second, I made him swear he would never divorce me and that he would always ensure his mistresses knew their place."

As he listened, Hiro thought of the way his kitten, Gato, toyed with bugs she captured in the yard. He wondered whether Netsuko, too, had a penchant for killing her prey when she tired of a game.

He smiled politely. "Your arrangement sounds reasonable."

Netsuko examined her teacup. "I think many people would find it strange." She looked up. "Most men believe a wife should not take an active role in her husband's affairs."

Hiro noted the double meaning and decided it was intentional.

"A wise man does not reject sound advice," he countered, "regardless of the source."

"And are you a wise man?" she asked.

The question caught Hiro off guard.

Netsuko laughed. "I wondered how far I would have to go to surprise you."

Her smile disappeared. "My marriage was a partnership based on convenience and mutual respect. I did not love my husband, as most poets use the word, but our relationship was acceptable and mutually beneficial. To that end, I considered my marriage a good one."

She set her empty teacup on the mat. "I want my husband's murderer punished. Put plainly, I want her dead."

"Her?" Hiro asked.

"My husband's mistress," Netsuko said. "She killed him because he refused to divorce me."

"You know this with certainty?"

As Hiro refilled Netsuko's tea, he realized he hadn't asked Ana to make the painkilling brew for Father Mateo. Etiquette didn't allow him to leave a guest alone, so unless the maid returned to the room the priest would have to wait a little longer.

Netsuko raised her cup with a nod. She savored the steam and sipped her tea, as relaxed as if they discussed a business transaction and not a murder.

Eventually she lowered her cup and continued, "Saburo told me everything. The relationship started innocently—as innocently as it could, anyway—but the girl became unreasonable. She wanted Saburo all to herself. He didn't know how to refuse without causing a scene, though he had no intention of acting on her demands.

"He asked me to help him discard her."

"Your husband asked you to end his affair?" Hiro asked.

"Why wouldn't he? I helped him with everything else." She sipped her tea. "The best lies always hold a grain of truth, so we decided that I would be his excuse. Saburo told the girl I suspected something and that he couldn't risk me making a public spectacle of the affair. He offered her money or to arrange a marriage for her outside of Kyoto."

"And she refused," Hiro said.

"She didn't just refuse, she murdered him."

"Why didn't you tell Matsunaga Hisahide about your suspicions?" Hiro asked.

"You think I didn't?"

"If you had," he said, "Hisahide would not have needed me."

"Hisahide doesn't believe a maid could kill a samurai."

"A maid?" Hiro asked.

Netsuko nodded. "My husband's taste in women was no better than his temper. Neither was very pleasant or well-controlled. I'm sure you've met the girl. Her name is Jun, and she conveniently discovered my husband's body." Netsuko tilted her head to the side. "Based on your expression she didn't admit the affair to you."

"No," Hiro said. "Would you, in her place?"

Netsuko smiled. "I would never allow myself to be caught in such a place."

A slip of the tongue, or another play on words? Hiro couldn't decide.

"What makes you believe Jun killed Saburo?" he asked.

"Her demands, and that Saburo was killed with a dagger. A man would have used a sword."

"But the dagger belonged to Ito Kazu, a fact you acknowledged yourself."

"I regret that accusation." Netsuko took her right hand off the teacup long enough to rub her left wrist. "I wasn't thinking clearly yesterday."

"Now that you have decided to accuse the real murderer, why come to me instead of Hisahide or the shogun?" Hiro asked.

She took a deep breath. Her shoulders sank slightly as she released it. "The foreign priests have a reputation for discretion. I thought, perhaps, since you work with one . . ."

She trailed off as if hoping Hiro would finish the thought. He didn't.

Just before the silence grew awkward Netsuko said, "I hoped you would punish the girl without revealing that I am the one who told you. Ichiro's future and mine depend upon our ignorance of the affair. A grieving widow receives assistance from her husband's clan, but a scheming woman who pandered to her husband's baser instincts always finds herself an object of disdain.

"I want Jun to pay for her crime, but I have no desire to suffer with her."

Netsuko looked at her tea. "Pity. It's gone cold."

She set the cup on the tray and stood up, ending the conversation.

Hiro escorted her to the door. To his surprise, no horse waited in the yard.

Netsuko saw him scan the street. "I rode as far as Okazaki Shrine and walked from there. No one questions a woman's need to pray at a time like this."

Hiro found the comment interesting. Grieving widows seldom thought their actions through so carefully.

"Thank you for your visit." Hiro bowed, the formal gesture echoing his words. "I will give your regards to Father Mateo."

"Thank you for the tea." She stepped off the porch and into her sandals. "And thank you in advance for your discretion."

Hiro watched her walk away.

As she reached the street the neighbor's akita began its furious barking. Hiro tensed, half hoping the dog would run into the street. He would have welcomed any excuse to kill it. But the dog did not appear, and Netsuko continued up the road without a backward glance.

The shinobi turned away and shut the door. Father Mateo still needed a painkilling tea.

Chapter 31

Hiro found Ana clearing the teapot from the hearth. He removed the twist of paper from his sleeve and pulled it open, revealing a sticky ball of resin. He pinched a tiny piece from the ball and extended it to the maid.

"Please brew a strong tea for Father Mateo and add this to the pot," he said.

Ana backed away as if he had offered a venomous spider. "I will not give him poppy tears."

Hiro hadn't thought she would recognize opium. "It will dull his pain and help him sleep."

"He doesn't even drink sake." Ana frowned. "Did he ask for this?"

"Do you want him to suffer?" Hiro's patience grew short. "He won't recover unless he rests and allows his wounds to heal. This slows the heart and brings on sleep. One taste cannot give him a permanent hunger for it."

The final part was a lie, but Hiro hoped Ana's knowledge didn't extend to single-dose dependency. Such addictions were rare enough that Hiro thought the need outweighed the risks.

He heard a loud sneeze and a painful groan from Father Mateo's room.

Ana glanced at the Jesuit's door and held out her hand. "All right." She narrowed her eyes at Hiro. "But I'm holding you responsible."

She accepted the bit of resin and hurried toward the kitchen.

"Hiro!" Father Mateo called, then sneezed again.

The shinobi slid open the Jesuit's door and stifled a laugh.

Father Mateo lay on his futon, blinking tears from his watering eyes. He held his bandaged hands aloft to keep them away from the tortoiseshell kitten sitting on his chest.

Gato leaned forward and licked the Jesuit's swollen nose.

"Hiro! Get it off me."

Father Mateo blew a puff of air in the kitten's face, but Gato just flicked her ears and kneaded her paws on his kimono.

Hiro laughed aloud.

"It's not funny," Father Mateo said, and sniffled to prove his point.

Hiro walked over and scooped the purring cat into his hand. "Come on, Gato. That's enough."

The kitten butted the shinobi with her forehead.

Hiro backed away from the priest. "How did she get in here?"

"I don't know." Father Mateo flinched as he laid his injured hands on his chest again. "I dozed off. When I woke up she was there."

"Most likely enjoying the warmth," Hiro said.

"Most definitely making me sneeze."

"We don't have to keep her," Hiro said. "I could find her another home."

"And upset Ana?" Father Mateo shook his head. "I'd rather sneeze. Besides, I like the cat when she's not shedding hair up my nose."

The Jesuit sighed. His lips wavered into a frown. "You mentioned medicine. Will it help the pain?"

"It will." Hiro fingered the twist of paper, wondering whether he should have opted for willow bark and horse chestnut seeds instead of the stronger opium. But he had used only a tiny amount—far less than a smoker used for a comforting high. He decided to watch the priest's reaction carefully. If the opium didn't give much relief, or if it worked too well, he would use something different the next time.

Hiro took Gato back to his room, set her down, and pondered Netsuko's visit. The woman's accusations, while superficially reasonable, had troublesome undertones. Mistresses didn't murder their lovers. They blackmailed or embarrassed them instead. Hiro found it more likely that Jun created the problem by accident.

Love made young men do rash things, and Den was in love with Jun.

None of which explained Kazu's refusal to talk or what Ozuru the carpenter really did after dark that night. Hiro even considered Netsuko a suspect. Her visit raised more questions than it answered. Hopefully talking with Den would do the opposite.

Hiro put on a pair of old *hakama* and a faded tunic, grabbed his swords, and hurried into the yard. He practiced katas until his muscles burned and his forehead dripped with sweat.

When he finished, Hiro retrieved his kimono from his

room and walked to the public bathhouse down the road. He bathed and spent an hour relaxing in the steam, returning home as the sky darkened from cloudy gray to charcoal. He hurried along the road, intent on arriving home by nightfall, the hour when shogunate workers headed home—and after which, a rival shinobi might pay the priest a visit.

Hiro reached the house exactly when he intended. He opened his mouth to call for Ana as he entered the *oe*, but the words dissolved like sugar on his tongue.

Kazu stood in front of the door to Father Mateo's room.

"What are you doing?" Hiro's hand flew to the hilt of his katana. He had the blade half out of its sheath when he froze, chilled by the realization that he really would kill anyone—even Kazu—to save the priest.

Kazu turned. "Looking for you." His lips curved into the charming smile that had melted women's hearts, and softened men's, since his early childhood.

It didn't work on Hiro anymore.

"That isn't my room," the shinobi said, "and you know it."

He pushed past Kazu and slid the door open just far enough to see Father Mateo sleeping and undisturbed. He slid the door closed and turned.

"What are you doing here? I won't ask again."

Kazu's smile faded. "You don't need to act like a mannerless ronin."

"Answer my question immediately."

Kazu stepped backward. "I found evidence. I thought you'd want to hear about it."

"What's too important to wait for tomorrow?"

"Forget it," Kazu turned away.

"You're here," Hiro said. "You might as well stay and tell me."

Kazu looked over his shoulder. Hiro thought the younger man might leave, but instead Kazu stalked to the hearth and knelt with a thump that made Hiro wince.

The shinobi forced his emotions away as he joined his guest at the hearth. Further hostility would not help him discern Kazu's real motives.

"May I offer you tea?" Hiro asked.

"Thank you, no."

As his thoughts cleared, Hiro doubted that Kazu had come to hurt the priest. Still, the younger man had no reason to enter the house without permission.

Hiro skipped the usual formalities. "What did you find at the shogunate?"

"Hisahide returned the ledger containing the schedules for the shogun's personal guards," Kazu said. "He claimed the shogun didn't need it any longer. The explanation seemed suspicious, so after he left I read the schedule.

"It's been altered since the night Saburo died."

Chapter 32

A ltered?" Hiro repeated.

Kazu nodded. "The guards originally assigned to the shogun's quarters tomorrow night have been exchanged for alternates."

"Alternates?" Hiro asked.

"Yes," Kazu said. "Shogunate guards, but not the men Saburo would have assigned for duty that night."

"How do you know?"

"Saburo had a system. The men on duty tomorrow night are not the ones the system would have named."

"And you know the changes were made by someone other than Saburo?" Hiro asked.

"The writing is similar, but it shows inconsistencies. I'm not certain."

"Could the shogun have changed the ledger?" Hiro asked. "The letter you found suggested a plot, and shifting the guards might stop an assassination attempt."

"It's possible," Kazu said, "but why tomorrow night? Lord Oda's men aren't due to arrive until the following morning."

"Do the changes continue through the ambassadors' visit?" Hiro asked.

Kazu looked at the floor. "I didn't look. I was so surprised about the change that I came straight here to tell you."

"You'd better go back and find out," Hiro said, "since it doesn't appear that you brought the ledger with you."

Kazu looked up, alarmed. "Of course I didn't bring it. The shogun would kill me if I took it outside the compound— and I don't mean that as a figure of speech. I won't be able to check tonight anyway. They've locked the gates, and no one goes in or out without an excuse. With everything that's going on, I'm not willing to risk the wall."

He looked at Father Mateo's door. "What happened to the priest? Does he always go to bed this early?"

"The neighbor's dog attacked him this afternoon."

Kazu leaned forward. "Is it serious?"

Worry weighted Hiro's chest. "Too soon to know."

"I hope he recovers." Kazu stood up and bowed formally. "It is a terrible thing to lose a brother."

Before Hiro could rise, the younger man left the room. Hiro heard the front door open and close as Kazu left the house.

The shinobi spent the night awake and listening for intruders. He doubted Kazu would return, but his thoughts made sleep impossible anyway. He checked on Father Mateo more than once and heard Ana do the same. Hiro found himself wishing the Jesuit would wake, even though the priest needed rest. The shinobi couldn't stop thinking about the murder, and he found himself wishing for Father Mateo's input.

Just before dawn, Hiro lay down on his futon and fell into restless sleep. He woke feeling bitter and unrefreshed. His knee ached, which made no sense until he realized Gato was sleeping on it.

He lifted the little cat off his leg and set her down on the futon. She yawned and stretched before curling into a ball and closing her eyes.

Hiro knelt on the veranda and meditated until his mind felt reasonably clear. Then he returned to his room, donned his usual smoky gray kimono, and fastened his swords through his obi.

Preparations complete, he went looking for Ana.

He found the housekeeper sweeping the *oe* floor. She looked up as he entered and raised a hand to her lips to warn him that Father Mateo was sleeping.

Hiro nodded and whispered, "How is he?"

"I warmed up more of your special tea at dawn."

"It's gone, then?" Hiro asked.

"There's still a cup left, maybe two."

"Give it to him when he wakes, along with the strongest broth you can make, but no rice unless he asks for it specifically."

"Hm," Ana said. "You think I've never tended an injured man?"

Hiro smiled. "If Father Mateo asks, I'll be back by noon."

The front door creaked and heavy footsteps thumped on the entry floor. Hiro turned, but without alarm. Only Luis sounded so much like a drunken bear.

The Portuguese merchant appeared in the doorway. His face was red and shone with sweat despite the cloudy morning.

Luis saw Hiro and raised a hand to his chest. "Don't sneak around like that!"

"I haven't moved," Hiro said.

"Well, make more noise. You'll scare someone to death."

"You should make less noise." Hiro gestured toward

the Jesuit's door and lowered his voice. "Father Mateo is resting."

"At this hour?" The merchant frowned, though Hiro noted Luis did lower his voice.

"How was your trip to Ōtsu?" Hiro asked.

"Miserable," Luis fumed. "I barely had time for a meal, and a poor one at that. I brought the weapons though. My servants are unloading them at the warehouse now. Lord Oda's men aren't due until tomorrow, so even Lord Matsunaga will have to admit I met his deadline."

"Matsunaga-*san* is not a daimyo," Hiro said.

Luis looked smug. "Every samurai fancies himself a lord. If he pays his bills, I'll call him one in the bargain."

"Did you see Miyoshi Akira on the road?" Hiro asked.

Luis wiped his forehead with a greasy hand. "How did you know? He passed me yesterday afternoon on the way to Ōtsu. He stopped just long enough to order me not to stay the night—and then galloped off without waiting for my response! Some nerve, addressing me as if I was some kind of servant."

The merchant opened his mouth to continue, but Hiro had no desire to entertain another of Luis's diatribes.

"Matsunaga-*san* ordered him to find you," Hiro said, "and also to return to Kyoto quickly."

"Well, he took it seriously," Luis said. "By the time I reached Ōtsu, he'd already left."

"Did you see Lord Oda's ambassadors?" Hiro asked.

"They hadn't reached Ōtsu yet. According to the inn-keeper, their messengers hadn't even arrived."

"You asked?" Hiro let his surprise show.

"Of course I asked," Luis scoffed. "I didn't want some

overzealous samurai trying to seize the shogun's weapon shipment."

Hiro considered this news. Samurai traveling parties often sent messengers ahead on the road to reserve sufficient space at the village inns. If the messengers for Lord Oda's embassy hadn't reached Ōtsu, the ambassadors must still be days from Kyoto.

Luis looked around. "You didn't answer my question. Why is Mateo sleeping at this hour? Is he ill?"

"The neighbor's dog attacked him," Hiro said. "He'll recover, but he needs to rest."

"I knew that beast would hurt someone," Luis scowled. "Did you kill it?"

"I wasn't here."

Luis's upper lip curled back from his teeth. "And you let that stop you? I thought you samurai understood revenge."

"Vengeance is taken for wrongful acts by men," Hiro said. "Samurai do not declare duels with dogs."

"The owner should pay an indemnity."

"A matter Father Mateo can address when he recovers," Hiro said, knowing the priest would neither demand nor accept any money for his injuries.

"If you'll excuse me," Luis said, "I can still get a few hours' sleep before I meet Lord Matsunaga at the warehouse."

He looked at Ana as if just noticing her presence. "Don't disturb me until noon."

As the merchant waddled to his room, Hiro left the house and hurried toward the shogunate.

According to Luis's estimate, Akira and Den would have reached Kyoto by midnight the night before. The boy would not have gotten much sleep, but Hiro wanted to hear Den's version of the events on the night Saburo died. More importantly, he needed to know if love for Jun was sufficient to turn the boy into a killer.

Chapter 33

A crowd of armored samurai lined the wooden bridge that led to the shogunate. At first they looked like petitioners waiting for entry, but as Hiro drew closer he realized the men all faced the street instead of the gates.

The samurai guards wore battle-scarred armor in place of their usual decorative pieces. Every man wore a helmet and several had *sarubo*, monkey cheek armor, protecting their lower jaws.

Hiro felt the charge in the air, as if the guards expected a horde of attackers to flood the street at any moment. Lord Oda's men must have bypassed Ōtsu and arrived in Kyoto ahead of schedule.

The shinobi slowed his pace and approached the gates with a casual stride that gave the samurai time to notice his approach.

"Halt!" a guard ordered. "Come no farther. State your name and business."

Hiro stopped about ten feet short of the wooden bridge that led to the gates. He bowed. "I am Matsui Hiro. The shogun ordered me to investigate Ashikaga Saburo's murder. I have come to continue my work."

"Approach," the guard said.

Hiro walked to the edge of the bridge. As he reached a more comfortable speaking distance the guard continued, "The messenger reached you quickly."

"Someone sent a messenger?" Hiro asked.

"Half an hour ago," the samurai said. "I didn't see the message, but I assume it requested your presence, given the suicide."

A prickling sensation ran down Hiro's spine and settled into his stomach. He hated being caught off guard, particularly when situations turned dangerous.

"I'm afraid I missed the messenger," Hiro said.

Samurai often used suicide to atone for a heinous crime. Yet Kazu, the only samurai suspect, hadn't seemed suicidal the night before. Women sometimes killed themselves over love affairs gone wrong, but the little Hiro knew of Jun made him doubt that option too. He wondered who had killed himself and why.

Seconds passed. Hiro wished the samurai guard would explain and save him the trouble of questions.

The guard looked up the street. "The messenger must have passed you on the road." He seemed uncertain how to proceed.

"May I see Miyoshi Akira?" Hiro asked.

"Since you're involved in the investigation, I don't think you need to wait for Miyoshi-*san*." The guard motioned to one of his companions. "Please escort Matsui-*san* to the stable."

"The stable?" Hiro asked.

"Yes," the guard said. "I'd explain, but it's not my place."

Hiro followed the second guard through the compound, silently cursing the samurai's leisurely pace.

The dead man had to be Masao or Den. No samurai would kill himself in a stable, and a commoner's death explained the lack of urgency in the escort's pace. Hiro tried not to guess which man was dead. He preferred to wait until he knew the facts.

$$\cancel{}$$

A pair of armored samurai stood guard at the stable doors. They shifted their feet as if wishing to leave the scene. Hiro found it vaguely amusing that most samurai felt uncomfortable near a corpse.

The shinobi glanced at the sky as he crossed the courtyard. Storm clouds smothered the sun and promised another day of rain. He could almost smell the droplets preparing to fall.

Akira emerged from the stable and bowed. "Good morning. I see you received our message."

Hiro returned the bow. "I'm afraid I didn't. I must have passed the messenger on the road. I was already on my way to speak with Den."

"I'm afraid that's impossible now." Akira gestured for Hiro to follow and turned back into the stable.

The moment Hiro passed through the doors he saw the body hanging from the rafters.

A rope ran around the corpse's neck, up over a ceiling beam and down to a wooden pillar at the edge of the platform where Den and Masao usually slept. The body dangled above the end of the platform, limp but already showing signs of the stiffness that followed death.

The corpse belonged to a boy of twenty, or thereabouts, with close-cropped hair and a scar on the bridge of his nose. Hiro noticed the scar particularly. It stood out, pale and shining, because the corpse's nose had turned a blotchy gray.

Masao sat on the far end of the wooden platform. He held his head in his hands and his shoulders slumped, though they did not shake. Masao looked up as Hiro entered. The shinobi saw despair in the stable master's red-rimmed eyes.

Still, Masao summoned the strength to stand and bow.

Hiro looked from the stable master to the corpse that twisted gently on its rope. He inhaled, but smelled only horses, hay, and leather. The corpse had not begun to putrify.

"This is Den, the stable boy?" he asked.

Masao clenched his jaw and nodded. He swallowed hard, but no words came. He turned pleading eyes on Akira. "Please, Miyoshi-*san*, may I cut him down?"

"No." Akira said. "Matsui-*san*, I would like you to confirm the death is a suicide."

Hiro looked from the samurai to the corpse. "Confirmation is required?"

"A formality, of course," Akira said, "but since you are here it would be impolite to conclude the matter without you."

Hiro stepped back into the doorway and looked carefully at the scene.

Three bales of hay lay at odd angles on the stable floor. The boy had apparently stacked the hay on the platform, climbed onto the bales to fasten the rope around his neck, and kicked the hay to the floor to finish the job.

Hiro mentally measured the relative heights and distances. Given Den's size, and the height of the rafter, three bales seemed the right number. The positioning also looked right for a suicide.

He asked Masao, "Where were you when this happened?"

"Sleeping." Masao pointed to a futon at the center of the platform. A pile of rumpled quilts lay discarded to one side.

A second futon lay beside the first, still neatly made. It must have belonged to Den.

"I'm not usually a heavy sleeper," Masao said, "but I stayed up late to have tea with Den when he returned from Ōtsu."

A teapot and two empty cups sat near the futons, confirming his story.

Hiro stepped up on the platform to look at the body. The rope was knotted around Den's neck with a simple hitch that tightened when pulled. Otherwise, the boy had no obvious injuries. His fingers had turned the same blotchy gray as his nose and ears. Hiro found the color interesting. Most corpses turned blue or purple instead of black.

"Did he say anything that suggested he planned to do this?" Hiro asked, without taking his eyes off the corpse.

"No." Masao said. "I had no idea . . ." His voice failed, but he tried again. "I would have stopped him. I swear it."

"I'm sure he knew that," Akira said, "so he didn't give you the chance."

"But why would he do it?" Hiro asked. As he turned, he saw the answer to his question.

A row of charcoal characters marched down the back of the beam where the rope was tied. The message wasn't visible from the stable entrance, but it was the last thing Den would have seen in life.

Akira pointed at the words. "His confession speaks for itself."

Chapter 34

Do not blame Masao, the words on the pillar read, *I acted alone.*

The second line of characters continued the message in bolder, thicker strokes, as if the writer drew strength from the opening words.

I killed Saburo to save the shogun, and kill myself to purge my guilty soul.

Hiro read the scrawled confession twice in silence. He saw no need to torture Masao by speaking the words aloud.

A burned stick lay at the base of the pillar, presumably discarded after writing the charcoaled words.

Akira pointed at the pillar. "You see? 'I killed Saburo'—a clear confession."

"Den knew how to write?" Hiro asked.

Masao nodded. "It is his hand."

Hiro studied the characters. "Every word?"

Masao looked at the ground. "Yes, every one."

"The wording seems to confirm the threat implied in Saburo's letter," Akira said, "unless there were two plots, which seems unlikely."

"I agree," Hiro said. "But how would Den have learned about a plot to harm the shogun?"

The confession seemed too convenient, given the altered ledger Kazu discovered the night before. Unfortunately, Hiro still didn't know who made the alterations or why.

"You saw the letter," Akira said. "Saburo needed to let his unnamed 'friends' into the compound. He must have enlisted Den to open the gates."

"Impossible," Masao said. "Den was a loyal servant of the shogun."

"So it appears." Hiro gestured to the characters on the pillar.

"But Saburo didn't know that," Akira said. "Perhaps Den pretended cooperation in order to kill Saburo and stop the plot."

"Why didn't he kill himself the night of the murder?" Hiro asked. "And why use Kazu's dagger? Most killers don't rely on finding a weapon at the scene."

"I can't answer the second question," Akira said, "but the first is easy. Den didn't think that anyone would suspect him. He invented the argument with Saburo—the one he used to convince Masao to help him escape—to make himself look like a victim. It gave him an excuse to leave Kyoto.

"When I brought him back from Ōtsu, he realized we would learn the truth and killed himself to escape the punishment."

Hiro glanced at the body. "Not the most effective means of escape."

Masao shook his head. "I don't believe it. Den would have told me about the plot, and last night he seemed eager to talk with Matsui-*san*."

"More deception," Akira said. "He knew you would in-terfere if you learned the truth."

Masao shook his head but didn't argue. As a commoner, he had no right to dispute with a samurai.

"We should cut the boy down," Hiro said. "There's no need to dishonor his body by leaving it hanging."

"He stays where he is." Akira started toward the door. "A murderer deserves dishonor."

Hiro's katana left its sheath and sliced through the air with a silent hiss. It severed the rope. Den's body fell to the floor.

Masao dropped to his knees with a muffled cry.

Hiro saw Akira whirl and heard the whisper of the sam-urai's blade. The shinobi raised his sword and blocked the strike that otherwise would have killed him.

Katanas rang as steel met steel.

Akira jumped back to block the expected counterstrike, but Hiro did not attack. The shinobi froze, sword high and eyes alert for any movement. He hadn't known Akira would respond to his action with violence, but drawing a sword at a samurai's back would always cause a fight.

Hiro didn't want Akira dead. If he had, he would have used the strike that cut the rope to sever Akira's neck.

But Akira didn't know that.

The stable darkened. The guards stepped into the door-way, swords in hand, but made no move to intervene.

Akira's katana quivered. His shoulders heaved and his eyes were wide.

Hiro waited, motionless.

After almost a minute, Akira lowered his sword. "How dare you disobey my order!"

"I am neither your retainer nor your servant," Hiro said. "I will not obey a dishonorable command."

Akira's nostrils flared. "You dishonor yourself by defending a murderer."

In a single motion, Hiro straightened and returned his sword to its sheath. "A samurai should show respect and mercy to the powerless, especially in the face of death." He didn't bother to hide his disdain.

Masao knelt beside Den's body, eyes wide and mouth open in shock.

The guards in the doorway looked at one another and then at Akira. A moment later, they sheathed their swords and left the stable.

Akira flushed. He sheathed his own katana and raised his chin. "I will overlook your impertinence this time, but do not think you can disobey me again without consequence."

Hiro nodded just enough to grant his opponent a modicum of dignity. The shinobi had made his point. Humiliating Akira further would only cause more trouble.

Akira puffed out his chest. "Hisahide will wish to hear your opinion about the suicide. Come with me."

Hiro had hoped to speak with Masao in private but saw no reasonable way to refuse Akira's command. A glance at Masao confirmed it wasn't an optimal time for interviews anyway. The stable master bent over Den's body, shaking as he tried to control his grief.

Hiro followed Akira from the stable.

"No one removes the body until I say so," Akira said as he passed the guards.

The men gave a nod of assent and resumed their watch on the stable doors.

Akira led Hiro across the compound to the samurai training yard. As they approached, the shinobi heard the distinctive clatter of *bokken* and saw Hisahide, wooden sword in
hand, facing off against the largest samurai Hiro had ever
seen. Both men wore baggy *hakama* and padded jackets that
bore the Miyoshi crest. They stood alone in the open yard,
most likely because of the early hour and threatening over-
cast skies.

Hiro and Akira stopped at a distance and waited for Hisahide to finish his match.

The shinobi found it interesting that Hisahide opted for
bokken rather than real swords. Samurai often used wooden
blades for solo practice but most preferred to use real ones
for sparring. As the bout continued, however, Hisahide's
reasons for wooden swords grew clear.

The giant samurai moved with startling speed. His blade
struck Hisahide's with a force that would have sent most
men to their knees.

To Hiro's surprise, Hisahide moved even faster. He blocked
the giant's strike and counterattacked with a flurry of violent
blows. The larger man backed away. But instead of pursuing,
Hisahide retreated.

The giant samurai paused, surprised by the reprieve. He
started forward and raised his sword for another powerful
strike.

He saw the trap a moment after Hiro did, but still too late
to avoid it.

Hisahide sprang sideways and thrust his wooden blade
at the larger man's stomach. The giant ran onto the point
with an audible grunt. Had the swords been real, the injury
would have killed him.

Hisahide withdrew his blade and bowed. His opponent

returned the bow with a deeper one that conceded the match.

Hisahide turned to Akira as the large samurai left the yard.

After exchanging greetings, Hisahide asked Hiro, "Have you seen the stable?"

"He has," Akira said, "and he agrees the boy's death was suicide."

Hisahide shook his head. "His expression says otherwise."

Chapter 35

"It looks like suicide," Hiro said, "but I'm not convinced. The boy had no reason to kill himself."

"He confessed in writing," Akira said. "He knew we would catch him."

"I would like to complete my investigation before I draw any final conclusions," Hiro said.

"Ordinarily I would agree," Hisahide replied, "but we have no time for protracted investigations. Lord Oda's men will arrive any day and the shogun insists we resolve this matter before they reach Kyoto."

"I have new evidence," Hiro said. "It suggests that the killer might not have acted alone." He watched Hisahide's reaction carefully.

"Another conspirator?" Hisahide frowned. "Do you have a name?"

"Saburo's mistress, Jun," Hiro said.

The altered ledger suggested that either Kazu or Hisahide was also involved, but Hiro knew better than to accuse a murderer when at a tactical disadvantage.

"The maid?" Akira laughed. "Are you serious?"

"The accusation is serious, though as yet I have no proof."

BLADE OF THE SAMURAI

"Where did you hear this?" Hisahide tapped his wooden sword against his hand.

"Lady Netsuko, Saburo's wife," Hiro said. "I believe she knows more, but I need to investigate the maid to earn her trust."

"Jun was really Saburo's mistress?" Akira grimaced. "The girl has a face like a dog and manners to match."

"She's prettier than Lady Netsuko," Hisahide said, then paused as though expecting the others to laugh.

They didn't.

"You saw Saburo's body," Hisahide said. "No woman could have inflicted such wounds. Besides, no woman is foolish enough to engage a samurai in hand-to-hand combat."

Hiro knew otherwise, but he also knew that arguing wouldn't change Hisahide's opinion.

"Masao did claim the boy was in love with Jun," Akira said. "Do you think he was jealous enough to kill Saburo?"

"I think I need more time to investigate," Hiro said. "The facts conflict. If Den killed Saburo because of Jun, why leave a suicide message claiming otherwise? Did Saburo's mistress know about the plot? And what else might Lady Ashikaga know?

"Until we know more, the shogun remains in danger."

"Cutting off the head of a snake will kill the body every time," Hisahide said. "Without Saburo, Lord Oda's men have no way to enter the shogunate. The plot will fail. The shogun is not in danger."

"Would you stake his life on your opinion?" Hiro asked.

The shogun's death would throw Kyoto into chaos. Rival daimyo would fight to claim the shogunate. Lord Oda would attack the city and no one in the capital would be safe. Until

Father Mateo had healed enough to flee, Hiro's oath required him to preserve the shogun's life as well as the Jesuit's.

"I have Portuguese firearms," Hisahide said. "Lord Oda's men have none. I have tripled the guards on the compound gates and put sentries on the walls. The shogun is safe."

Unless you're the murderer, Hiro thought, *in which case no one stands between you and the shogun.*

Before he could argue Hisahide continued, "The boy confessed that he murdered Saburo to save the shogun's life. The matter is resolved."

"No samurai conspiracy would depend on a stable boy," Hiro said, "even assuming Den actually wrote that confession. But what if he didn't write it, or what if someone forced him to write the words?"

Hiro suddenly realized why he doubted the authenticity of the message. Unfortunately, he needed Kazu's help to confirm his suspicions that the suicide was really a second murder.

Akira made a derisive sound. "What if Masao and Den are shinobi, with orders to kill the shogun and blame Saburo for the crime? That's no less ridiculous than your speculations."

"Akira is right," Hisahide said. "Masao has served the shogun for years. He has no motive to lie. His words and the evidence point to Den as the murderer. As far as I am concerned the killer is found. This investigation is over."

In the silence that followed, Hiro realized that the empty practice yard ensured no witnesses to the conversation. He remembered Kazu's warning about the Miyoshi ambassador, and Hisahide's determination to find the killer in time at any cost. Contradicting Hisahide would not end well for Hiro, regardless of the samurai's guilt or innocence.

"You are correct," Hiro said. "The confession was clear and Masao identified the writing as Den's."

"Then we agree—the investigation is over." Hisahide looked relieved. "You are released from your obligations. The shogun appreciates your service, as do I."

Hiro bowed, but without the rush of relief he expected to feel upon dismissal. Because the investigation wasn't over.

The shogun would now believe the murder solved. Kazu would not be punished. Father Mateo and Hiro were also safe, at least for the moment. But Hiro intended to risk it all by continuing the investigation in secret. He couldn't care less who claimed the title of shogun, but he would not allow a war in Kyoto until the priest had recovered enough to escape.

"Will you escort yourself to the gate?" Hisahide asked. "Akira and I have an errand outside the shogunate."

"If you please," Hiro said, "I would like to tell Ito Kazu that the murderer has been found. I am sure he would like to hear he's no longer a suspect."

"Acceptable," Hisahide said. "Can you find your way, or shall I call a guard to escort you?"

"Thank you," Hiro said, "I know the way."

He walked as far as the stable with Hisahide and Akira and then continued alone up the path that led to the *bakufu* mansion. He cut through a garden, intending to bypass the waiting room and enter the mansion through the door that led out to the kitchen.

As he approached the back of the mansion he saw a familiar kimono-clad form emerge from the kitchen. Fortune had smiled, and Hiro did too.

He moved quickly to intercept Jun in the courtyard.

"Good morning." He bowed. "Are you feeling better today?"

Jun startled but recovered quickly. She bowed, hands crossed in front of her. "I am. Thank you for asking."

She straightened and looked down at her hands demurely.

"I hoped to see you," Hiro said. "I wonder, was it very upsetting—finding Ashikaga-*san* facedown in a pool of blood?"

Jun leaned away slightly, as if confused by Hiro's graphic comment. Her smile wavered. "It was terrible. I had never seen a dead man before."

"Terrible, indeed," Hiro said, "especially considering your relationship."

"I am sorry." Jun's smile grew fixed. "I'm afraid I don't understand."

"I'm afraid you do. You lied to me about your affair with Ashikaga-*san*."

Jun raised a hand to her mouth. She lowered it slowly and shook her head. "No . . ."

Hiro lowered his voice to increase the threat in his tone. "Tell me the truth, right now, or I will tell Matsunaga-*san* that you killed Saburo in a lover's quarrel."

Her eyes flew wide. "No. That's wrong. I didn't . . ."

"Maybe you didn't. Maybe you did. Which one of us do you think Hisahide trusts?"

Jun looked around as if hoping someone would save her. The yard was deserted.

"I was Saburo's mistress," she said, "but I did not kill him. His wife, Netsuko, did."

Chapter 36

A n interesting accusation," Hiro said, "considering your previous claims of ignorance."

And even more so, given Den's confession.

"Why should I have told you?" Jun asked. "Saburo's wife will deny it, and no one believes a servant's word against a samurai's. More importantly, it would cost me all chance at a husband." She looked at the ground. "No one wants to wear a stained kimono."

"Then why tell me now?" Hiro asked.

"You know about the affair," she said. "Lying won't keep it secret anymore."

"What makes you believe Netsuko murdered her husband?" Hiro asked.

"No one else had a reason to want him dead."

"Most women prefer their husbands living," Hiro said. "Why would Lady Netsuko feel otherwise?"

"She was jealous because Saburo loved me. She ordered him to cast me away, and he let her think he would do it, but he secretly planned to divorce her and marry me." Jun's lower lip trembled. "He must have told her the truth."

"How do you know Saburo planned to marry you?" Hiro asked.

"He told me so, the night he died."

"Perhaps it was you he lied to," Hiro said. "Perhaps he loved Netsuko all along."

"No one could love such a wretched woman." Jun's eyes filled with tears. "She wasn't a real wife to him. She made him sleep in a separate room and claimed all the credit for his success. Saburo said I was the only woman who ever made him happy."

"Is that why you ran from him the night he died?" Hiro asked. "And why you asked Den to hide you?"

Jun dropped her gaze. "It was a game Saburo liked to play. He would chase me, and catch me, and . . ." She paused demurely, but Hiro noted the absence of a blush.

"He didn't catch you that night," Hiro said.

"I thought Masao had taken Den with him and left the stable empty," Jun said. "I intended to lead Saburo there . . . I thought he would find the change exciting." She raised her hands to her mouth as if ashamed of her forwardness, but once again her cheeks didn't darken or flush.

Hiro felt a spark of anger. Jun's innocent act had fooled him at first, but he would not tolerate further manipulation.

"Quit pretending embarrassment," he snapped, grateful that his samurai status allowed him to channel his anger into words when speaking with servants. "If you know enough to play such games, you can look at me when you speak of them."

Jun's humility disappeared like a stone cast into a river. She raised her face. Her hands fell to her sides.

"That's better." Hiro's anger retreated slightly. "Why did you let Den hide you instead of telling him the truth?"

"I didn't like deceiving him," she said.

"You did it often enough, if Masao's impression is accurate."

Jun shook her head. "You don't understand. Den was my friend. By the time I realized he felt something more . . . He was sweet. I didn't want to hurt him. But I decided long ago I would never be a commoner's wife."

"No, you opted for samurai whore." Hiro hoped the insult would provoke the girl into telling the truth. Angry people found it difficult to produce a consistent lie.

"I am not a whore." Jun's cheeks turned a mottled red. "Saburo intended to marry me."

"As you intended to marry Den?" Hiro paused to let the words sink in. "What happened after Den and Saburo argued?"

"Saburo left. A few minutes later Den walked me back to the kitchen. I hoped Saburo would find me there, but he didn't. I fell asleep in the servants' room.

"In the morning I remembered the dinner tray and went to retrieve it." She bit her lower lip. "That's when I found him."

"And also noticed your hair pin in his blood," Hiro said, "though you couldn't retrieve it until you thought no one would notice."

"That's not true." Jun met his eyes and shook her head. "I didn't see the pin at first. He must have pulled it out while he was chasing me the night before."

"What evidence do you have against Lady Netsuko?" Hiro asked.

"Who else could have done it?" The question sounded honest.

"Den loved you," Hiro said. "You made him think Saburo intended to hurt you."

"Den wouldn't kill a spider."

"His confession says otherwise."

"Confession?" Her forehead wrinkled with confusion. "What are you talking about?"

Hiro found her ignorance curious. "Den committed suicide and left a message confessing to the murder."

Jun stepped backward, shaking her head. "That's not possible. When? He was fine last night. I saw him . . ."

"You saw Den last night?" Hiro asked.

"After he returned from Ōtsu. It was late. Miyoshi-*san* came to the kitchen for a meal and told me to take a tray to the stable for Den. Nothing fancy, just rice and tea, though Den seemed glad to have it."

"A final meal," Hiro said. "He hanged himself in the night."

She shook her head. "He wouldn't do that. It doesn't make sense."

"Neither does your accusation of Lady Ashikaga."

"Maybe Den did it after all," Jun said.

Hiro found it interesting that she changed her story so quickly after hearing that the only two people who could confirm her actions on the night of the murder were dead.

"I've told you the truth," Jun said. "You have to believe me."

She glanced at the *bakufu* mansion behind him. "Are you going to tell Hisahide?"

"Do you mean, will I tell him you lied? Or are you concerned that I will expose your affair?"

"I've lost the only man I ever loved," she said. "If you don't mind, I would rather not lose my job and my life as well."

"If you've told the truth, you have no reason to worry," Hiro said.

She bowed.

Hiro turned away, slipped out of his sandals, and entered the mansion.

When he reached Saburo's outer office—now Kazu's office, at least for the moment—he slid open the door and stepped inside, catching a whiff of familiar wintergreen hair oil.

Kazu looked up from his desk with a welcoming smile that faded when Hiro entered. "I didn't expect to see you this morning."

"You invited me here to see evidence." Hiro slid the door closed behind him. "And I have another matter to ask about. The stable boy, Den, committed suicide last night."

Kazu nodded but didn't smile. "I heard the news when I arrived. The guards say he confessed to Saburo's murder."

"Hisahide just called off the investigation," Hiro said.

"You don't agree with his decision." Kazu's face reddened. "You still think I did it. If I killed Saburo, which I didn't, do you really think I would then kill an innocent boy to cover my crime? Canceling the investigation makes Hisahide look more suspicious than anything I've done."

Hiro agreed. Unfortunately, he wasn't convinced of Kazu's innocence either. He considered a lie, but Kazu spotted deception well, and if he recognized Hiro's falsehood their relationship could be injured beyond repair. That is, if Kazu's lies hadn't already done so.

The shinobi wished for Father Mateo. The Jesuit could

have explained in a way that Kazu would understand. But the priest was injured and Hiro's own words failed him.

This whole situation was Kazu's fault.

Hiro's anger flared. "If you don't want me to suspect you, then tell me where you were when Saburo died."

Chapter 37

Ican't tell you that." Kazu clenched his jaw.

"Can't or won't?" Hiro asked.

"In this case, they are the same." Kazu met Hiro's gaze with defiance.

Hiro recognized the look. It was the same one an eight-year-old Kazu had worn the day he took a beating that should have fallen on Hiro's back. Kazu hadn't confessed then, either, no matter how hard the bamboo cane had cracked against his spine.

The memory snuffed out Hiro's anger and made him wonder if Kazu was protecting someone else.

"What about last night?" he asked. "Where were you when Den returned from Ōtsu?"

"At home, sleeping," Kazu said. "I went there directly after I talked with you."

Hiro looked at the parchment on Kazu's desk. Tiny characters streamed down the page in perfect vertical lines. Kazu's calligraphy marked him as a highly intelligent, educated man. No person in Iga, and few in Kyoto, could match his skill with a brush. Words fell from the bristles as swiftly and lightly as snowflakes from a cloud, making it easy to underestimate the strength of the hand that formed them.

"There's no point comparing my letter to Den's confession," Kazu said. "I'm better at forgeries than you are at detecting them."

Hiro frowned. "That's not what I was thinking."

"Would you care to share your insight, then?"

"How much do you know about Den's confession?" Hiro asked.

"Only that he wrote one. I haven't seen it."

"The handwriting had a flaw that might interest you. The message contained two lines with different characteristics, almost as if two different people had written them. The first line exculpated Masao. The second confessed to Saburo's murder."

Kazu leaned forward, intrigued despite his frustration. "What kind of brush?"

"No brush," Hiro said, "charred wood. It lay on the ground beneath the message."

"Easy enough to add to the writing, then," Kazu said. "Which line had cruder strokes? Den was young and poorly educated. His writing would lack precision."

"The second line seemed larger," Hiro said, "and also less skillfully written, but not by much. If someone added to the message, he—or she—attempted to mimic the author's style."

"What did Masao say about it?"

"He claims Den wrote the entire thing."

Kazu shook his head. "Then Masao is the person who altered the message."

"Not necessarily," Hiro said, "but likely."

"You didn't need my help to figure that out," Kazu said. "Why come here instead of confronting Masao?"

Hiro gave Kazu a sideways look. "Hisahide considers the matter resolved. In fact, he ordered me to leave the shogunate."

"But you didn't," Kazu said. "You came here instead."

"Hisahide allowed me to tell you that you are no longer a suspect."

Kazu smiled wryly. "I wish you meant that—and also that you'd obey Hisahide's order and go home. You won't, though. You never give up until you win."

"This isn't about winning," Hiro said. "If Saburo's killer is working with Lord Oda, the shogun is still in danger—"

"When did you start caring about the shogun?" Kazu asked.

"I care about Lord Oda starting a war in Kyoto." Concern for Father Mateo made Hiro's stomach feel like a lantern beset by moths.

"There's not going to be a war," Kazu said. "The shogun is safe. Hisahide has doubled the compound guards and plans to add more this evening."

"That doesn't bother you?" Hiro asked. "After he altered the ledger?"

"Hisahide didn't do it. When I compared the writing it wasn't his." Kazu blushed. "The changes were made by the shogun himself. I'm sorry . . . I should have recognized the writing, but the shogun has never written in Saburo's ledgers before, and the alterations surprised me so much, it didn't occur to me that Shogun Ashikaga might have made them."

"You're positive?" Hiro asked.

Kazu nodded. "I'm sorry. I shouldn't have involved you in this at all. Would you like me to escort you to the gates?"

"No need to interrupt your work. I can find my way." Hiro bowed and departed, glad that Kazu didn't insist on walking him out.

The shinobi had no intention of leaving the compound.

As he slid the door shut behind him, Hiro heard the distinctive tapping of a chisel. He hurried quietly toward the sound.

Hiro felt certain Ozuru knew more about the night Saburo died than he had told them, and the stable boy's death presented an opportunity to renew the conversation.

The shinobi paused at the entrance to the audience hall and inhaled the slightly musky scents of cedar and fresh-cut pine. Ozuru stood halfway across the room with his back to Hiro. The shinobi saw no sign of the other carpenters. The new support beams were installed and partially covered with ceiling slats, though the southern end of the ceiling remained unfinished, presumably waiting for installation of the transom screen.

The screen itself lay sideways across a pair of wooden horses. Ozuru bent over it, focused on his work. He tapped his chisel with a wooden hammer, and delicate slivers of wood peeled off the screen and fell to the floor with no more sound than a maple tree shedding leaves.

Hiro started across the room. Just before he reached Ozuru, the carpenter turned and bowed. The shinobi struggled to hide his surprise that the carpenter heard his approach.

"Good morning, Matsui-*san*," Ozuru said. "Have you more questions for me?"

"I wondered about that transom," Hiro said. It wasn't what he intended, but it was the first thing that came to mind when he recovered from his surprise.

"This?" Ozuru followed Hiro's gaze to the wooden carving. "I should have finished it days ago, but the guards don't let me work late anymore. I am ordered to leave at sunset like everyone else."

He gestured to the empty room. "That's why my assistants aren't here today. I needed quiet to finish the screen."

Hiro looked at the carpenter's callused hands. "You like your work."

"Wood speaks to me." Ozuru smiled. "That probably sounds strange to a samurai."

"My father painted landscapes." It wasn't a lie. "He claimed the ink could speak to a man who developed the ears to listen."

Ozuru nodded. "He sounds like an artisan . . . as well as samurai." He brushed a hanging sliver of wood from the screen.

"He often said that painting reminded him of life's fragility."

Ozuru gave Hiro a knowing look. "I heard about the stable boy's suicide. Please forgive my directness. I appreciate the respect your politeness shows me, but the shogun will punish me if I do not finish this work today. Again, I apologize, but if you have questions for me please ask them plainly."

"Den let you out of the compound the night Saburo died," Hiro said.

"That is correct," Ozuru said.

"Before he killed himself, the boy confessed to Ashikaga Saburo's murder."

Ozuru glanced over Hiro's shoulder and then looked over his own as if to ensure that no one had entered the room. He lowered his voice.

"I don't care what the confession claims. That boy didn't kill the samurai."

Chapter 38

"How do you know Den didn't kill Ashikaga Saburo?" Hiro asked.

"Because Ashikaga-*san* was alive when the boy left his office that night," Ozuru said.

"Den was in Ashikaga Saburo's office? When? Why didn't you mention this earlier?"

The carpenter showed no emotion. "I didn't think it was my place to chronicle Ashikaga-*san*'s personal interactions the night he died."

"I'm making it your place," Hiro said, taking note of Ozuru's unusual phrasing. "Tell me everything you heard and saw that night.

"You may work while we talk, if you wish."

Ozuru rubbed his thumb idly along the handle of his chisel. "After my . . . conversation . . . with Ashikaga-*san*, I returned to work and tried to keep noise to a minimum. I hoped eventually Ashikaga-*san* would go home for the night and leave me to work in peace.

"About two hours after sunset, I heard voices from Ashikaga-*san*'s office. He was arguing with someone else."

"Who was it?" Hiro asked.

Ozuru shook his head as he set the chisel against the transom and raised his hammer. "I don't know. Ashikaga-*san* was the only one yelling. The argument lasted two or three minutes. After that, I heard nothing for a while. Almost everyone else had already left for the evening.

"An hour later, Miyoshi-*san* passed through, presumably on his way to the kitchen." Ozuru tapped the chisel gently and sent a flake of wood to the floor.

"Miyoshi Akira?" Hiro asked. "He passed through here?"

"Yes. He didn't speak to me. I doubt he even registered my presence." Ozuru made a gesture with the hammer. "If I'm not making noise, most samurai don't notice me at all.

"A while after that the maid ran through with Ashikaga-*san* close behind her." Ozuru shook his head. "A man his age shouldn't compromise his dignity by chasing foolish girls."

He paused as if expecting Hiro to chastise him for the inappropriate comment.

"What happened then?" the shinobi asked.

"Sometime later I heard Ashikaga-*san* returning, cursing under his breath." Ozuru ran a finger along the carving, checking for roughness. "I crouched behind the screen. I don't know what upset him, but I didn't care to be yelled at twice in one evening."

"What time was that?" Hiro asked.

"Four hours after sunset?" The answer sounded more like a question. "Maybe a little less. I worked for a while longer and then realized how late it was. Just before I left I heard footsteps approaching from Ashikaga-*san*'s office, but softly, as if the person didn't want to be heard. I hid behind the screen again—I know better than to be seen when I'm not wanted.

"It was the stable boy, and he was crying quietly. He passed through the room and disappeared."

"How could you tell he was crying?" Hiro asked.

Ozuru indicated the braziers near the door. "I keep the fires lit when I'm working. I saw the glint of tears in his eyes."

"What happened after that?" Hiro asked.

"I waited a few more minutes and went home. The stable boy opened the gates for me. I didn't mention seeing him in the mansion."

"He could have returned to Ashikaga-*san*'s office after you left," Hiro said.

"No," Ozuru said, "he was crushed, not angry. I believe he saw something he didn't want to see but couldn't change."

"What do you think he saw?" Hiro wondered how much the carpenter knew about Jun and Saburo.

"Rumor has it the boy was in love with Ashikaga-*san*'s mistress," Ozuru said. "That kind of infatuation never ends well. My guess is it ended that night."

"That's a very strong motive for murder," Hiro said.

"For a samurai, maybe. Not for a stable boy."

Hiro thanked Ozuru and hurried off to the stable. He had one more conversation to finish before he left the compound, and he hoped to conclude it before Hisahide returned.

Hiro found Masao kneeling beside Den's body. The stable boy lay on his back with his arms at his sides, clothing straightened in semblance of sleep.

Hiro noted again the unusual mottled darkness of the corpse's nose and fingers. He inhaled deeply but still smelled only the stable.

Masao turned at the sound of Hiro's sandals. He stood and bowed. As he straightened he glanced past Hiro as if making sure the shinobi had come alone.

"Thank you." Masao gestured toward the body. "You will never know how much it meant to me that you cut him down."

"Did Den know he was your son?" Hiro asked.

Masao stepped backward, startled. "He was not—" His shoulders slumped as he surrendered the argument. "He was my nephew. How did you guess?"

"Your behavior before his death suggested kinship," Hiro said. "Your grief confirmed it."

"He never knew." Masao shook his head. "I wanted to tell him, many times, but my sister made me promise. She did not want him to know his mother was a prostitute."

Hiro didn't ask why Masao's sister worked in the pleasure quarters. The question was inappropriate, and the answer easy enough to guess. Parents sometimes sold a daughter they couldn't afford to keep, especially when a poor harvest left them with debts they could not repay. Other girls went willingly, in search of fortune, though Masao's comments suggested his sister wasn't one of those.

"Den never asked you?" Hiro said.

"He thought he was an orphan."

Hiro looked at the body. "Does his mother know he's dead?"

"Not yet." Masao clenched his jaw and shook his head. "He was her only child."

Hiro shifted his gaze from the boy to the charcoal characters scratched on the pillar. "When did he learn to write? Who taught him?"

"I did," Masao said, "with sticks and scraps of wood. When we finished, we burned them in the fire."

"Why hide the evidence?" Hiro asked. "Commoners are allowed to read and write."

"We didn't hide it, though not many people knew," Masao said. "Only a fool brags of skills above his station."

Hiro understood the value of keeping talents secret. As he looked at the characters scratched on the pillar, he had no doubt that two people had written the message. He also suspected they both were still in the stable.

"I think there was more to Den's argument with Ashikaga Saburo than he told you," Hiro said, hoping indirection might yield results. "The scene you described would hardly justify murder."

"I've told you all I know," Masao said, "though Ashikaga-*san* was not a nice man when angered. Den may have killed him in self-defense."

Hiro pointed to the message. "That doesn't sound like self-defense to me. Did Den have a temper?"

"Not usually," Masao said.

"Not even over Jun?" Hiro asked. "Did she return his affections?"

Masao glanced at Den's body and quickly looked away. "She was kind to him, though I can't say she knew him well enough to understand what she felt about him. Den wasn't the type of boy who would speak before he could follow through, and he knew he couldn't marry until he completed his apprenticeship."

Hiro thought of Father Mateo's injuries and of Hisahide's imminent return. The shinobi couldn't afford to delay any longer. It was time to force the stable master's hand.

He stepped onto the wooden platform, picked up the teapot, and raised the lid. The musty odor of used-up tea leaves rose from the pot, along with the expected sweetness that told the shinobi exactly how Den died.

"Tell me," he asked, "what would you have done if the opium hadn't killed him?"

Chapter 39

O pium?" Masao looked startled. "What are you talking about? That's tea."

Hiro tilted the pot. An inch of tea still covered the bottom, but as it ran to the side he saw a dark brown smear on the porcelain. The cloying odor grew stronger as the remains of the opium resin met the air.

"There's opium in the tea," Hiro said. "An unreliable murder weapon, unless the killer can make the victim drink it, and you were the only one here with Den last night."

He didn't believe Masao had murdered his nephew, but Hiro also refused to make assumptions until he knew the facts.

"Where would I get opium?" Masao asked.

"Your cousin is an apothecary," Hiro said. "Did you get the resin the night Saburo died, or did you make Den carry his death from Ōtsu?"

"If you were not a samurai, I would kill you for saying that. Den was the closest thing to a son I will ever have." Masao looked at the body. "What made you think of poison? It looked to me like he hanged himself."

Hiro set down the teapot. He wanted his hands free

during the explanation, in case he needed to draw his sword. "The color of his nose and hands indicates death by asphyxiation, not by hanging. His throat doesn't show enough discoloration for that.

"Den was dead when someone put him on that rope. The question is, were you the one who tied it around his neck?"

Masao clenched his fists. "Accuse me again and I'll kill you, regardless of rank."

"Then why did you write the confession?" Hiro asked.

Masao unclenched his fists and looked at the pillar. "I didn't." After a brief pause he admitted, "I wrote the first sentence—the one about me. When I woke up and saw the words on the pillar I was afraid the shogun would blame me for Den's involvement in the crime."

"Are you certain Den wrote the part that confessed to the murder?" Hiro asked.

"I assumed . . ." Masao looked at the pillar again. "But if he was murdered . . . I thought the writing looked strange because he was frightened when he wrote it. In truth, it doesn't look like Den's, exactly, though I was afraid to admit it earlier. A wise man does not argue with samurai."

The stable master turned to Hiro. "I don't understand. I drank the tea too. Why am I alive?"

"You're substantially larger than Den. How much did you drink?" Hiro asked.

"Not much, maybe half a cup." Masao pointed to the egg-sized teacups sitting on the platform near the pot. "Mostly to keep Den company while he ate."

"You didn't ingest a lethal amount, though someone probably wanted you to." Hiro picked up the pot and smelled the remaining tea. "If you'd finished this, you would have died. You didn't notice the sweetness?"

"Den liked sweetener in his tea. Sometimes Jun would sneak him some. I'd been drinking sake at dinner—I didn't notice."

"Whoever killed Den may well have intended to kill you also. If you know anything that might identify the person who did this, I suggest you tell me now."

Masao seemed disinclined to answer.

Hiro set down the teapot and stepped off the platform. He looked at Den's body, knowing the stable master's gaze would eventually follow.

Death made the boy look pitifully young.

Hiro wished he knew whether Den was involved in the plot or just an innocent casualty.

"Den didn't return to the stable after walking Jun to the kitchen that night," Masao said slowly. "He hid in the yard to ensure that Ashikaga-*san* didn't bother the girl again. But Jun didn't stay in the kitchen. She went to the mansion, to Ashikaga-*san*'s office. Den followed and listened outside the door."

"I can guess what he heard," Hiro said.

Masao's eyes reddened with unshed tears. "It crushed him. He said he walked the grounds for hours, crying." The stable master shook his head. "That's why I believed the suicide and that Den had written the message despite the unusual writing. I sent him out of town because of the argument, but when I heard about the murder the following morning I did wonder whether Den had killed Ashikaga-*san* after all.

"Last night, when Den returned, he said he hadn't. But when I saw him this morning . . . and the message . . ."

Masao clenched his jaw, unable to finish.

Hiro decided not to increase the stable master's grief with more accusations. He couldn't rule out Masao's involvement

in the plot against the shogun and didn't want to say anything that might assist his adversary, whoever that adversary was. He felt a flash of dark amusement. Instinctively,
Hiro was treating the killer like a shinobi would treat a man
he intended to kill.

The key was closing the distance before the target knew
he was being hunted.

Hiro returned home hoping Father Mateo had recovered
enough to discuss the investigation. He wanted the Jesuit's
insight.

When he reached the house, he found Ana cleaning the
blood from the veranda. She looked up as he approached.
"Hm. Decided to come back?" She gestured toward the
house. "Father Mateo needs your help."

The Jesuit lay on his futon, wearing the same bloodstained
kimono he had on the day before. Hiro silently reprimanded
himself for not helping the priest change clothes. In a Japanese home that task would have fallen to the housekeeper,
but Hiro had forgotten the Jesuit wouldn't allow a woman to
see him naked.

Father Mateo forced a smile as Hiro entered the room.
"I'm glad you're back. I'm afraid the wounds are festering."

The shinobi inhaled deeply, seeking the scent of infection. He smelled only medicinal herbs and sweet green tea,
with a familiar opiate undertone that made him think of the
corpse in the shogun's stable.

Light footsteps approached behind him.

"Ana," he said without turning, "I need hot salted water,
clean bandages, and my medicine chest."

The maid's kimono rustled as Ana departed on nearly silent feet. The needs of her beloved priest would silence even Ana's ascerbic tongue.

Hiro knelt beside Father Mateo and inspected the gash on the Jesuit's neck. Father Mateo angled his head away, but the gesture stretched his skin and cracked the delicate scabs that covered the wound on his throat. A drop of blood welled up at the edge of the scab. Father Mateo winced, and the bloody droplet trickled down his neck.

"Don't stretch it," Hiro said. "You'll reopen the wound."

"I think I already did," Father Mateo muttered as he faced the ceiling.

Hiro noted the healthy color of the skin around the scabs. "At least there's no infection in your neck. If you keep it from bleeding too much more, it might even heal without a scar." He smiled. "On the other hand, many women find scars attractive."

"I'll keep that in mind." Father Mateo closed his eyes. "I'm more worried about my hands. Even with your tea, they hurt more than I think they should."

Hiro removed the bandages from Father Mateo's left hand, which had swollen to almost twice its normal size. The bite marks looked more inflamed than the day before, but Hiro saw no pus. Pale, soft tissue covered the wounds. Hiro's herbs and lack of air had kept the scabs from hardening, but the tissue itself looked normal on the surface.

Father Mateo opened his eyes. "Infected?"

Hiro shook his head. "Not yet."

He unwrapped the priest's right hand. It seemed less swollen than the left, but the flesh around the punctures felt unusually hot to Hiro's touch.

Father Mateo exhaled slowly. "That looks better than the other. Maybe there's no infection after all."

Hiro considered a reassuring falsehood, but remembered his promise not to lie to the priest. "This one concerns me. I need to remove the scabs and clean beneath them. It's going to hurt, but it's our only hope to prevent infection."

"Pain won't kill me," Father Mateo said. "Infection might. Do what you can to prevent it."

Chapter 40

When Ana brought the water and other items, Hiro opened the medicine chest and removed the twist of paper that held the opium.

Father Mateo shook his head. "No more of that."

"It helps your pain," Hiro said.

"I can handle pain. The relief is not worth the risk."

Hiro raised the twist of paper. "You know this drug?"

"I stopped in Macao on my way to Japan." Father Mateo glanced at the twist of paper. "I've seen what opium does to men. I would rather have pain than permanent hunger."

Hiro put the paper away and selected a pair of envelopes. He held them up for the priest to see. "Powdered willow and horse chestnut. Not as effective, but neither causes a lasting need."

He handed the envelopes to Ana. "Use a pinch of each in a pot of tea, with sugar to cover the bitterness. Keep the envelopes. He'll need them for several days, but he shouldn't have it more often than every four hours."

Ana nodded and left the room.

Hiro added an antiseptic to the water and swirled the

end of a cloth in the steaming brine. As he hoped, the water felt almost too hot to touch.

As Hiro lowered the cloth to the wounds, Father Mateo shut his eyes and clenched his jaw in anticipation of pain. The shinobi admired the Jesuit's strength.

Hiro inhaled the steam that rose from the cloth as he held it against the priest's right hand. He smelled only salt and medicine, with a metallic undertone the shinobi recognized as a combination of softening scabs and blood.

He inhaled again, seeking the slightly sweet odor that indicated putrefaction. He didn't find it. If an infection had started, it hadn't yet found a foothold.

Hiro held the cloth to the wound until the pale scabs had softened enough to wipe away without tearing the skin around them. Father Mateo flinched but didn't complain.

The reddened flesh beneath the scabs looked swollen but not infected. The shinobi dipped a fresh cloth in the water and pressed the dampened silk against the wounds. Father Mateo's breathing grew measured and even.

Hiro watched for a moment or two, surprised the Jesuit knew about breathing techniques to master pain. He finished cleaning Father Mateo's wounds and used the remaining silk for bandages.

Father Mateo opened his eyes as Hiro tucked the final strip into place.

"Have you found Ashikaga Saburo's killer?" the Jesuit asked. "I wish I could help instead of just lying here."

"I could use your help," Hiro said. "I think the murderer has killed again."

"What?" Father Mateo tried to sit up, but since he had no use of his hands the effort became a useless wiggle. "What's happened?"

Hiro folded a quilt across a wooden back rest and helped the Jesuit into a sitting position. As he did, he explained about the "suicide" at the shogunate and briefly detailed his talks with Ozuru and Jun.

Father Mateo gave Hiro a grateful look. "Thank you. It's nice to sit up." He frowned. "Since Den is dead, he can't confirm what he saw the night of the murder. That's suspicious and does make his death look more like murder than suicide. Besides, if Den intended to kill himself he wouldn't have poisoned the tea."

Hiro hadn't considered that, and the oversight surprised him.

"Assuming for the moment that Masao really drank it," Father Mateo continued. "Do we know who made the tea?"

"Jun delivered it to the stable," Hiro said.

"Lending credence to Lady Netsuko's suspicions." Father Mateo smiled at Hiro's surprise. "Paper walls and open rafters aren't the best for privacy. I heard part of yesterday's conversation before I fell asleep."

"But how would a maid obtain opium?" Hiro asked. "It isn't well-known as a poison."

"Any apothecary would know its properties," Father Mateo said, "and if he knows, his customer doesn't have to. The bigger question, for me, is whether the girl is strong enough to hang a body. From what I've seen, I doubt it."

"Which means she carried the poison for someone else," Hiro said. "But who? And who wrote the murder confession?"

"I know you doubt Masao as a suspect, but he has the strength to hang a body and could have poisoned the tea without Den knowing. We have only his word that he drank it, and he lied to us before."

"Masao is Den's uncle," Hiro said. "His grief was real."

"I'd like to think that changes things," Father Mateo said, "but if Masao was involved in Saburo's plot—or even trying to stop it—he might have needed someone to take the blame."

The Jesuit's eyes widened. "What if Saburo did recruit Den to his plot? Masao could have killed them both in order to save the shogun."

"Possible," Hiro said, "but complicated, particularly when we're not even sure what the plot entailed. I'd rather eliminate easier answers first."

"Like jealousy over a woman?" the Jesuit asked.

"Exactly."

"There's also the question of which woman." Father Mateo shifted his hands in his lap. "Jun and Netsuko accuse each other, and each one's story has elements of truth."

"No one saw Netsuko at the shogunate the night her husband died," Hiro said. "That and the poisoned tea shift suspicion to Jun. Also, the maid has lied to us, and from what I can tell Netsuko has not."

"Do we know that for certain?" Father Mateo asked. "What if Saburo did intend to divorce his wife and marry Jun, and Netsuko learned the truth? She could have promised Den a reward for killing her husband before he could follow through."

"That doesn't explain why Den was murdered," Hiro said.

"You're assuming the two are connected."

"The evidence connects them," Hiro countered, "and I don't believe Netsuko murdered Den."

"Jun isn't strong enough to hang a body," Father Mateo said. "If a woman was involved, she was working with someone else."

"I need to talk with Netsuko again," Hiro said.

"I'd like to come with you."

Hiro smiled. "You need to give those wounds more time to heal."

"Eliminating the women for a moment, who else is still a suspect aside from Masao?"

"For a while, I suspected Hisahide." Hiro explained about the ledger, concluding with Kazu's admission that the shogun had made the changes. "So now the leading suspects are Ozuru and Masao."

"There's still one you haven't mentioned," Father Mateo said.

Hiro knew what the priest was going to say and wished he didn't agree with the Jesuit's judgment.

Chapter 41

Hiro didn't wait for Father Mateo to say the name. "You mean Kazu."

"I'm sorry," Father Mateo said. "I know he's your friend."

"He is," Hiro said, "and for his sake I hope he's told the truth."

Ana returned, teapot in hand. As she knelt to pour the Jesuit's tea, Hiro caught a whiff of *ichibancha*. The grassy odor almost hid the bitter scent of powdered willow. Hiro hoped the expensive tea would suffice to mask the medicine's bite, since he caught no hint of the recommended sweetener.

The medicinal odor grew stronger as Ana poured the steaming liquid into an egg-sized porcelain cup.

Father Mateo frowned. "Ana, it's wrong to steal—even from Luis. That's his tea."

"Hm." Ana raised the cup to the Jesuit's lips. "He didn't refuse permission."

Hiro decided not to mention that lack of refusal wasn't exactly permission.

Father Mateo sipped the tea. He scowled. "That tastes terrible."

Ana's eyes widened. She picked up the teapot and hurried from the room.

"She forgot the sugar," Hiro chuckled.

"Not funny," Father Mateo said. "It tasted foul."

Hiro smothered a laugh.

Ana hurried back into the room, carrying a tray of sweetened rice balls. "This will take the bitterness away."

Hiro reached for the tray but Ana pulled the treats out of reach. "Hm. None for you. You laughed."

She laid the plate on the floor beside the Jesuit. "I'll bring more tea as soon as the water boils. You won't have to drink it tepid for my mistake." She glared at Hiro and left the room.

The shinobi shrugged. "I think I'll send a message to Lady Netsuko."

"Will she see you?" Father Mateo maneuvered a rice ball toward his mouth. His bandaged hands made the process awkward. "You said Hisahide dismissed the investigation."

"Netsuko seemed fairly certain that Jun was involved in Saburo's murder," Hiro said. "If she doesn't accept that Den acted alone, I think she'll welcome my visit."

"And if she accepts Hisahide's determination?" Father Mateo asked.

"As long as Netsuko believes I'm implicating Jun, I think she'll see me."

Hiro returned to his room and wrote a brief letter to Lady Ashikaga. He revised it twice before settling on a final version and setting the words to parchment. When it was finished and dry, he paid the neighbor's son a copper coin to deliver the message.

While he waited for her response, the shinobi sat down to review the evidence.

Saburo's letter suggested a plot against the shogun, as did Den's confession. The altered ledger indicated the shogun suspected something, though Hiro couldn't determine whether the guards were changed due to knowledge or merely caution. Unfortunately, he also didn't know if the shogun had really changed the names or if Kazu lied about that too.

He wished he knew who Kazu was protecting.

Hiro had barely finished the thought when he fell asleep.

Two nights without rest had finally taken their toll.

A knock woke Hiro from sleep. He raised his head from the desk and wiped a tendril of drool from his lip. He stood and straightened his kimono. Lady Ashikaga must have answered his message in person.

A moment later, he heard the front door open and then the mumur of Ana's formal greeting.

He crossed his room and opened the door just in time to hear Ashikaga Ichiro tell the housekeeper, "I have come to speak with Matsui Hiro."

Hiro stepped into the common room and bowed as Ana led Ichiro into the house.

Ichiro returned the bow with a deep one of his own, suggesting he viewed the shinobi as an equal. Given the boy's affiliation with the shogun's clan, Hiro found the respect surprising.

"Please have a seat." Hiro gestured to the hearth.

Ana bowed and left for the kitchen, doubtless intending to raid Luis's private stash of *ichibancha* for the third time in less than a day.

Ichiro looked at the hearth but shook his head. "Will you take a walk with me?"

Hiro hid his surprise at the adult phrasing. Whatever the boy intended to say, he wanted to say it where nobody else could hear.

"If you please?" Ichiro asked. "It isn't raining at the moment. Not much, anyway."

"I don't mind a little rain." Hiro gestured toward the door and followed Ichiro back through the entry and out of the house.

The shinobi stepped off the porch and into his sandals. Ichiro did the same, and they walked together down the gravel path toward the road. Hiro listened for the neighbor's dog but heard nothing. The wife must have recovered enough for her husband to return to work.

Hiro and Ichiro walked up Marutamachi Road toward the river. Clouds covered the sky, though here and there a wisp of blue peeked through, as if the storm could not decide between staying and moving on.

Hiro said nothing. Ichiro would speak when he was ready.

As they passed Okazaki Shrine the cloying odor of sandalwood incense rose from the braziers on either side of the gate, overwhelming the piny scent of surrounding trees.

Hiro stifled a cough.

"You don't like incense." Ichiro smiled. "I don't either." His smile disappeared. "My mother does. She burns it all the time, in the hope the kami will smell it and grant her prayers."

"What does your mother pray for?" Hiro asked.

"The same thing as always: my father. Only now she prays for his soul."

When they reached the river Ichiro turned onto the path that followed the eastern bank. Hiro matched the young samurai's pace without comment.

As they left the bridge behind Ichiro said, "Matsunaga Hisahide says that Den, the stable boy, killed my father and that he acted alone. Do you believe this?"

"Do you believe it?" Hiro asked.

"I saw your message. Why do you want to meet with my mother?"

"She asked me to keep her informed," Hiro said, deciding not to continue the question-for-question exchange.

"I don't believe you." Ichiro stopped walking. "Samurai do not report to women. Besides, the investigation is over and you are discharged from your duties. Matsunaga-*san*'s message mentioned that also."

"That is true," Hiro said, "but I didn't know that Matsunaga-*san* sent word to your family. I intended to tell your mother that the investigation has been canceled."

"You lie." Despite his diminutive stature, Ichiro looked every inch a samurai. "Do not patronize me because I am young. I am still my father's heir."

He paused. "Unless my father's mistress has borne another."

"Not that I know of." That much, at least, was true.

"But you know my father had a mistress." Ichiro searched the shinobi's face. Hiro wondered what the boy hoped to find there.

Hiro raised an eyebrow but didn't answer.

"My mother knew," Ichiro said. "She told me only after my father died. The mistress's name is Jun, and she is a maid at the shogunate. My mother says this woman killed my father."

Hiro blinked. Before he decided what to say Ichiro continued, "But I don't think Jun murdered my father. I think my mother killed him."

Chapter 42

Why do you suspect your mother?" Hiro asked.

"I don't think she held the dagger," Ichiro said, "but she dismissed her suspicion of Kazu too quickly, as if she knew that he was not to blame. She also didn't believe that Den confessed to my father's murder. She made Hisahide's messenger repeat the message twice.

"Later, when I asked why she didn't believe it, she refused to discuss the matter at all. That isn't like her. I think she knows who killed my father." Ichiro looked at the river. "But if she won't admit it, doesn't that mean she's involved in the crime?"

Before Hiro could answer, hoofbeats pounded on the bridge behind them. The shinobi turned, surprised by the sound.

The rider wore a dark-blue tunic emblazoned with the Ashikaga mon. His stallion's barding bore the shogun's crest. The samurai leaned over his horse's neck, urging the beast to maximum speed. Moments later, horse and rider disappeared down Marutamachi Road toward Okazaki Shrine—and the Jesuit's home.

Hiro started toward the bridge.

"Where are you going?" Ichiro asked.

"That rider is heading for Father Mateo's house."

Ichiro hurried to catch up. "How do you know?"

"No samurai wastes a horse's speed without reason, and the only home of interest beyond Okazaki Shrine belongs to the priest."

As Hiro expected, the messenger's horse stood in the street in front of Father Mateo's home. The samurai had disappeared, presumably inside, and left the horse alone with its reins dangling loose to the ground. Hiro had heard of horses that stood without tying but never seen it before. He wondered if Masao had trained the beast.

The shinobi hurried past the horse and up the gravel path to the Jesuit's home. Ichiro followed. Just before the shinobi reached the house, the door swung open.

Ana appeared in the doorway with the shogun's messenger right behind her. The housekeeper pointed at Hiro.

"That is Matsui Hiro," she said. "I told you he wasn't here."

The messenger stepped onto the porch and bowed. As he straightened he noticed the Ashikaga mon on Ichiro's clothing. He bowed again, more deeply.

"May I help you?" Hiro asked.

The messenger straightened. "Matsunaga Hisahide requests your presence at the shogunate immediately."

"I'll leave at once," Hiro said.

The messenger stepped into his shoes, bowed again, and hurried toward his horse. Hiro watched him swing into the saddle and canter away up the street.

"I'm going with you," Father Mateo said from the doorway.

Hiro turned to see the Jesuit standing next to Ana.

"No," Hiro said. "You haven't recovered. Besides, you seem to forget that Father Vilela barred you from the shogunate."

"For the duration of your investigation," Father Mateo said. "But unless I'm mistaken, Hisahide concluded that investigation this morning."

"I doubt Miyoshi Akira will find that persuasive," Hiro said.

"He can think what he wants." Father Mateo stepped off the porch and into his sandals. "We can argue the fine points later. I'm going with you."

Hiro looked to Ana for support, but the maid stepped into the house and shut the door.

Father Mateo started toward the street.

"I'd like to continue our conversation," Hiro told Ichiro. "May I send a message after I finish my business at the shogunate?"

Ichiro matched the shinobi's pace. "I'm going with you too."

"Hisahide may not admit you to the meeting," Hiro said.

Ichiro smiled. "If the meeting relates to my father's death, he has no legal right to exclude an heir who carries the Ashikaga name. If I have to, I will force my way in by rank."

At the shogunate, the guards admitted Hiro and the others without question. A messenger led them directly to Saburo's inner office, where Hisahide knelt at Saburo's desk.

A man and a woman knelt before the desk with their backs to the entrance. Hiro couldn't see their faces, but he knew them anyway.

Masao and Jun.

The stable master knelt with his hands at his sides and his face cast down in defeat. His shoulders slumped and he did not turn as Hiro and the others entered the room.

Hisahide looked from Hiro to the boy and the priest. A question formed in his eyes.

The shinobi bowed. "We came as quickly as we could."

"Speed necessitates companions?" Hisahide asked.

Father Mateo bowed. "Matsui Hiro is my retainer. Given your earlier dismissal of his services, your summons made me concerned that his performance was unsatisfactory. I came to apologize for his inadequacy."

Hiro gave the priest a sideways glance. It always startled him when the Jesuit lied.

"There is no need for apologies," Hisahide said. "I assure you, Matsui-*san*'s performance was acceptable. Miyoshi Akira would tell you the same, but he is away on other business this afternoon." He turned his gaze on Ichiro. "This is no place for a child."

"I am not here as a child," Ichiro said. "Your summons suggests new information about my father's death. I have come as his heir, to claim the right of vengeance against his killer."

Jun glanced over her shoulder at Ichiro and then looked at Masao. The stable master continued to stare at the floor.

"You guessed correctly," Hisahide said. "I have learned that Den did not kill Ashikaga Saburo. The stable master did."

"I did not kill anyone." Masao spoke without emotion, as if he knew the words would have no impact.

Hisahide gestured to Masao but looked at Hiro. "As you see, I have a problem. He will not confess, even when confronted with evidence of his guilt. The shogun commanded me to obtain a confession—it would be awkward to execute the wrong man, given our previous belief that Den was the killer."

After a long pause, Hisahide repeated, "It would be awkward."

"You want me to help you obtain a confession?" Hiro asked.

"Masao claims you can verify his innocence," Hisahide said. "He admits to changing the stable boy's suicide message, but says he didn't murder anyone."

"That is what he told me," Hiro said. "What makes you think he's lying?"

Hisahide pointed at Jun. "The maid saw him outside Saburo's office just before, or possibly after, the murder. Masao killed Saburo and took advantage of his apprentice's suicide."

Jun gave Hiro a pleading look. "It's true. I saw him sneaking around the mansion about the time Ashikaga-*san* died. I was afraid to admit it . . . after Den . . . I thought Masao would kill me too."

The stable master looked at Jun with revulsion. "She's lying. She didn't see me. I wasn't there."

Chapter 43

"I was at dinner with my cousin the night Ashikaga-*san* died," Masao continued.

"If you're innocent, why did you alter the stable boy's suicide message?" Hisahide demanded.

"I told you the truth about that to prove my innocence," Masao said. "Adding a line to his words doesn't make me a killer."

"Why did you see the need to add anything?" Hisahide asked. "An innocent man would not be concerned for himself."

"I was frightened." Masao looked to Hiro for confirmation. "When I saw Den, and the confession on the pillar, I worried that someone would hold me responsible. Den was my apprentice, after all." The stable master's voice took on a pleading edge. "Send to Ōtsu. My cousin is the apothecary there. He will verify I was with him when Ashikaga-*san* died."

"That only proves he will lie on your behalf," Hisahide said. "Confess! Do not dishonor yourself with lies."

"It was him." Jun pointed at Masao. "I saw him."

"Are you certain it was Masao you saw?" Hiro asked.

Jun nodded. Her cheeks flushed red.

"Why would I kill Ashikaga-*san*?" Masao looked from Hiro to Hisahide. "I have worked in this compound for thirty years. Why would I exchange an unblemished record of loyalty for a death sentence?"

"You have said it yourself," Hisahide said. "Your loyalty to the shogun was your downfall."

Masao leaned back, confused.

Hisahide lifted a parchment from the desk and held it up, though Hiro doubted Masao could read the characters at that distance.

"This letter reveals the existence of a plot against the shogun," Hisahide said. "It also proves Saburo had an accomplice, someone in a position to admit Lord Oda's assassins to this compound.

"At first I believed that accomplice was one of the guards, but I now see it wasn't a guard at all. Who better than the stable master, the man who controls the gates?"

Hisahide stared at Masao as if expecting the words to prompt a confession.

Masao said nothing.

"You are the traitor," Hisahide said, "and worse, you are also a coward. You learned that your apprentice conspired with Ashikaga Saburo, but you didn't report the crime. You feared we would hold you responsible, so you killed Saburo and persuaded your apprentice to leave Kyoto.

"When we brought the boy back, you ordered him to kill himself before he could implicate you in the crime."

Hisahide's explanation fit the evidence, but imperfectly, and it contained too many assumptions for Hiro's taste. Also, it didn't account for the handwriting, but Hiro decided not to mention that either, at least for now.

"That's not what happened," Masao said. "I added to the message, but none of the rest is true. I would have reported a plot immediately."

"If you didn't kill Saburo, who did?" Hisahide demanded.

"I don't know." Masao shook his head. His shoulders slumped. "Maybe it was Den."

"What kind of worthless coward blames a child for his crime?" Hisahide sounded disgusted. "His guilt does not render you blameless. He was your apprentice. By law you are responsible for his actions."

Masao took a deep breath. "That is true."

Hisahide raised his chin, triumphant. "At last, an admission of guilt." He clapped his hands. Two guards appeared in the doorway.

Hisahide nodded toward Masao. "Lock this murderer in the kitchen storehouse, under guard, until the shogun decides what manner of death best suits such a worthless coward."

Masao rose and followed the guards from the room.

Father Mateo opened his mouth, but Hiro spoke first. "How do you plan to keep the shogun safe from Lord Oda's assassins?"

The shinobi caught Father Mateo's eye and shook his head slightly, hoping the priest would understand not to argue. Samurai anger spread like fire and, like a flame, consumed whatever it touched.

"The shogun's guards will meet Lord Oda's men at the city gates," Hisahide said. "We cannot bar the embassy from Kyoto, but the shogun can provide Lord Oda's men an attentive escort. I have doubled the guards on the compound gates and posted archers in all the towers. I also purchased two hundred new firearms from the Portuguese and will spend the rest of the day preparing my men to defend this compound. Given the danger, and Saburo's plot, the shogun has requested support from loyal Miyoshi forces."

"Can a man be trained to use an arquebus in a day?" Hiro asked.

"They have trained with foreign weapons before," Hisahide said. "I just didn't have enough to equip them all. Under the circumstances, the shogun decided to cover the expense."

He looked at Jun. "You may go."

She stood up quickly, bowed to Hisahide, and scurried away.

Hiro watched her go. "Are you certain the girl is trust-worthy? She's changed her story more than once."

"The stable master has changed his story also," Hisahide said. "Between the two, the girl has more reason to tell the truth. The evidence doesn't implicate her in the murders."

Hiro decided not to mention the handwriting, the hair pin, or the tea. He had seen Hisahide jump to two conclu-sions based on assumptions and didn't want to endanger anyone else—including himself and the priest.

"When will the shogun execute Masao?" Father Mateo asked.

Hisahide looked surprised. "You wish to witness the ex-ecution?"

"In my country, the condemned are given the chance to see a priest before they die."

"I advise you not to interfere in this matter any further," Hisahide said. "The shogun will execute Masao in public, during the emissaries' visit, to show Lord Oda's men they are fish in a net."

As they left the shogunate, Father Mateo offered to escort Ichiro home. To Hiro's surprise, the boy accepted.

"I thought I would feel better when I learned who killed my father," Ichiro said as he turned south on the road that fronted the shogun's compound, "but I don't. Does that make me weak?"

"It makes you human." Father Mateo laid a reassuring hand on Ichiro's shoulder.

Hiro cringed inwardly at the breach of etiquette. Samurai did not touch without permission. Not unless they intended to start a fight.

Ichiro turned his face to Father Mateo and smiled. Saburo's son might look and act like a samurai, but in many ways he remained a child.

The smile faded as Ichiro's eyes turned red. He clenched his jaw and forced the tears away. "I wish it wasn't Masao," he said at last. "I thought he was my friend. But at least . . . at least it wasn't my mother."

Father Mateo gave Hiro a questioning look over Ichiro's head.

Hiro shook his head in response. They could discuss it later. He hoped the priest wouldn't make a comforting statement about emotions. Samurai didn't cry in public, and Ichiro needed strength to maintain his self-control.

Chapter 44

At the intersection of Marutamachi Road, Ichiro bowed to Hiro and Father Mateo.

"Thank you for your assistance," he said. "Please excuse me, but I would rather walk alone from here."

They returned the bow as Ichiro started west along Marutamachi Road.

Father Mateo turned east, toward home, and Hiro walked alongside him.

"Do you think Masao really killed Ashikaga Saburo?" the Jesuit asked after Ichiro was out of earshot.

"I wish I knew," Hiro said.

"Hisahide's explanation seems to fit the facts."

Hiro felt a drop of rain on his nose and glanced at the slate-colored sky. Apparently, the storm had decided to stay. "I think it's very convenient that Jun found her courage and implicated Masao just when it seemed that Den would be blamed for the crime."

"You said she didn't love Den."

"True," Hiro said, "but people would ask why a stable boy killed a samurai and that would bring Saburo's affair to light."

"Destroying Jun's chances of being a samurai's bride," the priest concluded.

Hiro nodded. "Masao may still be guilty, but I'm disinclined to condemn him based on a lie."

"We still have a few more hours to find the killer," Father Mateo said.

Hiro shook his head. "This is over. The arrival of Lord Oda's men will put the city on alert. The nail that sticks out gets hammered down, regardless of guilt or innocence. We are not going to risk our lives to save a man who might be guilty anyway."

"He might be innocent also."

Hiro refused to answer. It would only cause an argument that he didn't want the Jesuit to win.

By the time they reached the Jesuit's home, the scents of earth and rain had filled the air. Drops began to patter on the road.

Father Mateo stepped onto the porch but blocked the door so Hiro couldn't enter.

"This isn't over yet," the Jesuit said. "Masao's condemnation means Kazu is innocent, at least in the eyes of the law. He's claimed innocence all along, and although I suspected him before, I've changed my mind. I think you have too. If that's so, you owe it to Kazu—and yourself—to try to mend your friendship."

Hiro said nothing.

"There's no point in glaring," Father Mateo said. "You know I'm right."

"I'm not even sure where to find him." Hiro tried to edge

around the priest, but Father Mateo continued to block the door.

"It's almost evening," Father Mateo said. "You know where Kazu will go when he finishes work."

"Tomorrow," Hiro said.

"Reconciliations, like rice balls, get harder and less palatable with time."

"Why do you care?" Hiro asked. "He's not your friend."

"No, but he's yours—and you're mine—so get going."

Hiro sighed with frustration but stepped back into his sandals and retraced his steps along Marutamachi Road. The rain increased and the road grew muddy. The clouds continued to darken, promising heavier rain by nightfall.

Hiro fancied walking home in a downpour only slightly less than talking with Kazu. He wasn't entirely sure why he complied with Father Mateo's request. Perhaps because, having lost one friend, he felt disinclined to anger the Jesuit also.

When he reached the Kamo River, Hiro crossed the bridge and turned south onto the path that followed the river bank, where the overhanging second stories of houses along the river offered intermittent shelter from the rain. Between the houses, drops fell onto his face and spattered his oiled hair, cold but fresh and not altogether unpleasant.

He hurried along the path toward the business district. At Sanjō Road, he noticed someone fishing underneath the bridge. Ordinarily, Hiro would have ignored the fisherman, but something about the silhouette looked familiar. He paused as the shadowed figure turned to face the road.

It was Ichiro.

The boy waved and moved over, making room for Hiro beneath the bridge. At that moment, the clouds released an unexpected deluge, so Hiro changed his plans and joined Saburo's son to wait out the rain.

As he bent to crawl under the bridge, Hiro noticed that Ichiro's smile seemed nervous. The boy fidgeted with his fishing pole and the line twitched nervously in the water.

"Nice day for fishing," Hiro said to put the boy at ease. "Fish bite better in the rain."

"How do you know that?" Ichiro's eyes widened. "My father considered fishing an inappropriate pastime for samurai."

"But you do it anyway," Hiro said. He wondered if the boy had gone home at all.

"I guess there's no point in pretending otherwise." Ichiro tugged to make the line twitch again. "I keep my pole hidden under the bridge and sneak out to fish when I can— mostly at night when everyone thinks I'm sleeping. I've lost a couple of poles to thieves, and I think someone uses this one when I'm not here, but I'd rather share it than suffer another beating for disobedience.

"Not that my father can beat me anymore."

An awkward silence fell.

"My brother liked fishing when we were young," Hiro said.

Ichiro's mouth fell open in surprise. When he recovered he asked, "Does he still do it?"

"He hasn't much opportunity, but I doubt he's outgrown the enjoyment." Hiro looked at the place where the fishing line met the water. Concentric ripples flowed away from the line but broke apart almost at once in the turbulent river.

"Are you going to Ginjiro's?" Ichiro asked.

"How do you know about Ginjiro's?"

Ichiro smiled. "Kazu goes there. He won't take me. He says I'm too young for sake shops."

Hiro smiled at the boy's unguarded simplicity. "Kazu is right."

Ichiro's smile grew lopsided in a nearly successful attempt to hide disappointment. He looked at the river. "I'm glad you believed me that Kazu was innocent."

"It was good of you to have faith in him," Hiro said.

"I told you before, it isn't just faith. It's a fact. Kazu couldn't have done it."

Ichiro hadn't mentioned facts before.

"How do you know for certain Kazu is innocent?" Hiro asked.

"I can't tell you." Ichiro kept his eyes on the fishing line. "It would get me in trouble—and Kazu too."

Chapter 45

The obvious question seemed unlikely, but Hiro asked it anyway. "Was Kazu fishing with you when your father was murdered?"

"Kazu doesn't know about my fishing. I wanted to tell him, but I was afraid he would tell my father." Ichiro looked down at his hands. "The last time Father caught me, he beat me with the pole until it broke. That's when I started leaving my poles at the river."

"But you were fishing the night your father died."

Ichiro nodded. "Mother went to bed when the bells rang, three hours after sunset. I waited another hour to make sure she was asleep."

"You didn't worry about your father coming home?"

"Father rarely slept at home." Ichiro jiggled his pole and changed the subject. "I like fishing under this bridge. The lamps up there draw the fish at night, and the revelers from Pontocho are always too drunk to notice me."

"What do you do with your catch?" Hiro asked.

"There's a noodle vendor on Sanjō Road who buys them, if they're big enough to keep."

Hiro knew the man in question. The vendor bragged

about using only fresh-caught fish from the Kamo River.
All this time, the shinobi had thought him a liar.

"He buys from samurai?" Hiro asked.

"I don't usually wear my swords when fishing."

Hiro glanced at the samurai knot in Ichiro's hair and
considered what he knew of the boy's behavior. The vendor
knew who he bought from, he just ignored it—and with
good reason. Hiro doubted a boy who lied about fishing
bothered to bargain much for the price of his catch.

"I didn't intend to come fishing today," Ichiro said, "I
thought it might distract me, but it hasn't worked."

"Since the investigation is over, will you explain why
Kazu is innocent? I won't tell your mother or Hisahide."

Ichiro considered the request. "I will, if you also agree
not to get the girl in trouble."

Hiro raised an eyebrow at Ichiro. "What girl?"

"The one that Kazu brought to the river the night my
father died."

Couples often walked by the Kamo River on moonlit
nights. Although romantic, the setting was also public
enough to preserve a maiden's honor, provided the couple
was chaperoned and didn't stay out too late.

Hiro suspected Kazu and his companion broke those
rules.

"She was pretty and young and certainly not a prostitute," Ichiro said. "But not samurai either. She looked like
an artisan's daughter."

"Did you catch her name?" Hiro asked, though he thought
he knew.

Ichiro raised his face to look at the underside of the
bridge. The wood was strung with spiderwebs and the rem-

nants of swallows' muddy nests. Overhead, rain pattered on the timbers.

"Tomiko," Ichiro said at last. "Tomiko, I'm sure that's it." He grinned at Hiro. "Kazu tried to kiss her. She wouldn't let him."

"How long did they stay on the bridge?"

"They walked on the bridge and the bank for over an hour, maybe longer." Ichiro pointed to the path. "I started to worry they wouldn't leave. If my mother woke up and found me missing, she'd call the watch, and then I'd really be in trouble."

"But she didn't," Hiro said.

"She never even knew I'd left the house." Ichiro tugged on his pole. "Hisahide said someone killed my father shortly after midnight. But Kazu was here until at least an hour after that. He couldn't have done it."

Ichiro pulled in the fishing line. A grub hung limp on the hook, white and swollen from soaking in the river. "The fish aren't biting today. I should just go home."

He coiled the fishing line neatly around the pole. When he reached the hook he removed the grub and tossed it into the water.

"Do you have to tell anyone what I've told you?" Ichiro asked as he stowed the pole out of sight among the pilings. "I don't want Kazu's girlfriend to get in trouble. She seemed very nice and she didn't do anything wrong."

Other than falling for Kazu, Hiro thought.

Aloud he said, "I'll do what I can to keep her out of trouble."

Ichiro smiled and followed Hiro out from under the bridge. The rain had slowed to a drizzle. Hiro watched Ichiro walk away up the path. When the boy disappeared behind a tree, the shinobi started west along Sanjō Road toward Ginjiro's brewery.

As he walked, he felt his frustration mounting. He had chosen Ginjiro's to serve as a safe spot to pass information to Kazu when necessary, but Kazu's clandestine affair with the brewer's daughter compromised the meeting spot as well as Tomiko's honor.

Breaches of discipline made the shinobi angry, but Kazu's lack of respect for Tomiko's emotions made Hiro furious. Men who played games with women were part of the reason women could not be trusted.

A few blocks west of the river Hiro turned south into the commercial district. Sake shops and teahouses lined the street, their open storefronts bathing the drizzly road with inviting light and enticing smells.

The noodle vendor Hiro wanted had set up his charcoal brazier on the eastern side of the street near Sanjō Road. A lacquered umbrella shielded both the man and his smoking fire from the rain. As Hiro approached, the vendor called, "Fish noodles! Best in Kyoto! Fresh-caught fish from the Kamo River! Extra good today!"

The shinobi didn't miss the hopeful look in the vendor's eyes. Only regulars stopped for snacks on a rainy night.

Charcoal smoke stung Hiro's eyes as he approached the vendor's stall. He noted the salty odor of fish beneath the more pungent smells of smoke and rain. His mouth watered, anticipating the treat to come. As usual, he ordered the largest bowl.

"Extra onions?" the vendor asked with a gap-toothed smile.

Hiro nodded and traded the man a copper coin for a

heaping bowl and a pair of wooden chopsticks. He usually stepped away to avoid the smoke, but tonight the umbrella gave some refuge from the rain. He stood beneath it and savored the chewy noodles.

It seemed no time at all until the chopsticks clattered against the empty bowl.

"Another?" the vendor asked hopefully.

Hiro shook his head but held up a second coin. "Where do you get your fish?"

The vendor glanced at the boiling pot atop his brazier. He shuffled his feet. "From a vendor, sir, same as everyone else."

"Then how do you know they come from the Kamo River?" Hiro asked.

"You can tell they're fresh. None better in Kyoto!"

Hiro lowered his voice. "I think you buy them from a samurai boy. Not every day, but every day he sells them."

The vendor's eyes grew wide. "Your son?"

Before Hiro could respond the noodle vendor knelt in the muddy street. "I'm sorry, sir. I'll pay him fairly from now on. I didn't realize he was samurai. An honest mistake, I swear it!"

Hiro opened his mouth to correct the mistake but decided not to. A man who took advantage of children didn't deserve that courtesy. Instead the shinobi handed over the bowl and the second coin, and then continued his drizzly walk. He reached Ginjiro's brewery just before sunset, though the clouds allowed no evening beams to paint the sky.

The brewery was empty of paying patrons. Suke lay in his usual corner, snoring beneath his stained and ragged robe. Perhaps because of the early hour, Tomiko stood alone behind the counter.

Hiro entered the shop, drew his katana, and handed the weapon to the girl. She accepted it with a bow. "Good evening, Matsui-*san.*"

"Good evening, Tomiko." Hiro glanced at the indigo *noren* that hung in the kitchen doorway. As Tomiko placed his sword in the wooden cabinet behind the counter Hiro said, "I know where you were two nights ago."

Tomiko's hands flew up to cover her mouth. She lowered them slowly. "Are you going to tell my father?"

"That depends on whether you tell the truth."

Chapter 46

Tomiko met Hiro's gaze without pretense. "What do you want to know?"

"Where were you two nights ago?" Hiro asked.

"You said you already knew."

"I do, but I want confirmation." Hiro paused. "A life may depend upon the truth."

She rested her palms on the countertop. "I waited until my mother went to sleep and cleaned the kitchen, but I didn't go to bed when I finished. I sneaked away and went for a walk with Kazu." She shook her head slightly. "My father would be furious if he knew, but there is no reason to tell him. I promise you it was only an innocent walk."

"How long did you spend at the river?" Hiro asked.

"A couple of hours—I had to get back before Father closed the shop and noticed my absence." She tilted her head a fraction. "How did you know? Who told you? Kazu would never tell."

"Someone saw you at the river."

Panic spread across her features. "Does Father know?"

"No," Hiro said, "and the person who saw you has reasons

to keep your secret. But if I hear that you've done it again, I will tell your father myself."

Tomiko lowered her eyes to the counter. She nodded. "I won't. I promise." She looked up and startled. A crimson blush crept into her cheeks.

Hiro turned to follow her gaze, though the scent of wintergreen and the girl's reaction had already told the shinobi who stood behind him.

Kazu looked surprised to see Hiro and paused before returning the older man's bow.

"It's been a long day," Hiro said before Kazu could hand his sword across the counter. "I need a walk. Would you like to come with me?"

Kazu narrowed his eyes. For a moment, Hiro thought the younger man would refuse to comply with the coded instruction.

Eventually Kazu nodded. "Pour a flask for me," he said to Tomiko, "I won't be long."

Hiro retrieved his sword from the girl and led Kazu into the street. Together they walked south in the gathering dark. The drizzling rain made the lanterns sparkle and washed the street in a fresher scent than the quarter typically enjoyed. Kazu said nothing, waiting for Hiro to speak.

When they had left Ginjiro's far enough behind Hiro said, "I know about you and Tomiko."

"I don't know what you mean," Kazu said. "Tomiko . . . Ginjiro's daughter?"

"Ashikaga Ichiro saw you at the river," Hiro said. "He was fishing under the bridge at Sanjō Road two nights ago."

Kazu clenched his jaw and gave Hiro a sideways look.

The shinobi stopped walking. Kazu took two more steps

before he realized Hiro had stopped. He turned around, shoulders squared and ready to fight.

"Don't tell me what to do," Kazu said. "It's none of your business anyway."

Hiro swallowed the flush of anger that rose in his throat at Kazu's words and, with it, the scolding he intended to deliver. Instead he reminded himself why the priest had sent him.

When he finally answered Kazu, his voice was calm. "I apologize for accusing you of Ashikaga Saburo's murder."

"I told you I didn't do it," Kazu said. "You believe me now?"

"You would have thought the same if our places were reversed." Hiro struggled to keep his anger from returning.

"I thought you didn't make assumptions."

Hiro blinked, surprised by Kazu's bitterness. "You don't accept my apology?"

"Would you have accepted mine, if our positions were reversed?"

"You know I would," Hiro said. "I always do."

Kazu shook his head, still angry, but eventually he sighed. "All right, I accept your apology." He turned back toward Ginjiro's. "You always have to win."

Hiro shook his head at Kazu and wondered why the younger man saw everything as a contest.

As they started back toward the brewery Hiro asked, "How far has it gone?"

"With Tomiko?" Kazu shrugged. His anger had dissipated, leaving sheepishness behind. "Believe it or not, that was the first time I took her anywhere. I'd wanted to for a while, but I knew I shouldn't."

"You're right that you shouldn't," Hiro said. "She's an artisan's daughter. You're samurai."

Kazu returned Hiro's gaze without blinking. He didn't answer.

"Don't make her wish for what can never be," Hiro said.

"Yes, Father," Kazu mocked a childish response. He held up his hands. "You're ri—"

He stopped in midsentence and stared up the street.

Ichiro ran toward them, splashing through puddles as if he ran for his life. His swords stuck out at awkward angles. The hem of his kimono was dark with mud. He paused in front of a sake shop to read the name above the lighted space.

Kazu hurried toward him. "Ichiro!"

The boy looked weak with relief.

"Kazu," he gasped. "Help me. My mother is dead."

"Your mother?" Hiro asked. "What happened?"

As Hiro and Kazu reached him, Ichiro finally lost control. His lower lip trembled and tears welled up in his eyes. He hung his head. His shoulders shook.

Kazu laid a hand on Ichiro's shoulder. Hiro wouldn't have dared it, but Kazu was the closest thing Ichiro had to a father now.

They waited while the boy regained control. He managed it faster than Hiro expected.

Ichiro raised his face to Kazu. "Someone killed her and tried to make it look like a suicide."

Chapter 47

"How do you know it was murder?" Hiro asked.

Kazu shot the shinobi an angry look over Ichiro's head.

"We have to know." Hiro glanced at the boy. "If it really wasn't suicide he's in danger."

Ichiro forced his tears away and sniffed to clear his nose. "My mother would never kill herself. Not before, and definitely not now. She had control of my father's money. She had no reason . . ."

He paused, unable to finish but determined to keep control.

"How did it happen?" Hiro asked.

"Poison, I think," Ichiro said. "Her mouth was foaming, but she was dead. I didn't know what to do . . . I was looking for you at Ginjiro's. I don't have anywhere else to go."

"You can stay with me tonight," Kazu said. "We'll talk to your relatives in the morning."

"But first we need you to take us to your mother," Hiro said. "You don't have to see her again, but I need to know whether this was murder or suicide."

"It was murder," Ichiro said. "She would never leave me."

"I believe that," Hiro said, "and I will find the person who did this."

"And I will kill him," Kazu added.

"I'm coming with you." Father Mateo stepped from the shadows at the edge of the road.

"What are you doing here?" Hiro asked.

"I know a thing or two about mending dams," the Jesuit said. "I followed you—by a different route—in case my help was required."

Kazu looked at Hiro. "What is he talking about?"

"He doesn't trust me to apologize properly," Hiro said.

Kazu gave the priest an appraising glance. "He knows you well."

"We can discuss that another time." Hiro nodded at Ichiro. "Let's go."

※

Ichiro's home lay on Marutamachi Road, in the expensive residential ward that surrounded the shogunate. The two-story wooden house had painted lintels and cedar beams. A pair of snarling statues guarded the path that led to the entrance.

The house was dark except for a muted glow that spilled onto the porch from the open door. Ichiro had left it ajar in his flight.

Hiro felt a pang of sorrow for the boy, bereft of father and mother in less than a week. The Ashikaga clan would look after its own, but the knowledge did little to soothe the shinobi's regret, or his rising frustration. The man—or woman—who murdered Ashikaga Saburo, and probably Den, had almost certainly killed Netsuko too. With Masao under guard at the shogunate, the list of suspects was very short indeed.

Part of Hiro hoped Netsuko had killed herself after all.

Ichiro paused at the edge of the veranda.

"You don't have to go in," Kazu said.

"Yes, I do." The boy stepped onto the porch and approached the door. "A samurai does not shirk his duty, especially to his parents. If you're going to catch her killer, I'm going to help you."

Inside, the dark foyer gave way to an *oe* lit by a single brazier near the door. Ichiro must have lit it, or added charcoal, when he returned, illuminating the grisly scene within.

Ashes covered the coals of a near-dead fire in the sunken hearth. A kettle hung from a chain above the fire pit. On the tatami beside the hearth, a single porcelain teacup sat to the right of the host's position, as if waiting for a guest who had not come. A second teacup lay on its side a little way from the hearth, just beyond the outstretched fingers of the woman lying dead beside the fire.

Netsuko was sprawled on her back, with her left arm over her head and the right flung out to the side, almost touching the empty teacup that she had been holding when she fell. Her empty eyes stared into the distance, devoid of spirit and slightly glazed by exposure to the air. Her nose and fingers had the grayish hue that Hiro expected, and the vomit on the floor and around her mouth gave off the distinctive odor of opium. Hiro smelled it even over the charcoal smoke from the dying fire and the pervasive wintergreen of Kazu's hair oil.

"Stay here." The shinobi crossed the room and knelt beside Netsuko. As he expected, the sour-sweet odor grew stronger and more familiar as he approached.

He lifted the teapot, removed the lid, and turned his head away from the smell that assaulted his nostrils.

"Opium?" Kazu asked from the doorway.

Hiro tilted the pot and saw a half-melted lump of resin the size of a peach pit. "Yes. There's no doubt she ingested a fatal dose. Far more than Den consumed."

"I don't understand," Kazu said. "Saburo's death left the family better off in many ways. I'm sorry, Ichiro, but your mother was probably glad that your father was dead."

"She was," Ichiro said. "She told me so."

"But she would have tasted the poison," Father Mateo said. "It has a distinctive flavor."

"Small quantities can be hidden with sweetener," Kazu said.

"That's what happened with Den," Hiro said, "but Den's pot held a fraction of what's in here." He picked up a nearby poker and stirred the coals. They collapsed in a pile of ash, sending a handful of sparks into the air.

He looked at the room and then at Kazu. "What do you see?"

Kazu studied the scene for a minute or two. "The fire's old, and almost dead—this happened a couple of hours ago. Also, Netsuko had a guest—the second cup at the hearth."

"Not bad," Hiro said. "And since there isn't a second body, the visitor brought the poison and made her drink it."

"Or slipped it into the pot when she wasn't looking," Ichiro said.

"Not that much opium," Father Mateo said. "Even if she didn't see it, she would have smelled it—or tasted it in the tea. But why would she drink poison voluntarily?"

Hiro looked at Ichiro. "She was trying to save her son."

"Where's the logic in that?" Kazu asked. "She had no assurance the killer wouldn't murder Ichiro too."

"What if that was the bargain?" Hiro set the pot on the floor beside Netsuko. "She drinks the opium, making the murder look like a suicide, and in return the killer lets Ichiro live. He is only a boy. To the killer, he seems no threat, especially if Netsuko claims that she hasn't shared her suspicions with her son."

"You think she knew who killed Ashikaga Saburo," the Jesuit said.

Hiro nodded. "Or, at least, the killer thought she knew."

"You know who did this," the Jesuit said.

"I think so," Hiro answered, "and if I'm right, the shogun's life is very much in danger."

Chapter 48

"The same person killed Saburo and Netsuko?" Kazu asked.

"Den also," Hiro said.

"Who did it?" Father Mateo asked.

"It's still an assumption," Hiro said, "and assumptions have killed enough people already. I need to return to the shogunate. There's evidence there that confirms or disproves my theory. When I have it in hand, I'll tell you who killed Saburo—and Den, and Netsuko too."

"The gates are closed," the Jesuit said. "Will the evidence wait until morning?"

"I doubt it," Hiro said, "and I want to save Masao if I can, which means retrieving the information tonight."

"I want to go with you," Ichiro said.

Hiro shook his head. "It isn't safe. Go with Father Mateo."

The Jesuit nodded. "I'll take him home with me."

Ichiro looked at his mother's body. "I don't want to leave her like this."

Hiro started to object but Kazu said, "You'll want a priest to take care of her, with proper prayers and rituals for her

soul. We shouldn't move her—you don't want to anger her
ghost."

Ichiro frowned. "I don't believe in ghosts."

"Your mother did," Kazu said, "and she wouldn't want
you defiled by touching a corpse—especially hers. Would
you disturb her body against her wishes?"

Ichiro hesitated. "I suppose no one else will see her tonight."

Kazu nodded. "Let's go for now. Tomorrow morning I'll
summon the priests myself."

When Father Mateo and Ichiro had disappeared down
Marutamachi Road toward the river, Hiro asked Kazu, "Did
Ashikaga Netsuko believe in ghosts?"

"I have no idea," Kazu said, "but it got Ichiro out of
the house. What evidence are we looking for at the shogunate?"

"The shogun didn't alter Saburo's ledger," Hiro said, "the
killer did."

Kazu's mouth fell open. "You knew that I lied? Why
didn't you say so?"

"There was no point at the time," Hiro said. "You wouldn't
admit it. You knew the killer had changed the schedule, but
you didn't recognize the writing. If you had known who did
it, you would have said so.

"You knew the shogun was in danger, along with anyone who got too close to revealing the killer. A person willing to kill a shogun will kill any lesser man who gets in his
way." Hiro smiled. "You thought your lie would keep me
safe. Instead, it made you a suspect."

"How did you figure all that out?" Kazu asked.

"I've known you all your life," Hiro said. "And, as you say, I always have to win."

"Why get the ledger tonight?" Kazu asked. "The gates are closed, the ledger is safe in my office, and Masao will still be alive first thing in the morning."

"But the shogun won't be," Hiro said, "and I'm not so sure about Masao either."

"Lord Oda's men don't arrive until tomorrow," Kazu protested.

"So we were led to believe," Hiro said. "But if that's true, why did the schedule changes impact only the guards for tonight? The killer was putting his men in position. They're already here."

"Then why bother with the ledger?" Kazu asked. "We need to get out of Kyoto now."

"It's too late for that," Hiro said. "The barricades at the city exits are certainly closed for the night. The shogun's enemies may have already seized them.

"We need the ledger as evidence. If the plot succeeds, that proof may save our lives. At a minimum, it gives us the power to bargain."

Kazu looked at Hiro's kimono. "You're not getting over the shogunate wall in that. I have extra *hakama* at home. Let's go."

They stopped at Kazu's rented house just long enough for Hiro to exchange his kimono for midnight-blue *hakama* trousers and a matching surcoat. Kazu opted to stay in the formal *hakama* and trousers he normally wore to work at the shogunate.

"I haven't got any special weapons to loan you," Kazu said. "My landlord is nosy and since a samurai clerk has no excuse for keeping shinobi items, I've gone without."

"That's all right." Hiro withdrew a pair of star-shaped *shuriken* from the inner pocket of his kimono. "I brought my own."

He transferred the weapons to the inside pocket of his borrowed surcoat. "I'm ready," he said as he thrust his swords through his obi. "Time to go."

Hiro and Kazu hurried through the darkened streets and approached the shogunate from the west. When they reached the walls, Kazu led Hiro onto a narrow thoroughfare that bordered the northern side of the shogun's compound.

Hiro noticed extra guards in the towers along the compound wall. He leaned toward Kazu and slung his arm around the younger man's neck.

"We're drunk," he whispered. "Make a good show."

Kazu laughed as if Hiro had told a brilliant joke. He wobbled and pulled Hiro sideways in a convincing imitation of drunken revelry. Hiro pulled against him, and they wandered together down the street like a pair of besotted comrades.

A snicker from overhead told Hiro the ruse was working. He smiled. No one remembered a passing drunk for very long.

A couple of minutes later, Kazu guided their weaving pace toward the side of the road. Hiro followed. They wobbled closer and closer to the wall. Hiro expected a warning shout from the guards but it never came. The men in the towers considered the drunks no threat.

On the opposite side of the nine-foot wall, a cluster of ancient trees stretched into the air. Their questing branches extended across the wall and into the road as if reaching for the houses on the other side of the street.

Hiro smiled. The shogun took such care to clear the branches around the mansion. He would have done well to watch the walls as closely.

The two shinobi passed under the branches and out of sight of the guards. Without a word, Kazu let go of Hiro and leaped for the lowest branch. He caught the limb and swung himself upward, disappearing into the tree with barely a sound.

Hiro followed a moment later. Concealed in the branches, he waited.

No alarm split the air. Their movement into the trees had gone unnoticed.

Kazu tilted his head toward the wall and started climbing. Hiro followed him up the branch and over the palisade that surrounded the compound. Together, they dropped to the ground on the opposite side. Kazu landed more loudly than Hiro, but not by much. A passerby would have thought them nothing more than a house cat hunting mice.

Hiro crouched defensively, smelling the loamy odors of woods and rain.

To the south, the trees gave way to landscaped yards. The *bakufu* mansion lay out of sight on the opposite side of the landscaped gardens that covered the northern part of the shogunate grounds. From here, Hiro would have to trust Kazu to lead him.

He hoped he had judged correctly that Kazu wasn't involved in the plot.

Chapter 49

Pine needles crunched under Hiro's feet and released an evergreen scent that competed with Kazu's hair oil.

"The ledger is in my office," Kazu whispered. "We're headed there?"

"Not yet," Hiro said. "I'd like to get Masao to safety first."

"Are you crazy?" Kazu asked. "We owe him nothing. If you're right, we'll be lucky to get the ledger and save ourselves."

"He doesn't deserve to die any more than Netsuko . . . or Ichiro."

Hiro hoped the boy's name would have the desired effect. He needed Kazu's help to find and free the stable master.

"Let's get the ledger first and help him later," Kazu said.

Hiro was not going to fall for that. "They're holding Masao in a kitchen storehouse. Freeing him will be faster than getting the ledger."

And assure your compliance with both, Hiro thought.

"Unless we're spotted," Kazu said.

"In which case, we won't need the ledger."

Kazu made an exasperated sound but didn't argue.

They made their way through the gardens toward the mansion. Stone lanterns lined the paths, but they were dark and cold that night. Hardly surprising, given the inclement weather.

Kazu led the way without hesitation. He knew exactly where and when to move to avoid the guards that patrolled the compound. Not that there were many guards to avoid.

"I expected better security," Hiro whispered.

The two shinobi crouched behind a decorative hedge at the edge of the yard that separated the gardens from the kitchen. On their journey from the wall, they had seen only four patrolling guards, none of whom seemed overly alert.

Kazu shrugged. "Lord Oda's men aren't due until tomorrow. Most of the guards are posted at the gates or on the towers. The shogun doesn't expect anyone to breach the walls unnoticed."

"Foolish," Hiro said.

Kazu snorted. "Him, or us?"

Hiro looked at the storehouses near the kitchen. The boxy wooden structures stood a few feet apart and on wooden stilts to discourage rats. There were two, of roughly equal size, but only one had a bar across its doorway.

"That's it." Hiro nodded. "He's in that one."

A bored-looking samurai leaned against the back of the kitchen building, apparently guarding the storehouse, though Hiro considered "guarding" too active a word.

"We need a diversion," Kazu whispered.

"You are the diversion," Hiro replied. "You work here. Circle around and distract him."

Kazu grumbled but disappeared into the darkness. A few minutes later he reappeared around the corner of the kitchen. He walked briskly, as if bearing important news.

"You!" Kazu startled at the sight of the guard. "What are you doing here?"

The samurai jumped and snapped to attention. "Matsunaga-*san* ordered me to guard the prisoner."

"Nonsense!" Kazu snapped. "The entire compound is on alert and you're lazing behind the kitchen, shirking your duty!"

"No, sir, I swear it. Matsunaga-*san* wanted the prisoner guarded."

"Do you know who I am?" Kazu demanded. "How dare you question me!"

The guard's eyes widened. "No sir . . . I'm sorry . . ." He bowed three times and straightened, trembling like a sapling in an earthquake.

"Lord Oda's men may already have entered Kyoto," Kazu snarled. "You have better things to do than guarding an aging stable boy. If he gets loose, we'll kill him. Until then . . . get back to your regular post!"

The samurai hurried out of the yard, tripping over his sandals in the process. He righted himself and hustled away.

Kazu watched him go. When he was certain the guard had departed he gestured to Hiro and crossed the yard to the storehouse.

Hiro met him there. They slid back the bar and opened the door but saw only darkness within.

"Masao," Hiro whispered, "It's me, Matsui Hiro."

Masao's face appeared in the darkened doorway. A layer of rice dust grayed his clothes and hair.

"Matsui-*san*?" The stable master looked confused. "I don't understand . . ."

"We know you are not the killer," Hiro said. "We've come to free you."

Masao backed away from the door. "No . . . no samurai frees a commoner. It's a trap."

"It will be, if you don't get out here right this second," Kazu hissed. "We're not waiting around while you make up your mind."

Masao's face appeared again. "Ito-*san*?" His face went slack as he took in Hiro's baggy trousers and darkened coat. His eyes widened with fear and recognition.

Most Japanese had heard of shinobi, but few expected to see one.

"We have to go," Hiro said. "You're not our only errand here this evening, and time is short. If we get you out of the compound, can you hide until the city gates open tomorrow?"

"I can." Masao stepped out of the storehouse and glanced toward the kitchen building. "But I can do better than that. There's a path through the compound that leads to a hidden exit near the stable. The previous stable master showed me the place. If the shogun is ever in danger and has to escape, I'm supposed to meet him there with his fastest horse."

"Is the exit locked?" Hiro asked.

Masao smiled. "Of course, but I know how to open it." He bowed to Hiro and then to Kazu. "Thank you for helping me. I owe you my life."

As the stable master hurried off into the darkness, Hiro closed the storehouse and slid the lever back across the door.

He turned to Kazu. "Let's get that ledger and clear the wall before anyone knows we're here."

Stone lanterns burned in the yard between the kitchen and the northern entrance to the *bakufu* mansion. More lanterns ringed the mansion itself, their flickering glow creating overlapping pools of light intended to foil the stealthy approach of thieves or shinobi assassins.

Fortunately, Hiro had no intention of sneaking anywhere. He walked across the yard and into the mansion as if he, not Kazu, had worked there for several years.

Kazu followed with silent strides.

For once, they didn't bother to remove their shoes before going inside. Hiro had no intention of needing to leave the way they came.

They entered the mansion and made their way to the outer office where Kazu worked. Light flickered through the hallway from the reception room where the carpenters had been working. Hiro paused and listened, but heard nothing. Ozuru must have been sent away with the others.

As he laid his hand on the door to Kazu's office, a tapping echoed through the hall. He looked over his shoulder. "Is that a chisel?"

Kazu nodded. "Sounds like Ozuru is working late."

That seemed odd, since the carpenter claimed he couldn't stay after sunset anymore.

The door to Kazu's office slid open with barely a sound, releasing a wave of parchment-scented air into the hall. The smell of the new tatami and the piles of ledgers had long since overpowered the smell of death. Not even Hiro's sensitive nose could catch a trace of the crime in the air.

Kazu grasped a pair of tongs from the charcoal bucket by the door and stirred the coals in the brazier near the entrance. The coals returned to life with a puff of sparks and a few small licks of flame. Hiro slid the shoji closed behind them as Kazu added charcoal to the fire.

"Wait here," Kazu said, and walked off into Saburo's

inner office. He reappeared in the doorway a moment later, holding a ledger. "This is the one you want."

Behind him, a shadow moved.

Akira stepped into the light and laid a dagger at the base of Kazu's neck. His eyes were locked on Hiro. "If you yell—if you even move—I'll kill him."

Chapter 50

"You're going to kill him anyway," Hiro said. "It's in your plan—or was, when you believed 'he'd return alone. Now that I'm here, you can't afford to kill him."

Akira narrowed his eyes. "I could kill him right now if I wanted to."

"And then I'd kill you," Hiro said. "See the problem? You need him if you want to stay alive."

"Is that Akira?" Kazu tried to see behind him but stopped as Akira pressed the blade against his flesh. "What are you doing here?"

"He came to plant evidence that will implicate you in Saburo's plot," Hiro said, "and he probably intended to murder you too. I thought he would have left, since you went to Ginjiro's."

Akira sneered. "I knew he'd be back. He left a fire in the brazier."

"Not intentionally." Kazu sounded remarkably conversational, given the knife at his neck.

Hiro recognized the tactic. The moment Akira lowered his guard, Kazu would try to disarm him.

Akira looked at Hiro. "I didn't expect you to come back

with him. This works even better than what I originally planned."

"You'll claim you found me standing over his corpse with a knife in my hand," Hiro said. "You'll kill us both and call it a 'conspirators' argument ending in murder.' Believable, as far as it goes, but even if you survive to try it, how will you explain the shogun's death if everyone in the conspiracy is either dead or captured?"

"What are you talking about?" Kazu asked.

Hiro looked at Akira. "Would you like to tell him, or shall I?"

"Go ahead." Akira smiled smugly. "You seem to have everything figured out. But before you do, both of you drop your swords to the floor. And don't try anything foolish. I'll kill this man before you can strike, and then I'll kill you too. A ronin translator is no match for a trained Miyoshi swordsman."

"If you say so," Hiro said. "Kazu, drop your swords."

Kazu narrowed his eyes in displeasure but eased his katana from its scabbard and dropped it to the floor. His *wakizashi* followed a moment later.

Akira kicked the swords out of reach and nodded at Hiro. "Your turn, and slide them away. I don't want them where you think you can retrieve them."

Hiro took off his swords and lowered them to the matting. After a moment's hesitation he pushed the weapons out of reach. They slid across the room and came to rest against the veranda door.

"Stand up," Akira said, "and keep your hands where I can see them."

Hiro obliged.

Akira nodded. "Now, let's hear you tell your tale."

"You should kill us now," Hiro said. "If you don't, I'm going to kill you."

Akira laughed. "Not likely. In a few hours I will be shogun and you will be dead."

"If you say so," Hiro said, "but you're mistaken."

"Talk," Akira said, "before I get bored and kill you like the others."

"He's the killer?" Kazu asked. "I thought it was Hisahide."

"It had to be one or the other," Hiro said, "though I didn't think Hisahide would kill Netsuko. He's too professional for that."

"She suspected me," Akira said. "She had to die."

"Actually, she didn't," Hiro said. "She suspected the mistress."

"Jun?" Akira sneered. "Impossible. Netsuko would have said so before she died. All she did was beg for the life of her son."

"Saburo was plotting with the Miyoshi?" Kazu shook his head a little—as much as the knife allowed. "That isn't possible. He hated the Miyoshi daimyo—and his heirs."

"Saburo knew nothing about the plot to murder the shogun," Hiro said. "The letter was a diversion, no doubt written after his death to distract the shogun from the real plot. That's why you didn't find it until the morning after the crime."

"Correct," Akira said. "I wrote it and left it in his office. I knew about the letter box all along. We needed permission to increase the number of Miyoshi guards in the compound, to dilute the shogun's forces with samurai under our control. Nine-tenths of the men on duty tonight are loyal to the Miyoshi. The letter made that possible."

"You're seizing the shogunate now?" Kazu asked. "On the night before Lord Oda's men arrive?"

"Lord Oda never sent any men to Kyoto," Hiro said, "the ambassadors were a clever ploy to distract the shogun's attention from the traitors within his walls."

"How did you know?" Akira asked. "Everyone else believed it."

"Blame the merchant," Hiro said, "the Portuguese. He checked at Ōtsu. The innkeeper there knew nothing of the embassy, but official delegations always send a man ahead to ensure the inn has rooms available. No messenger making reservations, no delegation from Oda.

"I think Saburo discovered it too—that's why you killed him."

"A mistake at last!" Akira gloated. "Saburo was an ignorant fool. He had no idea about our plans. In fact, he'd still be alive if he hadn't walked in on me copying from his ledger.

"I needed to know which men he assigned for duty tonight, and how many, so we could plan the final attack. I sneaked in here to check the ledger, but as it happened Saburo hadn't left. He was locked in an embrace with that ugly maid.

"They didn't see me, so I hid in the shadows and waited for them to finish."

"But Jun saw you when she left," Hiro said. "That's why she claimed Masao was here. She saw your silhouette, and Den's. She recognized him but mistook you for the stable master."

Akira nodded. "Den was just outside the door. I saw him arrive, though I didn't know the girl had seen me too. After everyone left I sneaked back into the office to get the ledger. But Saburo returned before I finished with it.

"I pretended I was looking for Ito Kazu and tried to leave. If he had let me, I might have let him live. But he followed me into this outer office, accusing me of stealing. He called me names." Akira scowled. "No one insults Miyoshi Akira and lives."

"So you took the dagger off my desk and killed him," Kazu said.

"You wouldn't expect me to use my own," Akira said. "I moved so quickly he barely had the chance to raise his hand in self-defense. He never even tried to draw his sword."

"But covering your tracks proved more difficult than you expected," Hiro said, "especially when Hisahide didn't believe that Kazu was to blame."

"Wait," Kazu said. "I thought Hisahide was part of the plot."

Hiro shook his head. "Against the shogun, yes, but I don't think he sanctioned Saburo's murder, or Den's, or Lady Netsuko's either. Killings would put the compound on alert and make seizure of the shogunate more difficult. Akira had to invent the letter, and Saburo's plot, to keep Hisahide from learning the truth—that Akira made a mistake."

"He didn't suspect anything until you pointed out that Kazu wouldn't have used his own dagger," Akira said. "Then I had to explain what really happened. Fortunately, he considered Saburo's death an accidental boon. It gave us an excuse to move more of our men inside the shogunate."

"You must have been relieved to learn Masao sent Den away," Hiro said. "So the stable boy couldn't accuse you either. He saw you do it, didn't he?"

"Not the murder," Akira said, "although I think he guessed. Thank you for finding him for me and for giving me an excuse to bring him back."

"How did you get the opium into the tea?" Hiro asked.

"When we returned from Ōtsu, I told Jun to take some food and tea to the stable. I even gave her permission to add some sweetener. I checked the pot on a pretense of making sure the water was hot enough. It was. For tea, and also for dissolving opium."

"I'm guessing you intended to kill Masao as well as Den," Hiro said. "A double suicide, no questions asked."

"I don't know why it didn't," Akira said, "I used enough."

"Masao didn't drink it," Hiro said. "But you didn't know that, so you doubled the dose for Netsuko. Did you stay to watch her die?"

"I've explained enough," Akira snapped.

"Why stop now? We're almost finished," Hiro said.

"We're finished now." Akira tilted the dagger.

A bead of blood appeared on Kazu's neck.

Chapter 51

H iro," Kazu said, "quit helping."
Hiro kept his eyes on Akira. "You killed Netsuko
and Den for nothing. They didn't know you murdered Saburo. Netsuko even believed Den wrote the suicide message
in the stable. Good thing you knew the boy could write."

"I found out on the way back from Ōtsu, in order to arrange the scene," Akira said. "And I only did what I had to
do. I saw a problem and solved it—the way a shogun would."

"Not even a shogun has license to murder the innocent
without cause," Hiro said.

"No ronin understands what it means to be shogun,"
Akira said. "By morning, all of Japan will answer to me."

"You really think Hisahide will make you shogun?"
Hiro laughed. "By morning, you'll be dead. I guarantee it."

"Do not laugh!" Akira snapped. "Matsunaga Hisahide is
a Miyoshi retainer, a glorified servant. He has no claim to
the shogunate."

"Curious that you feel the need to say so," Hiro said. "If
Hisahide seizes the shogun's compound and gains control
of Kyoto, some people might think his claim to the shogunate rather strong."

"Including the emperor," Kazu said.

"Even the emperor answers to the shogun." Akira looked down his nose at Hiro. "And Hisahide remembers who pays his salary."

"Not you," Hiro said. "If Hisahide kills the shogun, he'll kill you too."

Uncertainty flickered across Akira's face. "That's not true. You just want me to let down my guard so you can escape."

The door behind Hiro rattled open.

Akira startled. He jabbed Kazu's neck with the dagger.

It was the opening Hiro needed. He pulled the *shuriken* from his tunic and leaped across the room. As he landed, his free hand knocked the dagger away from Kazu's throat. His other hand drove the sharpened point of his star-shaped weapon through Akira's eye.

The *shuriken* sliced through the eyeball like a knife through a melon. Blood and bits of eye spurted over Hiro's hand and onto his face. Hiro didn't flinch. He pushed the *shuriken* further into Akira's eyeball, stopping only when the metal star lodged deep in the samurai's skull.

Akira's good eye widened with shock. A moment later, the spark of life disappeared.

The moment Akira died, Hiro pulled the *shuriken* free. He tucked it into his sleeve as he spun around.

Hisahide stood in the doorway, watching them from the opposite side of the room.

Hiro heard a thump as Akira's body hit the floor.

"Thank you." Hisahide smiled. "You've saved me the trouble of killing him."

"Hiro was right?" Kazu stepped to Hiro's side. Aside from a trickle of blood on his neck, he seemed unhurt. "You intended to kill Akira all along?"

"Only if he refused to cooperate," Hisahide said. "He was foolish, but his rashness helped my cause. The murders made the shogun believe Lord Oda really did plan an assassination. He was so focused on that plot that he never suspected the real one."

"Your phrasing suggests the shogun is already dead," Hiro said.

"That depends who you mean by 'shogun.'" Hisahide smiled again. "Ashikaga Yoshiteru committed seppuku an hour ago, at my invitation. I promised to let his family live in return for his suicide, and abdication. I am shogun now." He searched Hiro's face, and then Kazu's, for a reaction.

Hiro heard Kazu's clothing rustle in a bow. The shinobi kept his eyes on Hisahide.

"Congratulations, Shogun Matsunaga," Kazu said.

"A wise decision," Hisahide said. "The question now is what becomes of you."

"I would willingly serve your administration," Kazu said. "Your predecessor found me a competent clerk."

"I think not," Hisahide said. "Men with secrets are dangerous, and men who know other men's secrets even more so. You know too much about the shogun's suicide. I have a letter naming me successor shogun—or regent for the former shogun's infant cousin, if the emperor won't confirm me directly. But Ashikaga Yoshiteru's brother might find your knowledge useful if he decides to dispute my claim."

"Yoshiteru's brother is a monk," Kazu said. "He surrendered his attachment to this world years ago. Even if he changed his mind, I've never met him and have no loyalty to his cause."

"Every man has a price," Hisahide said, "and I have no

assurance that yours is beyond my rival's grasp. It seems wiser to eliminate you now."

"Banish him to Iga," Hiro said, "on penalty of death if he leaves the province. Iga is loyal to the shogun, an ally of Kyoto. That will neutralize Kazu's usefulness to your enemies."

Hisahide transferred his gaze to Hiro. "You're in no position to negotiate." He looked at Akira's body. "Though I admit you did me a favor tonight, and favors merit reward."

"Kill me if you want to," Kazu said, "but you have to let Hiro go."

"I don't have to do anything." Hisahide straightened his shoulders. "No one in Japan commands the shogun."

"True enough," Kazu said, "but the Portuguese control the flow of firearms. Matsui-*san* is a friend of the Portuguese merchant who arms your soldiers—a merchant who would sell to Lord Oda as happily as to you, if you give him reason."

Kazu fell silent, letting the threat sink in.

"I have hundreds of firearms," Hisahide said, but Hiro caught the hint of uncertainty in his voice.

"Enough to seize Kyoto, perhaps," Kazu said. "But enough to defend it? And you're assuming the Portuguese won't call in foreign soldiers to avenge the translator's death. The foreigners consider their servants much like a daimyo's retainers—they will not allow a killing to go unpunished."

Hisahide frowned. "The Portuguese priest did accompany him to the compound today to ensure he hadn't displeased me."

Kazu nodded. "Have you sufficient strength to defeat Lord Oda and the Portuguese?"

Hisahide drew a deep breath and let it out slowly. He

looked at Hiro. "If I allow you to live, you must ensure that the foreigner sells no weapons to Lord Oda and that the Portuguese support my appointment as shogun."

"I am merely a servant," Hiro said. "I cannot guarantee—"

"You will make it happen," Hisahide said, "or I will kill not only you but the foreign priest and the merchant also."

"Then I have no choice, Lord Shogun." Hiro glanced to his side. "Let's go, Kazu."

Hisahide shook his head. "Not Kazu. Only you."

"I will do what you ask," Hiro said, "but only if Kazu goes with me. If you kill him you will start a war for which you are not prepared."

Hiro thought of Hattori Hanzo and the shinobi of the Iga *ryu*. A man who killed both Hiro and Kazu would have more to fear than the Portuguese.

"An intelligent man would accept his freedom and go," Hisahide warned.

"An honorable man will die to protect his friends," Hiro said. "Do what you must. I will not leave him."

"A bold statement for a man without a sword." Hisahide crossed the room and picked up Hiro's katana and *wakizashi*. He examined the scabbards and tested the heft of the weapons.

Just when Hiro thought Hisahide would call for his guards, the samurai turned the scabbards sideways and offered the swords to Hiro.

"I, too, am a man of honor," Hisahide said. "It was never my intention to seize the shogunate by unnecessary force, and I would rather have the foreigners on my side. I will let you go on the following conditions. Hiro will ensure that the Portuguese support me without question. Kazu is banished to Iga at once and permanently. If I see his face again it will leave his shoulders."

Hiro accepted his swords with a nod.

Kazu bowed. "Thank you, Shogun Matsunaga."

"May I ask a question?" Hiro asked.

Kazu gave him a disbelieving look, but Hiro continued, "Jun, the maid—she wasn't involved in Akira's plot, and I doubt she knew about yours."

"She did not," Hisahide said, "but she suspects too much to remain in Kyoto. I intend to find her a husband well outside the city limits. A farmer, perhaps—a man who presents no threat."

"She won't like that," Kazu said.

Hisahide smiled slowly. "She will prefer it to the alternative." He looked over his shoulder and called, "Ozuru!"

"Yes, Shogun Matsunaga?" The carpenter appeared in the doorway too quickly for coincidence. Chagrin burned Hiro's chest like flame as he realized Ozuru was a spy.

"Escort my guests to the gates," Hisahide said. "They are not to be harmed."

Ozuru bowed. "It will be done, Lord Shogun."

"One final question," Hiro asked, "before we go?"

Hisahide nodded.

"How did you know you would find us here tonight?"

Chapter 52

"I didn't," Hisahide said. "I came to this office to kill Akira. I told him to wait for me here and to send Kazu home if he returned before we seized the shogunate. Mainly, it was an excuse to keep Akira out of the way and alone. He would not have survived this night, though you have improved my position by taking care of the problem for me."

Hisahide joined Ozuru in the outer doorway. "Now, if you will excuse me, I must go. I have a lot to accomplish before dawn."

He nodded and departed.

Ozuru gestured to Hiro. "We need to get going."

As Kazu retrieved his swords, the carpenter crossed the room and looked down at Akira's body. He shook his head. "Poor fool. He assumed his Miyoshi blood made him important."

Ozuru escorted Hiro and Kazu through the *bakufu* mansion. When they encountered guards, Ozuru nodded and said, "Miyoshi Summer."

The guards accepted the code word and let them pass.

In an empty audience hall near the front of the mansion, Ozuru paused and looked at Hiro. "Iga *ryu*, I presume?"

"I'm sorry?" Hiro said. "I don't understand."

"I think you do." Ozuru lowered his voice and continued, "I recognize a *shuriken* strike to the eye when I see one. I know what you are."

Hiro noted the change in the carpenter's accent. "You're from Koga."

The Koga *ryu* was the largest shinobi school aside from Iga. No one knew exactly which was larger. Few men had seen both *ryu* and lived to tell it.

Ozuru nodded. "Yes, currently in the employ of Matsunaga Hisahide."

Hiro felt a twinge of concern. The Iga *ryu* and the Koga *ryu* were tentative allies but also fierce competitors, and now Ozuru could betray Hiro's identity at will.

"But you've been here for years, as a carpenter," Kazu protested. "Hisahide only came to Kyoto recently."

"The *ryu* sent me to Kyoto years ago, to await the day when someone needed an agent inside the shogunate. The most convincing spy is the one who isn't—until he's needed."

"Why admit your affiliation and surrender your advantage?" Hiro asked.

"I had to tell you," Ozuru said, "to repay a debt my family owes your clan. An Iga shinobi saved my father's life ten years ago, placing the Koga—and me—under obligation.

"I swear, on the honor of the Koga *ryu*, that I will never reveal your identy or your profession to any man," Ozuru said. "You tell Hattori Hanzo that the debt of Yoshida Bashō has been repaid."

Hiro had no doubt of Ozuru's sincerity. The shinobi code was stronger and more closely held than any other. However, that didn't make Ozuru a friend or mean that he could be trusted beyond his silence.

Hiro and Kazu raced the rain to Father Mateo's home. They approached the veranda just as chilly drops began to fall.

Inside, they found Father Mateo and Ichiro at the hearth. Loud snoring from the direction of Luis's room said the merchant had already gone to sleep.

The boy sat cross-legged on the tatami with Gato in his lap. The sight of the child stroking the sleeping cat made Hiro smile. Though feisty, Gato seemed to know when someone needed comfort.

Father Mateo looked up expectantly as Hiro and Kazu entered but waited for the men to share their news.

Hiro didn't waste time or words. "Saburo's killer is dead, but so is the shogun."

Ichiro's head snapped up. His eyes went wide with terror. "Lord Oda has seized Kyoto? We heard nothing!"

"Not Lord Oda." Kazu knelt beside Ichiro. "Matsunaga Hisahide."

Kazu briefly explained the events at the shogunate, though he didn't mention Ozuru or the way Akira died. In Kazu's version, Hiro killed the murderer with a sword and Hisahide allowed them to live because they discovered Saburo's killer.

Father Mateo listened without comment, though he shot Hiro a look that showed he expected a better explanation after Kazu left.

When Kazu finished, Ichiro looked down at his lap and stroked the ridge of fur along Gato's spine. "I wish you had let me go with you."

He looked up with tears in his eyes. "I will never have

vengeance now, and since the Ashikaga have lost the shogunate, I don't even have a home to go back to."

"You do, if you want one," Kazu said. "I will take you to
Iga with me."

Hiro was shocked, though the offer made a strange sort
of sense. The boy already looked up to Kazu, and Hisahide
would probably kill any Ashikaga male who threatened his
rule, despite his alleged promise. Taking Ichiro away was
the only effective way to ensure his survival.

"Iga?" Ichiro asked. "You're going away?"

"New shoguns always change the administration," Kazu
said. "I'm going home to my family. I'll take you with me."

"Are you sure you want to do this?" Hiro asked.

Kazu stood up and turned to Hiro. "You know how badly
Mother grieved for Ichiro." He gestured to the boy. "His
name is also Ichiro. Mother will consider that a sign. She'll
take him in, as one of us. I know it."

Father Mateo looked from Kazu to Hiro. "Mother? One
of *us*?"

Hiro looked at the Jesuit. "May I introduce my brother . . .
Hattori Kazu."

Chapter 53

Hattori?" Ichiro shook his head. "Your surname is Matsui, and his is Ito."

"A shinobi never uses his real name when on assignment," Kazu said.

"Shinobi?" Ichiro's eyes grew even wider. "Will I be allowed to become a shinobi also?"

"If you would like to." Kazu grinned.

"Cousin Hanzo may not approve of your decision," Hiro warned.

"Forgiveness is asked as easily as permission," Kazu said, "and I'm fairly persuasive when I want to be. Besides, if the Ashikaga ever recover the shogunate, they'll owe the Iga *ryu* for saving the boy."

Kazu pulled a folded parchment from his tunic. "I slipped a map of the shogun's compound, and also one of the city, out of the office when we left. That, and the information in my head, is worth at least the care of one small boy."

"I want to go with you," Ichiro said. "I always wanted to be your brother anyway."

Gato stretched, jumped to the floor, and started to clean her coat. Raindrops pattered on the roof.

"Then it's settled," Kazu said. "We'll leave at dawn."

Ana laid extra futons on the floor of the common room for Kazu and Ichiro. No one wanted dinner, though when the housekeeper insisted Father Mateo eat soup and rice to help him heal, the others had some too to keep the Jesuit company.

They went to sleep soon afterward.

It felt to Hiro as if he had barely closed his eyes when the shoji rustled and Kazu entered the room. The younger shinobi crossed the floor and crouched by Hiro's futon. "We're leaving now—Ichiro and I."

Hiro sat up and pulled his feet from beneath the sleeping cat. He tried to sense the time. "It isn't dawn. The gates are closed."

"It's close enough. The barricades will open when we get there."

"What about passes?" Hiro asked.

Kazu drew a folded paper from his sleeve. "I haven't been without it since you made me return to the shogunate. Just in case. Both Ichiro and I can travel on it."

"He's too old to pass without documentation," Hiro said.

Kazu smiled. "His only family died in a fire. Their documentation burned. As a courtesy, I'm escorting the boy to his relatives at Iga." He shrugged. "That and a gold koban should solve any problems. He won't be wearing his swords on the road, and no one cares very much about a boy."

Hiro laid a hand on Kazu's shoulder. "Travel safely. And tell Mother our new brother is entirely your fault—but that I welcome him to the family nonetheless."

Kazu chuckled. "I'll send word of our arrival when we get there." The smile left his face and voice. "Please tell Tomiko I'm sorry I had to go."

"If I can."

Kazu nodded. "Don't kill the priest."

Hiro frowned. "Don't kill yourself."

"I've done all right so far." Kazu patted Gato, stood, and made his way to the door.

Hiro followed.

As Kazu and Ichiro left, Hiro stood on the veranda and listened to the muffled crunch of their feet on the gravel path. The neighbor's dog began barking as the boy and the shinobi reached the street. Ichiro startled, but Kazu put a reassuring hand on the youngster's shoulder and together they hurried off down the darkened road.

Clouds drifted across the heavens, blocking out the stars and moon. The air held the damp-earth smell of grass and trees still wet with rain.

Hiro inhaled deeply, enjoying the freshness and the charge in the air that promised a lightning storm by morning. He stood on the veranda and considered the past few days. Father Mateo's hands were healing and with proper care would avoid infection. Kazu and Ichiro were closer to safety with every step.

Hisahide would be a dangerous shogun, but probably no worse than the one before him.

A warlord was a warlord, after all.

A flash of lightning lit the sky. Moments later, thunder cracked. Raindrops pattered on the roof like tiny paws. The sound made Hiro think of Gato, sound asleep at the end of the futon quilt.

The shinobi yawned. Like the cat, he needed to sleep while he had the chance.

With a satisfied smile, he turned and went inside.

Glossary of
Japanese Terms

B

bakufu: Literally, "tent government." Another name for the shogunate and the shogun's administration.

bokken: A wooden practice sword, used for sparring or solo weapons practice.

Bushido: Literally, "the way of the warrior." The samurai moral code, which emphasized loyalty, frugality, and personal honor.

C

chogin: a type of silver coin, used as currency in medieval Japan.

chonmage: The traditional hairstyle of adult samurai males. After shaving the pate, the remaining hair was oiled and tied in a tail, which was then folded back and forth on top of the head.

D

daimyo: A samurai lord, usually the ruler of a province or the head of a samurai clan.

dōshin: The medieval Japanese equivalent of a beat cop or policeman.

F

futon: A thin padded mattress, small and pliable enough to be folded and stored out of sight during the day.

G

genpuku: A traditional samurai coming-of-age ceremony, after which a boy was allowed to wear swords and take on the responsibilities of an adult.

geta: Traditional Japanese sandals (resembling flip-flops) with a raised wooden base and fabric thongs that wrap around the wearer's big toe.

gyokuro: Literally, "jewel dew." A high-quality green tea that is grown in the shade rather than in the sun.

H

hakama: Loose, pleated pants worn over a kimono or beneath a tunic or surcoat.

I

ichibancha: Literally, "first-picked tea." Tea leaves picked in April or early May, during the first picking of the season. *Ichibancha* is considered the highest quality, and most flavorful, kind of tea.

inkan: A personal seal, used in place of a signature on official documents.

J

jitte: A long wooden or metal nightstick with a forward-pointing hook at the top of the hand grip; carried by *dōshin* as both a weapon and a symbol of office.

K

kami: The Japanese word for "god" or "divine spirit"; used to describe gods, the spirits inhabiting natural objects, and certain natural forces of divine origin.

kanzashi: A type of hair pin worn by women in medieval Japan.

kata: Literally, "form(s)." A detailed pattern or set of movements used to practice martial skills and combat techniques, performed either with or without a weapon.

katana: The longer of the two swords worn by a samurai. (The shorter one is the *wakizashi*.)

kimono: Literally, "a thing to wear." A full-length wraparound robe traditionally worn by Japanese people of all ages and genders.

koban: A gold coin which came into widespread use in Japan during the later medieval period.

komusō: A mendicant monk of the Fuke school of Zen Buddhism.

kunoichi: A female *shinobi*.

M

maiko: A novice or apprentice entertainer who has not yet earned the title or rank of geisha.

mempo: An armored mask that covers the wearer's face, with holes for the eyes and mouth.

miso: A traditional Japanese food paste made from fermented soybeans (or, sometimes, rice or barley).

mon: An emblem or crest used to identify a Japanese family or clan.

N

noren: A traditional Japanese doorway hanging, with a slit cut up the center to permit passage.

O

obi: A wide sash wrapped around the waist to hold a kimono closed, worn by people of all ages and genders.

oe: The large central living space in a Japanese home, which features a sunken hearth and often serves as a combination of kitchen, reception room, and living space.

otosan: Father.

P

Pontocho: One of Kyoto's *hanamachi* (geisha and courtesan) districts, containing geisha houses, teahouses, brothels, restaurants, and similar businesses.

R

ronin: A masterless samurai.

ryu: Literally, "school." *Shinobi* clans used this term as a combination identifier and association name. (Hattori Hiro is a member of the Iga *ryu*.)

S

sake (also *saké*): An alcoholic beverage made from fermented rice.

-sama: A suffix used to show even higher respect than *-san*.

samurai: A member of the medieval Japanese nobility, the warrior caste that formed the highest-ranking social class.

-san: A suffix used to show respect.

seppuku: A form of Japanese ritual suicide by disembowelment, originally used only by samurai.

shakuhachi: A type of flute, normally made from bamboo and blown from the end. *Shinobi* sometimes concealed weapons inside flutes or other benign objects.

shinobi: Literally, "shadowed person." *Shinobi* is the Japanese pronunciation of the characters that many Westerners pronounce "ninja." ("Ninja" is based on a Chinese pronunciation.)

Shinto: The indigenous spirituality or religion of Japan, sometimes also called *kami-no-michi*.

shogun: The military dictator and commander who acted as de facto ruler of medieval Japan.

shogunate (also *bakufu*): A name for the shogun's government or the compound where the shogun lived.

shoji: A sliding door, usually consisting of a wooden frame with oiled paper panels.

shuriken: An easily concealed, palm-sized weapon made of metal, often shaped like a cross or star, that *shinobi* used for throwing or as a handheld weapon in close combat.

T

tabi: An ankle-length Japanese sock with a separation between the big toe and other toes to facilitate the use of sandals and other traditional Japanese footwear.

tanto: A fixed-blade dagger with a single or double-edged blade measuring 6–12 inches (15–30 cm) in length.

tatami: A traditional Japanese mat-style floor covering made in standard sizes, with the length measuring exactly twice its width. Tatami usually contained a straw core covered with grass or rushes.

tengu: A supernatural demon ("monster-spirit") from Japanese folklore, often depicted as a human-avian hybrid or with a long, hooked nose reminiscent of a beak.

tokonoma: A decorative alcove or recessed space set into the wall of a Japanese room. The tokonoma typically held a piece of art, a flower arrangement, or a hanging scroll.

torii: A traditional, stylized Japanese gate most commonly found at the entrance to Shinto shrines.

W

wakizashi: The shorter of the two swords worn by a samurai. (The longer one is the katana.)

For additional cultural information, expanded definitions, and author's notes, visit www.susanspann.com.

L AD
12/14 -   2/15

6/15 - 6